ASH TOUGH

SEASON ONE

"I think I had a normal childhood. Well, maybe it's better to say that I had a relatively normal childhood. I mean, I was adopted by parents who, at their best, were emotionally distant. So, I guess I'm grading on a curve.

"Anyway, as I grew up, my parents would read bedtime stories to me about beautiful fairy queens, mischievous leprechauns, and merrily scampering water babies. I would pretend that I was invited to tea parties and balls with the fairies. As I grew older, I started to read stories about the legendary deeds of Achilles, Odysseus, Beowulf, and Arthur. I came across tale after tale filled with magic and wonder. Story after story where good always triumphed over evil.

"I filled my life with stories that made me believe the world was a magical, wonderful, and essentially good place. I believed that the forces of good would always be honest, stalwart, true, and ultimately victorious. I believed that the forces of evil would be despicable, repulsive, and—well, for want of a better word, evil. I believed that as long as you were good, you would persevere, find your white knight, and have your own happy ending. These tales made me believe that life would be simple, or at least straightforward.

"But then I grew up, and while the world might not have lost its wonder, it lost its magic. Not only did the lines between good and evil become blurry, but so did what it meant to be good. It wasn't a world of black and white but one filled with various shades of gray. When I met my white knight, her armor was dirty and battered. For a while, though, that was okay. She wasn't perfect, and neither was I. But then she died. Before we ever really had our happily ever after, everything we had been building was shattered in an instant.

"If the real world had been like the stories I grew up reading, I would have stayed to pick up the pieces of my broken life and put them back together. But I am not one of those great heroes, or any kind of hero. So, instead, I ran. I ran across the entire country. I ran to escape my demons before they swallowed me whole.

"But the problem with running away from something is that you don't always see what you are running toward. And I ran headfirst into a world of problems I didn't even know I had. A family, and a sister, that I never knew I had.

"And, as it turns out, I might not know as much about the world as I thought I did. Maybe, just maybe, magic and Faeries really exist. But, relatively speaking, that's a good thing, because every mythical or magical creature you can think of, and a lot that you can't, are being drawn to Seattle to kill me. So, if I'm going to survive what is coming, I'll need all the help I can get."

—*Kate Matthews*

EPISODE ONE: HOLLY

Twins: two unique souls united by birth.
—Unknown author

PROLOGUE

A dark SUV pulled to a stop outside of a two-storey, Greek Revival Colonial-style house. The house had been converted into four condominiums several years earlier. It was perfectly situated in Capitol Hill on a quiet, tree-lined street between several other beautiful homes.

Rowan Ashley stepped out of the car and onto the curb, swinging her long, dark brown hair over her shoulder. The twenty-eight-year-old woman was slimly built with a strong jawline, alabaster skin and a charming smile. She wore dark blue jeans and a dark gray shirt under a leather jacket with knee-high black boots.

Rowan had, at various times in her life, been described as the human equivalent of a Golden Retriever. While she had initially been offended, she had grown to appreciate that the sentiment was a testament to her loyal, and positive nature, which was accompanied by a tendency to be a little goofy and overly eager at times.

Just as Rowan shut the car door, her phone rang. She stopped to lean against the car as she fished it out of the pocket of her form-fitting jeans. The screen read *Captain Tomas Montoya*—her boss at the Seattle Police Department.

Rowan enjoyed working under Captain Montoya. On most days, she appreciated his no-nonsense, by-the-book approach. Today was not one of those days, though. She needed more than platitudes about how she'd followed procedure. Following procedure meant nothing when it resulted in her partner in the hospital, fighting for her life. Rowan needed someone to tell her the truth, or at least what she saw was the truth: that there was something more she could have done.

Rowan sighed and rubbed the nape of her neck, walking toward the door of her ground-floor apartment as she answered her phone and placed it on speaker.

"Hello, Captain."

"Detective," said Captain Montoya by way of greeting. "Are you still at the hospital?"

"I just got home." She fished for her keys. "I needed to grab a change of clothes before I head back."

"Was there any news on Eddie before you left?"

Detective Edana Caulfield, or Eddie, as she was more commonly known, had been Rowan's partner for the last eighteen months. Rowan had only just, albeit reluctantly, left the hospital where Eddie was fighting for her life after what had started as a routine canvass of witnesses before going drastically sideways.

"Yes." She spun her keychain around her index finger. "She has three broken ribs, a punctured lung, a lacerated spleen, and a severe concussion. They were taking her into surgery when I left."

Even Rowan, with all her positivity and optimism, knew that Eddie's prognosis sounded grim. However, it was much better than her own initial assessment. There had been several seconds when she'd first seen Eddie on the ground where Rowan had been sure it was going to be a lot worse. She had never been as scared as she was in the moment where she struggled to find Eddie's pulse. The relief of Eddie's prognosis had been short-lived, though, when the gravity of her situation sank in.

As Rowan turned the doorknob to open her front door, she sensed someone coming up behind her. Before she could react, her head was slammed into the doorjamb. Dazed, she dropped her phone and keys as she fell to her knees.

"Detective? Rowan?" asked Captain Montoya with concern as Rowan reached for her service weapon.

Before she could pull it from its holster, the figure behind her stabbed her twice in the back: once between two ribs into her lung, and once between two other ribs into her liver. Rowan dimly heard Captain Montoya asking whether she was okay as she fell forward.

The weight of her body pushed the door open, revealing her living and dining room. It was filled with the assortment of furniture she had cobbled together over the years. As Rowan tried to place a hand against her back to stanch the bleeding, her gaze landed on the two things that were more about design than function: large black-and-white photos of New York's Brooklyn Bridge and Flatiron Building. She had purchased them when she first felt something calling her to New York.

She hoped she would survive to see them in person one day.

SIX WEEKS LATER

Another twenty-eight-year-old-woman with the same slim build, as well as the same long, luxurious dark brown hair, captivating emerald eyes, strong jawline, alabaster skin, and charming smile, walked across the ground floor of the converted condominium apartment in the Greek Revival Colonial-style house. The space was empty of all furniture and belongings.

Katherine Matthews moved through the living and dining room to look out of the large windows. Kate knew that people perceived her, and rightly so, to be a motivated and determined perfectionist with unrealistic expectations of herself. She also knew that people misconstrued her introversion and guardedness for an aloof detachment. She felt that this could not be further from the truth, as she had an incredible capacity for kindness, loyalty, and compassion. But she preferred to display such traits through everyday actions instead of more ostentatious grand gestures. She also measured these qualities against a responsible and dutiful nature.

"As I was saying," said the realtor from behind Kate, "this apartment just exudes warmth. It has nine hundred and thirty-one square feet of living space. It has a classic open floorplan with oak hardwood floors, high ceilings, large picture windows, and pocket doors. The owners would like to have a new tenant as soon as possible. They updated the kitchen about two years ago. It's through to your left."

Kate turned to look at the agent. She had introduced herself as Agatha Truman. Agatha was only half an inch shorter than Kate and had warm brown eyes and wavy blonde hair that came to just past her shoulders. Kate would have guessed that Agatha was of a similar age to her, in her late twenties or early thirties. Even in the short time that she had been around the agent, she had realized that the other woman was highly motivated and determined, bordering on stubbornness. Admittedly, Kate thought, those were traits that suited Agatha to her profession.

She wandered away from the window to glance in the kitchen as Agatha continued.

"The master bedroom is back this way. It has double glass French doors, which open to a rounded balcony."

Slowly, Kate turned back toward Agatha. The apartment suddenly darkened. The empty spaces filled with an eclectic array of furniture that materialized out of thin air. It looked like that odd mix one would normally see in someone's first apartment. On the wall between the foyer and the doorway to the master bedroom was a large black-and-white photo of New York's Brooklyn Bridge. Behind the couch was one of the Flatiron Building.

A woman wearing a rain jacket, jeans, and rubber galoshes walked into the living room. She dropped a bag next to the doorway then sat down on the couch. She picked up a remote from the coffee table and turned on the TV. In the low light from the screen, Kate finally saw the other woman's face.

It was identical to her own.

The darkened room filled with furniture suddenly dissolved, leaving her standing in the empty, sunny apartment, facing Agatha.

"Ms. Matthews?" Agatha cocked her head slightly. "Is everything all right?"

Kate offered her a tight smile to cover her surprise before she walked past her to look at the master bedroom. "What can you tell me about the owners?"

"An older couple owns the property," said Agatha after a brief pause.

Kate assumed the other woman had been waiting on some explanation as to why she had suddenly spaced out, and was slightly disconcerted when she found that it was not forthcoming.

"They purchased the property about four years ago when it was converted into a condo," Agatha continued. "From memory, they were downsizing. They lived here until two years ago when they moved to a nearby retirement community. They've been renting it out to their daughter ever since."

"Please tell me they didn't evict their daughter," said Kate, tilting her head in confusion.

"No, they didn't," said Agatha softly. "She died. She was killed about six weeks ago. The owners aren't sure whether they want to hold on to the property, but they're relying on the rental income until they can decide."

"Hence the highly motivated part?" asked Kate.

"Exactly."

"Should I be concerned about my safety here, or in this neighborhood?"

"No." Agatha's brows knitted together in a frown. "Why would you ask that?"

"You did just say that the woman who lived here was killed less than two months ago."

"Right—no. She was a cop killed in the line of duty. Her death had nothing to do with how safe this building or this neighborhood are." Agatha paused. "So, would you like a rental application?"

"Yes, I'd appreciate that," said Kate. "I'd also like to be notified if the owners are interested in selling."

"Would you be interested in buying the property if they are?" asked Agatha in surprise.

Kate only smiled, more genuinely, in response.

CHAPTER ONE

Kate looked around the apartment. It had been two weeks since she'd signed the lease and the furniture she had brought with her from New York was now sitting around the room. Compared to the eclectic array that had filled the apartment in her vision, Kate's furniture was all matching, of much better quality, and looked expensive without being ostentatious. She had unpacked most of her belongings, but there were still several boxes scattered across the living and dining room waiting for her. As Kate began to unpack more boxes, she played the voicemail messages that had accumulated over the last two weeks while she had been finalizing the details of her move.

The first box contained several books. She started pulling them out of the box one by one as the first message, from her lawyer, began to play in the background.

"Kate, this is Kelly from Blackburn and Slater Lawyers. I wanted to confirm that we have received all the paperwork to finalize the sale of your townhouse. I'll call you again in a couple of days to discuss the final steps of the transaction."

Despite Kate legally holding the title to the townhouse, she had felt conflicted about selling it. It had sentimental value, as it had been the first place that she and her wife had lived after their wedding. But while they may have bought it together, it had never really felt like home, particularly because she had spent so little time there. Kate also did not like holding on to a property in which she and Alex had planned on building their family together.

She started to break down the box while the second message played. This one was from her mother. Lillian was a person who appreciated the finer things in life, but was incapable of dealing with her emotions and refused to show any vulnerability. Kate often struggled with her mother's lack of affection and compassion. She could not help but sigh as she listened to the message.

"Katherine, it's your mother. I received your message. Please tell me that selling your townhouse and moving to Seattle is some kind of joke. I don't believe you would have done something so foolish. It's bad enough that people at the club are talking about you turning down both Princeton and Columbia's job offers. I will not become a laughingstock because of your poor decision-making."

"Yes, Mother," said Kate, rolling her eyes as the message ended. "By all means, make my personal tragedies about you."

She sighed again in frustration as she ripped off the tape sealing another box. This one contained a collection of small photo frames showing Kate with her friends at various times throughout her adult life. She started placing these on a side table as the next message began to play.

"Katherine, it's your father. I think you should call your mother."

Kate viewed her father as a product of his time and societal upbringing. Edward was a stern, hard-working man who had spent more time at work than at home when she was growing up. It meant he knew very little about his daughter and had never shown much motivation to change this. He was also an imposing man who rigorously adhered to the traditional values of the upper-class life into which he'd been born.

The message had been exactly what she was expecting from him. No—she had *actually* expected him to have his secretary call, but this was a close second. Their conversations had long been entirely predictable.

The next message played as she placed the last photo frame onto the table and began breaking down the empty box. It was from her younger brother Robert, or Robbie, as he was more affectionately known. It had only been about twelve months after Edward and Lillian had adopted Kate that Lillian found out she had finally fallen pregnant with Robbie. As he was the son her parents had always wanted, they had always doted on him.

Kate had struggled not to let her jealousy of their overt favoritism color her relationship with her brother. She had always loved him deeply and relied on his support throughout their lives. But that was not to say that his devil-may-care, privileged, entitled approach to life was not a frequent annoyance to her. Kate firmly believed that if Robbie ever found himself in hot water, he had the charm and guile to talk his way out of it.

"Katie, it's Robbie. Can you please call Mom and Dad? They are really freaking out. Or at least, Mom is freaking out, and she's convinced Dad to freak out too. I know you're hurting, but Mom believes that you're doing this for attention. Realistically, I know you probably won't be able to convince her that she's wrong, but I think you should try. And yes, I know trying the same thing over and over again is the definition of insanity, but under all the hairspray and neuroses, she is still our mother."

Kate couldn't help the slight chuckle that escaped her at his description. The next message started to play as she opened a box containing throw pillows that she pulled out and arranged on her couch.

This message was from her former supervisor, Greg Spinda, from the Niehaus Center for Globalization and Governance at Princeton University, where Kate had been a postdoctoral research associate. Kate had always found Greg to be a considerate colleague and a supportive mentor. He was just one of the many reasons that she had enjoyed her time at Princeton as much as she had, despite the problems it caused in her relationship with her wife.

Alex had not taken it well when Kate had agreed to work at Princeton, as she had wanted Kate to take a role in New York. It had not mattered that Princeton offered a better opportunity for Kate at that time in her career.

"Kate, it's Greg. I know I said that I thought you should take some time and get out of the city to write your book. This isn't exactly what I had in mind, though. I kind of assumed you would rent a house in the Hamptons for a couple of weeks." He paused. "I can't even imagine what you're going through, but I want you to remember that there are people who love you and want to support you through this."

Kate was pulling a throw out of the box as her phone beeped again. She started draping it over her couch as a message from her brother-in-law, Erin Quinn, played.

Kate had always found Erin to be warm, supportive, and giving. He was the friend everyone wished they had by their sides when the going got tough. Despite his own grief, Erin had been Kate's port in a storm since Alex had died five months earlier in a car accident. He also had a unique ability to always make her laugh, particularly when she needed it or when the chips were down.

"Katie, it's Erin. I won't ask how you are, because I'm guessing you're handling things about as well as I am. Dad and I were surprised to hear that you decided to move out here, but I would love to catch up for coffee or dinner or whatever. I just want you to know that you don't have to go through this alone."

Kate had just started to break down the final box when she paused, her head tilted to one side with interest as she listened to the next message.

"Hi, Kate, my name is Ainsley Cooper. I'm an Associate Professor at the University of Washington. Greg Spinda mentioned that you had just relocated to Seattle. I'm interested in discussing a potential role for you at the university. You have my number, so I would appreciate it if you could call me back when you get a chance."

Well, thought Kate, *that could be interesting. Unexpected, but interesting all the same.*

Detective Eddie Caulfield was in her early thirties, very tall and strikingly attractive with a finely curved athletic figure. She had dark red hair, currently cut to just below her ears, and warm, chestnut-colored eyes. Her friends in college had always categorized her as a cinnamon roll due to her gentle, kind nature. She had always laughed this off and had spent most of her working life endeavoring to demonstrate her bravery, sense of justice and honor, and hardworking nature.

It was those traits that had driven her to pursue a career within Seattle's Police Department. Most days, she loved strapping on her gun and badge and catching bad guys.

Today was not one of those days.

Instead, Eddie was currently pacing from one side of the room to the other in the office of Dr. Daryl Wong. The room itself was about what one would expect from a therapist's office, complete with the almost mandatory counseling couch. Eddie assumed that therapists used couches to help their patients feel comfortable. All things considered though, the couch was not helping her current comfort levels. She was sure her therapist was having a field day interpreting her flushed face and pressed lips, but she couldn't help it. She was grappling with a unique combination of anger, annoyance, and impatience.

"It's not fair," said Eddie almost petulantly as she continued to pace across the room. "My partner has only been dead for eight weeks. I haven't even been cleared for active duty yet."

"As the one who hasn't signed off on your return to duty, I'm aware," said Dr. Wong.

Dr. Wong was the psychiatrist the Police Department had ordered that Eddie see following not only her physical injuries, but also the death of her partner. He was very calm, softly spoken, and even-tempered. He even looked the part with his glasses and sweaters.

Eddie stopped and turned toward where Dr. Wong was sitting with an ankle squared over one knee. He had a slight smile on his face.

"Funny." She dropped into the seat across from him with a huff.

"The reason I haven't yet agreed to you returning to duty is that I don't believe that you have fully dealt with the trauma of losing your partner," said Dr. Wong. "Start dealing with that and I can get you back to work."

"Trust me when I say that I have dealt with my trauma," said Eddie earnestly.

"Really?" asked Dr. Wong. "Then explain to me why you don't want a new partner."

"It's just too soon." Eddie picked up one of the couch's small pillows and turned it over in her hands.

"You're a cop. You had partners before Rowan. If you're to continue being a cop, then you will need a new partner." Dr. Wong leaned back in his chair. "Do you want to hear why I think you don't want a new partner?"

"Enlighten me." Eddie punched the pillow in her hands softly.

"You are blaming yourself for Rowan's death. I have spent the last eight weeks trying to get you to tell me why that is. Maybe you don't know, or at least you don't want to admit why. Regardless, until you're willing to acknowledge that for yourself, you won't be able to move past this."

Eddie crossed her arms in front of her chest. "And why shouldn't I blame myself for what happened? Why shouldn't I blame myself for not protecting her?"

"You think your partner died because you couldn't protect her?" asked Dr. Wong. "Let's set aside all the troubling and condescending connotations of that statement, which suggests your partner was somehow less capable of protecting herself than you were, for a moment. Instead, just answer me. How were you supposed to protect her when you were lying in a hospital bed with three broken ribs, a collapsed lung, and a lacerated spleen? You're only human. What more could you have done? Were you supposed to be with her at all times of the day and night? Because if that's the case, either your partner was incompetent or you have some control issues that we should be addressing."

Eddie looked away without answering. It wasn't like she could tell him she was not human, but a Faerie. She couldn't tell him that she had lost her parents and spent most of her life exiled from her home due to a civil war that had engulfed their royal family. She couldn't tell him that she should have protected her partner because Rowan had been one of the two rightful heirs to the throne currently held by Rowan's usurping great-uncle, Cornelius, who had seized it after the death of Rowan's mother.

The Broadway Coffee House was a bright, airy, well-lit store in Capitol Hill's Pike/Pine corridor. It was a bustling but casual bookstore cafe. On one side of the front half ran a counter, while a collection of wooden tables filled the other side. A long wooden bench ran along the glass storefront. Several bookshelves filled the back of the store, with even more in the loft area above the cafe.

Kate was seated at a table partially hidden toward the back, just in front of the bookshelves. She had a half-empty cup of tea and a half-eaten sandwich in front of her while she worked on her laptop. The cafe provided the right amount of white noise to prevent her from going stir-crazy, but was not so loud as to distract her from her work.

Kate also found the proximity to so many books to be very comforting, but also a bit tempting. She had been coming here every day for almost a week now and there was yet to be a day that she had not bought a new book for her collection. She was definitely of the view that one could never have too many books. She was even using the spare room in her new apartment as her own personal library.

Suddenly Kate's table was bumped as another customer accidentally backed into it, stepping out of the way of one of the cafe's employees.

"Sorry about that," said the woman without turning around.

Kate looked up and noticed that she was very tall with short red hair. "Totally fine," she said, turning back to her laptop.

The other customer dropped her cup of coffee.

"Rowan?" she asked, brown eyes wide and eyebrows raised in shock.

"Uh, no," said Kate. "I think you have the wrong person."

"Seriously?" The woman's hands settled on her hips. "Rowan, this isn't funny."

Kate narrowed her eyes. "Look, no offence, but I have no idea who you think I am. I don't know who this Rowan is, but I'm not her."

"Show me your ID," the woman demanded.

"Not a chance in hell."

"My name is Detective Eddie Caulfield." She flashed Kate her police credentials. "So show me your ID."

"Fine." Kate pulled out her license and handed it to Detective Caulfield. "Here. See? My name is Kate Matthews. Now, I don't know what your problem is, but I would prefer it if you left me alone."

Kate snapped her laptop closed in frustration, picked up her bag, and slid it inside. She took her license back from the detective before walking out of the cafe.

Kate did not notice that as she left, Detective Caulfield's eyes slammed shut as she sagged forward and braced herself against the table.

Erin Quinn was in his bioengineering research lab at the University of Washington bright and early each morning. He was thirty-two years old, tall with short brown hair, blue eyes, and a slight but deliberate stubble along his jaw and upper lip. He was slim with a muscular build. People like his sister-in-law tended to gravitate to his warmth, positivity, and optimism. He made sure to show each person who found themselves within his circle that he was a loyal, trustworthy, and dependable friend. He also knew that his slightly flamboyant nature made it easy for casual observers to overlook the intelligence and determination that had shaped his professional career.

His laboratory was on the smaller side, but it was well-funded for him to perform experiments, take measurements, and gather data. To Erin, it only mattered that the lab was equipped with everything he needed for his research. Admittedly, most days he still felt like a kid who had been given the key to a candy store.

He had not always wanted to go into bioengineering research. He had spent most of his life wanting to help people as a doctor. But when his mother had been diagnosed with a rare terminal lung disease when he was in college, his aspirations changed. Watching her suffer had compelled him to find a cure for the disease that ended her life. There was nothing he could do to change what had happened to her, but maybe one day, another family would not have to lose their mother like he had lost his.

Erin was looking through the lens of a microscope when his phone rang. The display showed the name *Katie Matthews*. He smiled widely as he answered, "Hey, honey. How are you?"

"Hi, chicken," said Kate warmly. "I'm as good as can be expected in the circumstances. What about you and your dad?"

"Honestly? About the same." His smile turned sad. "It's surprising how often I pick up the phone to tell her about my day and have to stop myself."

"You know that you can always call me instead, right?" said Kate quickly to fill the silence.

"You're going through enough," said Erin softly. "I don't want to add to that."

"But you want to always be there when I need it?" asked Kate. "We both lost Alex. We're both grieving her. I don't want to do it alone anymore. I think that's part of the reason that I wanted to move here. I don't want to be alone in this."

"You were never alone, honey."

"I know. But if we're going to find a way through this, it should be together."

"I like the sound of that."

Erin paused as a petite Asian woman walked into the lab. Akiko Shimizu was bright, bubbly, lively, and almost annoyingly perky. Erin had never asked her age, as a gentleman never asks those kinds of questions, but he had always assumed that she was in her mid-twenties.

This morning, she was wearing a tank top that briefly revealed a tattoo on her shoulder before she pulled on her lab coat. Erin had always found the tattoo, a triskelion within a nonagon, unique and fascinating. Despite him asking several times, Akiko had never told him about the inspiration behind it.

"Sorry, sweetheart, but I have to go," he told Kate. "How about we do drinks?"

"Tonight?" she asked. "You can see my new place?"

"That sounds great. I'll see you later." He hung up the phone. "Hi, Akiko."

"Morning, Erin," said Akiko cheerily. "Was that a new boyfriend? Have you been holding out on me? You know I live vicariously through you."

"No, there is no new boyfriend. I would have told you if there was." He rubbed his forehead. "It was my sister."

"Sister?" She frowned. "I thought Alex was your only sister."

"Alex's wife, Kate. She just moved to Seattle."

"Moving from New York to Seattle five months after burying her wife?" asked Akiko. "Talk about impulsive decisions in the wake of grief."

"Actually, it's surprisingly in character," said Erin.

Akiko raised her eyebrows in surprise. Erin offered a small smile in return and turned back to the microscope.

The office of the Chief of Staff to the Mayor of Seattle looked exactly like what Eddie would have expected of a senior-level bureaucrat, with a lot of polished wooden furniture, including a large, ostentatious mahogany leather-top desk. The huge room occupied the corner of the building with floor-to-ceiling windows that provided spectacular views of downtown Seattle. One of the remaining walls had several floor-to-ceiling mahogany bookshelves, while the other had a large oil painting of some landscape in an expensive frame.

The man seated at the desk looked to be in his fifties, with wavy but perfectly coiffed dark brown hair that was graying slightly at his temples. He had blue eyes and a charming smile. In his crisp and perfectly tailored suit, he exuded confidence and power. He was the very definition of a man behind the curtain. On the desk was a nameplate that read Nolan Fitzroy.

"This whole 'Master of the Universe' thing really seems to work for you, Nolan," said Eddie as she leaned against the doorjamb.

Nolan had rescued her from the conflict that had engulfed their home when Cornelius murdered his brother, King Regulus, and attempted to seize control of the throne from its rightful heir, Queen Titania. Eddie was sure that Regulus and Titania's Chief Advisor had had other plans than becoming an adoptive parent to a five-year-old grieving not only the loss of her home, but also her parents, who had fallen victim to Cornelius' ruthless rise to power. But in Eddie's eyes, Nolan had more than risen not only to that challenge, but also to the challenge of rallying the fragmented factions that had remained loyal to Queen Titania and her heirs.

"Thank you," said Nolan as he looked up at Eddie. He smiled kindly and gestured for her to come into his office. "How are you feeling?"

"I'm going into the station tomorrow to discuss returning to work with Captain Montoya," said Eddie as she sat down in front of Nolan's desk. "And before you say anything, all my injuries have healed and my doctors have signed off on me returning to work, at least in an administrative capacity."

"That was not what I asked, and you know it," said Nolan.

"Well, that's the only answer you're going to get."

"If you don't want to talk about that, then what brings you downtown at this time of night?"

Eddie straightened her back and squared her shoulders. "I ran into someone interesting in a coffee shop today."

"Did you come here to talk about your dating life?"

"Seriously?" Eddie frowned and shook her head. "No. Trust me, that is something we will never talk about."

"Thank goodness for that."

"Moving on," said Eddie. "The woman I ran into—I could have sworn she was Rowan."

"Eddie," said Nolan cautiously, "are you still speaking to that therapist?"

"Why would you even ask that?"

"I know grief can do strange things to people, and if you're seeing things—"

"I was not doing a Haley Joel Osment impression," interrupted Eddie.

"A what?"

It was an easy assumption for Nolan to make, that her grief had been clouding her judgment. She'd been so distraught on learning of Rowan's death that the hospital staff had needed to sedate her to prevent her from injuring herself. She had almost thought she was seeing things when she first saw the woman who was a doppelganger for her late partner. It had thrown her for a loop.

But surprisingly, her discontent had only been short-lived. Instead of the grief, loss, and guilt she had carried for the last several weeks, Eddie had quickly found herself filled with hope—hope that their cause was not lost, and that one of Titania's daughters remained alive.

"You're the one who has spent almost thirty years telling me I need to blend in with humans more," said Eddie. "You know—'Do as the humans do, Eddie' and 'You should only ever be ordinary, Eddie, and never extraordinary.' One would think that in all that time, you would have taken your own advice, embraced human pastimes, seen a movie or two."

"Do you think I am working as the Mayor's Chief of Staff just for kicks?" asked Nolan.

"Well, with a job like this, you can probably buy a lot of really nice shoes." Eddie laughed as Nolan rolled his eyes. "Hayley Joel Osment was in *The Sixth Sense*. You know, 'I see dead people'? Which, for the record, I didn't. But I confronted the woman and got her to show me her ID. Her name is Katherine Matthews."

"Her name is Katherine?"

"Interesting, don't you think?" asked Eddie. "Particularly considering Rowan had a twin sister named Catriona who we haven't been able to find since you organized her adoption twenty-eight years ago."

Chapter Two

Kate and Erin were in her living room, Kate at one end of the couch and Erin reclining against the armrest at the opposite end. They each held a glass of wine and there was an open bottle on the coffee table. Both the glasses and the bottle were already half empty.

"What did you do?" asked Erin.

"Well, she was a police officer, so I had to show her my license," said Kate with a slight shrug. "Although, it concerns me that someone like that is responsible for protecting the people in this city. I mean, she seemed a little unhinged."

"Maybe she was less unhinged than you think."

"What is that supposed to mean?"

"Well, you were adopted," said Erin.

"Don't tell me you think I somehow have a twin sister that I've never met?" asked Kate, slightly exasperated. "I mean, how clichéd can you get?"

She was not willing to acknowledge, either to herself or to Erin, how many years she had spent hoping for just such a sibling to show up when she was younger. But Kate had long since dismissed any such thoughts as the foolish musings of a lonely child.

"Clichéd as it may be, you have never looked into your biological parents." He tapped his foot against Kate's knee. "And I'm not judging you for not doing that, but have you never wanted to know?"

"Know what?" asked Kate. "Who my parents were? Why they gave me up? Why they didn't want me? What if I follow this down the rabbit hole and I find out something I don't want to know? What if I find out they wanted her and not me?"

"No one can guarantee that the answers you find will be ones that you like or want to hear," said Erin. "But you will get answers. In my book, knowing is always better than not knowing. Okay?"

"Okay," said Kate. "Okay. I'll see if I can find that police officer and hear her out."

"Good," said Erin. "Does your planning for the future mean that you're planning on sticking around?"

Kate relaxed back against the arm of the couch. "Shouldn't the apartment have given that away?"

"Please," said Erin. "We both know that you could afford to buy apartments in at least a dozen cities across the world and still not need to work a day for years."

"I suppose that's fair," said Kate. "I needed a change, though. And that isn't because of losing Alex."

"Seriously, sometimes getting you to open up is like pulling teeth."

"You're lucky that I love you."

"Oh, I know," said Erin. "This would be so much more difficult if you didn't. So, why did you decide to leave New York?"

"I can't say that it was ever my favorite place to live in," said Kate. "I would have preferred to stay at Yale or Princeton, but Alex ... she was the one who wanted to live in New York."

"What about Columbia?" Erin rested his chin in his palm. "I thought you were looking forward to that job."

"I was looking forward to Columbia because Alex wanted me to love Columbia," said Kate cautiously. "Since our first date, she never stopped talking about how much she wanted to work on Wall Street and teach at Columbia. So, I knew going in that if we were to stay together, we would always end up in New York. And before you say anything, I was completely okay with that. I wouldn't have agreed with Alex's plan for our life if I wasn't. But Columbia and New York only made sense when I was with her. At the end of the day, the thing I love is teaching, and I can do that here. I even got a call from someone at the University of Washington about a job there."

"Well, I would love to have you on campus," said Erin.

Kate smiled at him and refilled both wine glasses.

Agatha sighed as she looked around Ainsley Cooper's office at the University of Washington. It was in its usual state of half-organized clutter. In one half were several floor-to-ceiling bookshelves. About two-thirds were lined with books and textbooks, the other third with paperwork and manila folders. In the other half of the office was Ainsley's desk with piles of paperwork stacked on top, alongside a laptop. In a corner behind the desk was a TV, currently switched off.

Agatha was sitting in one of the two seats in front of the desk while Ainsley sat behind it. While Agatha had known Ainsley for most of her century-long life, Ainsley's youthful appearance meant she easily passed for a woman in her early thirties. Her long blonde hair, with slightly darker brown roots, was cut so that it was just touching her shoulders, with a long fringe that fell just below her eyebrows to frame her wide, heart-shaped face. She had warm blue eyes set above highly defined cheekbones.

Agatha had always known Ainsley to be a courageous, self-assured, independent person who faced danger head-on. As much as she loved how caring Ainsley was, Agatha was equally frustrated with her tendency to be overly headstrong, selfless, and dutiful. Admittedly, Ainsley had never been as committed to her duty to Prince Regent Cornelius before the civil war that had engulfed their home almost thirty years earlier. But that was a time that had changed so many Faeries Agatha had known. It had torn families and friendships apart as her people found themselves forced to choose between Cornelius and his niece, Titania.

Like many other loyalists, Agatha had hoped that after the deaths of Titania and her husband, Oberon, the wounds left behind would have an opportunity to heal. But her hopes had been short-lived as Titania's remaining rebel factions continued to promote their cause even after their queen's death, allowing the wounds to fester and infect their people. Despite being pragmatic enough to know the one thing that would extinguish the rebels' last hope, Agatha was unsure whether she was callous enough to hope for the death of Titania's last remaining heir. That was something she had never felt comfortable sharing with Ainsley, though, as the other woman's thoughts on the issue, much like Cornelius', were set in stone.

Agatha sighed again as she looked at the picture of Rowan Ashley that Ainsley had placed on the desk between them.

"So, are you sure it was Rowan who rented the property?" asked Ainsley.

"I guess her hair was styled a little differently," said Agatha. "Plus, the clothes were different. The woman I met was more East Coast preppy as opposed to Rowan's more classical Seattle street style. In saying that, the new look definitely works for her—"

"Agatha," interrupted Ainsley. "Please. Focus. Was it the same person?"

"It definitely could have been." Agatha looked up at her. "But if it was, she was a good actor. Not even a flinch or glimmer of recognition at any point. So, what do you think it means?"

"I'm not sure. There are a few possibilities."

"Like what? Rowan faked her death, assumed the name of the twin sister she never knew existed, and decided to rent her own apartment?"

"As opposed to the twin sister that Rowan never knew about not only deciding to move to Seattle, for some as yet unknown reason, but also somehow deciding out of all of the available apartments in this city to rent Rowan's?" asked Ainsley.

"Well, the simplest explanation is the best explanation," said Agatha.

"And which out of *faked own death* or *mystically drawn to Seattle* is the simplest? They are both equally absurd."

Agatha shrugged. "I don't know."

"Then why did you say that?"

"I thought it was a good idea."

"Yes, well, at this stage, I'm hoping for a third option," said Ainsley. "Neither makes sense. We must be missing something."

Agatha looked away. There was one option that Ainsley was overlooking. Agatha was unsure whether it would hold any more water than the others, but she felt it needed consideration.

She and Ainsley had never been able to determine whether Rowan was aware of her parentage, but Agatha had always thought it suspicious that several of the leaders of the rebel faction had been calling Seattle their home for some time. Consequently, Rowan's connection to the rebels was never something she felt comfortable ruling out. Rowan's sister, though, presented an even greater uncertainty. If she discounted the absurd, the only option left was that the rebels had brought Kate here to fill the void in their organization left behind by her sister.

Agatha's darkening thoughts were interrupted as the sharp ringing of Ainsley's phone broke the silence that had settled between the women.

Ainsley looked at the screen. "Sorry, do you mind if I take this?" she asked. "I'm happy for you to stay here while I'm on the phone."

"No need to apologize. Go ahead."

Ainsley reached for her phone. "This is Ainsley Cooper speaking."

"Hi, Ainsley, it's Kate Matthews. I'm just returning your call from the other day. I apologize for the delay in getting back to you."

"Kate," said Ainsley. "Your ears must have been burning."

"Excuse me?"

"Sorry—I was just mentioning you to a colleague, telling them what a valuable addition you would be to the university. Please tell me you're interested?"

"Yes, actually," said Kate. "I've decided that Seattle could be a much-needed change for me, so I was hoping to discuss that position with you in more detail. Perhaps over coffee?"

"Coffee sounds like a great idea. How about I take a look at my calendar and find a time that we could meet?"

"That would be great," said Kate. "Thank you so much for reaching out in the first place."

"I can't take all the credit there, unfortunately. Greg was quite insistent."

"He can be like that."

"It seemed like he really cared about you," said Ainsley. "Anyway, I'll let you know later today about coffee."

"Thanks," said Kate. "I'll wait to hear from you."

Ainsley hung up her phone and placed it back on her desk, then leaned back in her chair and looked up at Agatha.

"So, does that mean she's the real Catriona?" asked Agatha.

"Maybe."

"Maybe?"

"If this Kate Matthews is really Catriona, why would she decide to move to Seattle after Rowan's death?" asked Ainsley.

"You said that Kate's wife was killed. Could it be that simple?"

"I would understand her moving, but she could have gone anywhere," said Ainsley. "Why Seattle, and why did she find herself drawn to Rowan's apartment? What are we missing?"

Captain Tomas Montoya stretched his neck to the side as he picked up another report that required his attention. He was a forty-five-year-old Latino man with brown eyes, slightly graying black hair, and an athletic build. He knew the detectives and officers that worked under him at the Seattle Police Department viewed him as a no-nonsense, humorless, by-the-book straight-shooter. He supposed it was just a natural assumption when they saw how seriously he took his job and his vow to protect Seattle's citizens.

He was also self-aware enough to know that he came across as harsh and intolerant of humor when engrossed in a case. While he did everything he could to encourage this perception, he cared very much for those under him in the Police Department, assisting them if they got into a pinch, diverting the resources at his disposal if required. In reality, Tomas knew that he used his tough exterior as a coping mechanism to help him handle the day-to-day stresses of his line of work and his responsibilities as a captain.

He had spent most of the morning so far sitting at his desk, working his way through a mountain of paperwork that he had contemplated just throwing out the window on more than one occasion already. It was only his tireless dedication and his commitment to professionalism that prevented him from doing so. However, he was seriously rethinking that commitment when he heard a knock on the door.

"You can come in."

The door opened and Detective Eddie Caulfield stepped inside. "Is now still a good time, Captain?"

"Yes, it is. Take a seat." Tomas waited as Eddie closed the door and took a seat in front of his desk. "Now, I wanted to apologize. I had wanted to be the one to talk to you about your new partner. I didn't want you to find out how you did."

"I am actually kind of glad I found out how I did. Not that I wouldn't have liked to hear it directly from you, but..." Eddie fell silent.

"I know from experience that losing a partner is incredibly difficult," said Tomas. "I also know that you are still recovering from the physical and psychological trauma you suffered on that evening before adding that loss into the equation. So I'm happy for you to take things slow."

"It probably helps that at this stage I'm only cleared to return to administrative duties," said Eddie.

"That it does," said Tomas, "but I would still like you to start working with your new partner as soon as you feel up to it."

"I understand, and I appreciate it."

"Would you feel up to meeting him now?"

"Okay," said Eddie hesitantly, "but first, is there any update on finding the person responsible for Rowan's death?"

"I've assigned the case to your new partner, Detective Hunter Lowell," said Tomas. "That way, when you come back, you can be involved in the investigation."

"That isn't exactly within regulations," said Eddie.

"I am choosing to make an exception." Tomas smiled as he picked up his phone. He dialed Detective Lowell's extension and asked, "Can you come into my office?"

There was a knock on Tomas' office door only moments later. Detective Lowell was an attractive man, who looked like he was in his thirties. Tall, with curled dirty-blonde hair and dark blue eyes that contrasted with his fair skin, he was well-built with a delicate yet masculine face. He was well-dressed in slacks, a dress shirt, and a vest. He walked into the room carrying a case folder and closed the door behind him.

"Detective Caulfield, this is Detective Lowell," said Tomas.

Detective Lowell stepped forward and offered his hand to Eddie. She shook it firmly as he said, "I wish we were meeting under different circumstances, Detective. I'm sorry for your loss."

In the short time that he had worked with Detective Lowell, Tomas had gleaned that the man liked to pretend he was some combination of the Grinch who stole Christmas and the Tin Man without a heart. However, there were brief instances, such as this, when Tomas got the sense that Lowell was really more like a piece of rocky road—hard on the outside, soft and gooey in the middle, and just a little bit nutty.

"Thank you," said Eddie.

"Any update on the investigation of the death of Detective Ashley?" asked Tomas.

"Unfortunately, we haven't made any progress," said Detective Lowell. "While the perpetrator left behind the knife they used, they didn't leave any prints, DNA, or anything else we can use."

"Can we trace the knife to the manufacturer?" asked Eddie.

"It appears custom-made, but at this stage, we haven't been able to trace it back to a commercial manufacturer."

Detective Lowell opened the file he'd brought with him and spread out the contents on Tomas' desk. There were several photos of the knife used to stab Detective Rowan Ashley. The blade was double-edged and about ten inches in length. It lacked any ridgelines and was flat. The handle had a triskelion within a nonagon etched into it.

"Any chance you've seen this before?" Detective Lowell asked Eddie.

Eddie pulled her car to a stop just down the street from the Broadway Coffee House. She was parked close enough that if she were to look in that direction, she could see patrons through the window.

Just as Eddie got out of her car, her phone started to ring. Nolan was calling her. Eddie closed the door and leaned against it as she answered.

"Thanks for getting back to me."

"It sounded urgent," said Nolan.

"A shape-shifter killed Rowan," said Eddie.

"Excuse me?"

"I asked for an update on the investigation into Rowan's murder when I was at the station," said Eddie. "The blade used to kill her had the shape-shifter insignia etched into the handle."

"Are you sure?" asked Nolan.

"I saw the pictures myself. The insignia was clear," said Eddie. "Why would a shape-shifter kill Rowan?"

"You know that they're mercenaries, Eddie," said Nolan. "Unless you can identify the specific shifter, find them, and get them to reveal their employer, you will struggle to find a motive."

"Are you suggesting that I should just give up?"

"No, but you need to be realistic. It's important that you come to terms with the simple reality that you may never know why Rowan was targeted."

Eddie sighed in frustration. She knew Nolan was only looking out for her in the way that he always had, but she wished he would be more decisive. Whether he was prepared to admit it or not, they both knew that the only one responsible for Rowan's death could be Cornelius. He was the only person who would benefit from the death of one of the two legitimate heirs to the throne on which he sat.

Eddie sighed again as she looked toward the Broadway Coffee House. She noticed Rowan's doppelganger sitting inside near the window. Eddie straightened, tracing Katherine Matthews' figure with her gaze. At that moment, she promised that she would not let Katherine down as she had her sister. She would do everything that she could to protect her.

"Eddie?" asked Nolan.

"I have to go. I'll call you later," said Eddie abruptly, ending the call and walking toward the cafe.

Kate was sitting at a table with a half-empty cup of tea in front of her, once again focused on the book proposal currently open on her laptop. Someone placed a coffee cup on her table, and she looked up. Detective Caulfield took a seat across from her.

"You again," said Kate.

While she had promised Erin that she would speak to the detective, she had hoped she would have longer to think about what she was going to say before she tracked the other woman down. She also would have preferred that such an encounter took place on her own terms. It seemed that she would need to wing it, even if the thought of doing so made her skin crawl.

"Me again," said Detective Caulfield, offering Kate a warm smile.

"So." Kate rested her chin in her palm. "Who is Rowan to you, and why do you think I look like her?"

"Has anyone ever told you that you are very perceptive?" asked Detective Caulfield. "And also very direct?"

"People have a tendency to tell me that just after they finish lying to me," said Kate, rolling her eyes. "So, are you going to tell me why you looked like you saw a ghost when you saw me the other day, or are you going to lie to me?"

"I want you to look at something for me." Detective Caulfield pulled out her phone and swiped through the photos.

Just as the detective was distracted, something over her shoulder caught Kate's attention. She watched as someone who looked just like her, but in very different clothes, walked across the cafe and sat down. As Kate blinked, the other woman suddenly disappeared.

Kate frowned in confusion, but found her attention pulled away as Detective Caulfield sighed.

"What?" asked Kate as she finally processed the detective's last statement. "Why?"

"Just trust me."

"Trust is earned."

Detective Caulfield finally looked up from her phone. She sighed once more as she looked at Kate across the table. Kate's heart ached at the sight of her biting down on her lip to stop it from trembling. Detective Caulfield hesitated for a moment before she rubbed a watery eye, turned her phone around, and offered it to Kate.

"So give me the chance to earn your trust. This is Rowan."

Kate looked at the photo the detective had selected. It showed Detective Caulfield with her arm around another woman who looked exactly like Kate.

Hunter was standing on the sidewalk across the street from the Broadway Coffee House. To the other pedestrians, he was sure he looked like he was waiting for someone as he leaned against the wall, one leg crossed in front of the other and his hands in his pockets. He was dressed in jeans and a dark T-shirt with a baseball cap to complete the look of feigned casualness.

Even if someone gave him a second look, his nondescript clothing would make it difficult for anyone to provide much of a description of him. If he needed to, Hunter could disappear in plain sight. It was a skill he had spent decades perfecting. He often believed that it was one of the main reasons he had managed to survive as long as he had. Shifters who did not develop such skills tended not to live too long.

He had also long since learned to school his face into the neutral, bland expression he was currently adopting. It would take a keen observer to notice the tension in his body and the tightness in his jaw. It would take an even keener observer to notice that his gaze never left the window of the cafe that he watched, waiting patiently.

He had followed his new partner, Detective Caulfield, from the precinct down to the coffee house. Something about her reaction to the photos of the blade used to kill Detective Rowan Ashley had raised a red flag. As much as Caulfield had denied any knowledge of the markings, he had seen the sudden change in her demeanor when he had asked her whether she knew the meaning of the insignia. She had shuffled slightly, avoided eye contact, and tugged on her ear.

The signs were subtle, so Hunter doubted that Captain Montoya had noticed, but Caulfield's behavior had concerned him. He had assumed that someone close to Ashley had been feeding personal information to the forces that had conspired to eliminate the young Faerie princess. Although beyond either of his current job descriptions, he was genuinely curious as to whom that was, and his new partner had, unfortunately, been at the top of his list of suspects since he took over the case.

He had not shared this suspicion with Captain Montoya or anyone else in the Department. Not that he was actually planning on doing anything other than satisfying his own curiosity, but he didn't want to besmirch someone's good name unnecessarily. He also didn't want to reveal that he too knew the meaning of the insignia on the blade used to kill Ashley.

Hunter watched Caulfield as she sat down across from another woman inside the cafe. His face showed a flicker of confusion for an instant as he recognized the woman, before he once again schooled his expression into neutrality. The woman had the same slim build, alabaster skin, dark brown hair, emerald eyes, and strong jawline as Caulfield's former partner.

It occurred to Hunter that maybe Caulfield was holding back more than just the fact that she knew who had attempted to kill Ashley. Maybe she was also holding back that Ashley had somehow survived the attack. He was sure that it would be news to many people that Ashley could still be alive.

If anyone would want to fake her death, it would be the rebels. Only those who wanted to use her as a pawn to restart the civil war between Prince Regent Cornelius and Queen Titania's heirs would benefit from Detective Ashley being shielded from her great-uncle.

Hunter reached up to remove his cap and riffle his hand through his hair. As he did so, his shirt sleeve pulled up, revealing the triskelion tattoo on his inner bicep for a brief moment.

He was glad that he owed no fealty to the Faerie Orders. They seemed to spend more time fighting one another than they did anything else. That benefited him, though. Hunter was a shifter who made his living as a mercenary, so the more conflict that existed between the Faeries, the more he got paid.

He took a deep breath as he reminded himself that he needed to keep things as simple as that, as black and white as that. As much as his inquisitive nature was screaming at him to investigate whatever was brewing here, he did not want to become embroiled in this mess. But for some reason, he couldn't help himself. He needed to understand who the woman with Detective Caulfield was, and if it was Detective Ashley. He needed to know who had helped her survive the attack that he'd been sure had claimed her life.

Hunter watched as Caulfield slipped her phone back into her pocket. Both women picked up their coffee cups, stood up, and left the cafe through the front door. Hunter continued to watch as they walked down the sidewalk, heading toward a nearby park. He was too far away to hear what they were talking about, but he could see that his new partner was doing the majority of the talking.

He followed the two women, keeping his distance, staying in the shadows.

Kate and Eddie walked across a park near the Broadway Coffee House. Cal Anderson Park was a large, wide-open space bordered by trees. Eddie had fallen silent not long after they entered. There was more that she wanted to say, but she had sensed that Kate needed time to process what she had told her about Rowan. She got the feeling that if she told Kate everything she needed to hear in one go, Kate would shut down, and that was something she wanted to avoid as much as possible.

They walked past the sports field and the park's shelter house. Eddie did not like the silence stretching between them. As much as she knew that Kate needed it, it was difficult for her to keep quiet. She could not help fiddling with the takeaway coffee cup in her hand to keep herself occupied. She wished she hadn't finished her coffee so quickly. Kate was still sipping from her cup. Eddie hoped it was helping to reassure her.

As the two women walked past the park's fountain, texture pool, and reflecting pool, Eddie noticed a bench and gestured for Kate to take a seat, then sat beside her.

"Do you ever have those moments when you wonder how your life turned out like this?" asked Kate.

"I take it that finding out you possibly had a twin sister wasn't part of the plan?" Eddie shifted to face her, placing an arm along the top of the bench behind Kate's back.

"Leaving New York and moving here," said Kate as she looked away. "Turning down a job offer from Columbia. None of that was part of the plan. In fact, it's all so far away from the path I thought my life was going to take that I don't even know how to find my way back. I don't know that I would want to, even if I could."

Eddie hesitated for a moment. She had been so taken with finding Kate here in Seattle that she had not stopped, even for a second, to ask what had brought this woman into her life. She had been so relieved that she had a second chance to make up for her past mistakes, she hadn't asked any questions of Kate, hadn't taken the time to get to know this woman and find out just how similar she was to her sister.

"So, what makes a wealthy, successful, well-educated woman leave her job and move all the way across the country? What was it that got you so far from where you planned to be?" Eddie drew small, comforting circles on Kate's shoulder with the hand she had draped along the bench.

Kate frowned at the familiar gesture. She inched slowly away from Eddie, twisting to face her. Eddie's hand dropped back to the bench.

"Loss of a loved one does strange things to people," said Kate softly.

"But you didn't know Rowan—did her death really impact you that much?"

"I wasn't talking about Rowan."

Eddie frowned, but before she could ask Kate who she was referring to, a large animal resembling a fox landed heavily in front of the bench. It was far larger than any fox Eddie had ever seen, closer in size to a large wolf. Also unlike a normal fox, it had three tails.

It opened its mouth, showing sharp teeth. It snarled at the two women sitting frozen in disbelief—then lunged suddenly toward them.

CHAPTER THREE

Kate instinctively threw her half-empty coffee cup at the fox's face as it lunged toward the bench. The creature landed even closer to the two women, blinking in surprise before it shook its head, clearing the hot liquid from its eyes. Kate saw several sharp teeth and felt its hot breath on her face as it snarled at them. It smelled more like mint than the smell of decaying meat she had been expecting.

Detective Caulfield grabbed her and pulled her over the back of the bench. Kate landed heavily on the ground, looking up to see the detective crouched down beside her, watching the fox pace from side to side, snapping its jaws. Kate pulled herself up into a crouch, mirroring Detective Caulfield's position.

"What exactly is a bench supposed to do against that?" she asked.

"Is this how you respond when something is trying to attack you?" Detective Caulfield turned to look at Kate, then reached out to squeeze her hand.

"I guess so," said Kate. "It's never exactly happened before."

The fox snarled again. Both women turned toward the sound. Suddenly, the fox stilled. Its muscles tensed before it vaulted the bench, landing behind them.

Detective Caulfield reached for her service weapon, quickly removing it from the holster on her hip.

"*Now* you go for the gun?" asked Kate.

"I couldn't exactly shoot it through the bench, could I?"

She raised her weapon to aim at the fox. It stilled again, its muscles tense as a loaded spring. Kate closed her eyes, anticipating that within moments, the fox would have either herself or the detective in its jaws.

Instead of pain or screams, she heard a heavy thud. She looked up to see that a wolf, even larger than the fox, had barreled into its side, knocking it away from the two cowering women. Both animals were now tangled in a heap several feet away.

Detective Caulfield scrambled to her feet and pulled Kate up beside her. She positioned herself between Kate and the two large animals, pointing her weapon toward them as they snapped and clawed at one another.

Suddenly, the fox lunged at the wolf, knocking it to the ground. The fox turned instantly and advanced on the two women again. Eddie squeezed the trigger on her service weapon just as the wolf slammed into the fox's back.

With the change in the fox's position, the bullet grazed its right shoulder before it plowed into the ground. The fox let out a loud howl before it turned and fled. The wolf turned to chase it, leaving the women standing next to the bench.

"If being attacked by huge foxes and wolves is par for the course in Seattle," said Kate, "I may want to reconsider my decision to move here."

Detective Caulfield holstered her weapon before she wrapped an arm around Kate. "I'm sure there's a completely reasonable explanation. Like, maybe the circus is in town."

"Seriously? The circus?" asked Kate incredulously.

"What's wrong with the circus?"

"Well, the only thing more terrifying than the fox and wolf we just encountered would be if we were to be attacked by clowns," said Kate. "And now I can't stop thinking about being attacked by clowns."

"Don't worry," said Detective Caulfield as she pulled Kate closer. "I'll protect you from any stray clowns we come across."

Agatha was sitting in Ainsley's office at the University of Washington again when Ainsley's phone vibrated with an incoming message. Ainsley frowned in concern as she read it.

"Is everything okay?" asked Agatha.

Instead of responding, Ainsley switched on the TV behind her desk to a local news broadcast.

Both women watched as the news reporter said, "Just recapping our earlier story: two women escaped injury after being attacked by two large animals in Capitol Hill's Pike/Pine Corridor. The animals are believed to have escaped from a truck headed to the Woodland Park Zoo. Police officers have assured us there is no ongoing risk to the public from the animals."

Ainsley muted the TV and turned back to Agatha. "One of the women involved was Kate Matthews."

Agatha inhaled sharply. "So, that means that Kate was just attacked?"

"Yes, it does," said Ainsley, twisting the ring on her middle finger.

"And I'm assuming the two large animals that escaped from the zoo are code for something Fae-related? That or two shape-shifters?"

"Yes," said Ainsley as she leaned back in her chair. "Which means we have a very serious problem, as we appear to have one more shifter who appears hell-bent on interfering in our plans."

Kate opened the door to her apartment, ushering Detective Caulfield inside and closing the door behind them. She only wished it would be that easy to shut out the events of the day.

The plush couch softened Kate's impact as she flopped herself down. The detective was still hovering in the doorway. Noticing Kate's gaze on her, she asked, "Are you sure you're okay?"

"I'm feeling as okay as I can be in the situation."

"I suppose that's fair."

"You can come over here and sit down if you want to," suggested Kate.

Detective Caulfield bit her lip, blushed, and looked down coyly before she walked over and joined Kate on the couch. "It looks different in here."

Kate frowned. "You've been here before?"

"You don't know?" The detective glanced sideways at Kate, then turned to face her fully.

"Know what?" asked Kate.

"This is Rowan's old apartment."

Kate narrowed her eyes and tilted her head. "Wait, what?"

"I'm sorry. I thought you knew."

"Could my life get any weirder?"

"Um," said the detective, "I'm not sure I know how to answer that."

"Don't worry, it was a rhetorical question," said Kate. "I mean, who else would move to the other side of the country and rent the apartment previously occupied by the dead twin sister she never knew about?"

"Rhetorical again?"

"I wasn't expecting an answer, but if you can, please go ahead." Realizing that the detective would not fill the silence, Kate continued, "Okay, then. Moving on. Of course the apartment looks different. Just because we look the same doesn't mean we are the same."

"I know that. Or at least, I do in theory," said Detective Caulfield. "I guess part of me was expecting this place to look exactly as it did when I was last here."

"When was that?"

"Now that I think about it, I'm not sure. I guess it's one of those things I did so often, I can't quite remember when the last time was."

"Sometimes that happens. Like with something you do one last time without even knowing it's the last time."

"Exactly," said Detective Caulfield.

It was something that Kate had wondered about so many times since her wife's death. She had wondered when their last kiss had been, the last time she had said she loved Alex, and the last time they had just been happy and content with one another. She assumed it had been months before Alex's death, maybe even as early as the alumni drinks at Columbia. Their relationship had been strained in the months since then, but she had always been unable to pinpoint when that last moment was, and what had transpired between them.

Kate blinked as she reorientated herself. She shook her head slightly to dispel the thoughts of Alex. "You said it looked different in here. What was different?"

"The furniture was more like the mix of IKEA flat-pack stuff and mismatched hand-me-downs you'd expect to see in someone's first apartment," said the detective, smiling warmly for a second. It looked to Kate like she was also lost for a moment in memories of another. "She also had two nice black-and-white prints," Detective Caulfield went on. "She had a thing for New York landmarks. Don't ask me why."

"New York?" Kate was suddenly filled with a sense of yearning. She had not realized how much she'd wanted to have something in common with this identical-looking stranger until that moment. But it was more than just New York that they had in common; they also had Seattle.

"Does that mean something to you?" asked Detective Caulfield.

As Kate opened her mouth to answer, the detective's phone vibrated. She smiled before she looked down to read the message. After a moment, she looked back up at Kate with an apologetic look.

"I guess I'll have to tell you about New York some other time, then," said Kate.

"Very perceptive again," said Detective Caulfield. "I'd like that, though."

Hunter stood looking at the bench where his partner and the woman calling herself Katherine Matthews had been attacked earlier that day. The two women had long since left. The area around the bench was now surrounded by yellow crime scene tape.

The uniformed officers standing just inside the tape kept the handful of onlookers a decent distance away. Light from several portable floodlights illuminated the area. Hunter watched as crime scene investigation technicians combed for any forensic evidence.

He grimaced slightly as he rotated and rubbed his right shoulder. One of the first lessons he had learned since he joined the police force was to always keep clear of the technicians while they were working. Once they had scoured for clues, he could start putting those clues together, or at least pretending to. He could make his oblivious human superiors believe he was spinning his wheels for months, trying to figure out where the animals had come from and why they had attacked. Humans were by far the least observant creatures that inhabited the mortal realms. They would never know that he knew exactly what had happened—or at least half of it.

"Sore shoulder?" asked Captain Montoya as he walked over and stood beside Hunter.

"Huh?" asked Hunter, confused for a moment. "Oh, yes. I think I overworked it at the gym earlier today."

"Just try to take it easy, then."

"Will do, boss."

"What can you tell me?" asked the captain.

"The two witnesses, Detective Caulfield and a"—Hunter looked down at his notes, feigning ignorance—"Katherine Matthews, reported being attacked by a large fox. They mentioned that there was also a large wolf. However, this wolf appeared to intervene to scare the fox away."

"And the press is running with the story about it being escaped animals from the zoo?"

"Yes, it seems so."

"That's good. Do we have any other explanation as to how a wolf and a fox appeared in a park in the middle of the city?" asked Captain Montoya.

"Unfortunately, not yet," said Hunter. "However the two animals got here, they appear to have now disappeared without a trace."

"Anything else I need to know?"

"There is one thing," said Hunter. He signaled to a crime scene technician, who started to walk toward them. "About five yards from where Detective Caulfield was attacked, we found a knife. Normally, I would assume that this was just a coincidence, because animals tend not to carry weapons. But you should take a look."

The technician handed Hunter a translucent plastic tube marked *EVIDENCE*. Hunter held it out to Captain Montoya. The knife inside the tube was a double-edged blade about ten inches in length. The blade lacked any ridgelines and was flat. The handle had a triskelion within a nonagon etched into it.

Captain Montoya frowned. Hunter assumed that he recognized the blade as identical to the one used to kill Detective Rowan Ashley.

Kate was curled up on the couch, staring off into space as she hugged a pillow to her chest.

She was a little relieved that Detective Caulfield had left. While she did not want to be alone with her thoughts tonight, she needed more than just company. She was sure the detective was a pleasant conversationalist, but an evening of light chit-chat would be Kate's definition of torture, particularly at a time like this.

She had always needed more from her interactions; she needed a meaningful connection. She wanted to get to know the people around her deeply, and she wanted those people to know her deeply in return. She wanted to know their passions, desires, and motives, and she wanted them to know hers. But she knew from experience that getting to know someone like that was an exhausting process, and after the day she'd had, Kate did not have the energy for that.

She was also not sure whether Detective Caulfield would even want to be that open with her. She had sensed that the detective was not telling her the whole truth about Rowan and her family. There had been something in the other woman's tone of voice that screamed that she was hiding something monumental.

Maybe Kate was misjudging her. Maybe she was being paranoid and letting her trust issues get the better of her. But she was not usually wrong, and someone who kept monumental things from her would probably be reluctant to be as open as Kate wanted.

She knew that she was asking a lot of someone she had just met. But she had very high, if not unrealistic, expectations. She didn't mean to, but sometimes she couldn't help but impose these expectations on those around her.

Alex had struggled with that when Kate had first met her. In time, though, she understood. And once she understood, she supported Kate unconditionally. Kate had always loved that about her.

Kate was the kind of person who was rarely satisfied with her achievements; she did not take compliments well, and she did not believe the praise that came her way. Alex had always made sure that Kate stopped, even if just for a moment, to celebrate her successes. Alex could always get through to her when she was beating herself up for falling short. Alex was the one who had taught her that she should not compare herself to others.

Kate's friends, colleagues, and family did not understand just how much she had lost when Alex had died. She did not just lose her wife. She did not just lose the woman that she loved and that she had planned on building a family and a home with. She had lost one of the few people in this world who understood her, contradictions and all. She had lost her greatest supporter. The person who made her feel safe. The one she could always rely on and the one who was always there. Even if things had been complicated between them, Kate had lost her home.

The ringing of her phone broke her concentration. Kate blinked away the tears developing in her troubled and melancholy mood. She saw the name *Greg Spinda* on her phone's display.

"Hey, you," Kate answered.

"So, you do have a working phone," joked Greg. "I was almost beginning to take it personally that you hadn't called me back yet."

"Yes, sorry. The move has kept me busy."

"I figured," said Greg. "I heard that you at least returned Ainsley's call."

"Yes, I have plans to meet her in a couple of days to discuss a role at the University of Washington."

"Its Politics and International Studies Program isn't the most highly rated of the universities that offered you a position, but U.W. receives a lot of research funding, and there is a lot of opportunity for growth. It will probably provide opportunities that you wouldn't necessarily get at another university."

"So, you approve?" asked Kate cautiously.

"You don't need my approval," said Greg.

"But if I was asking for it?"

"It wouldn't have been what I would have recommended for you if you had asked six months ago."

"But it isn't six months ago," said Kate.

"No, it's not," said Greg. "Things have changed. You have changed, and so have your priorities. This will be good for you."

"Thanks."

Kate paused as she searched for the words to convey her appreciation. Before she could say anything further, she heard a knock on the door.

"Sorry, I have to go. Someone just knocked. How about I call you in a couple of days?"

"That's fine," said Greg. "I'll speak to you then."

Kate hung up, dropped her phone on the coffee table, and unfolded herself from the couch with a groan. There was another knock on the door.

"Someone needs to learn to hold their horses," she mumbled at the third knock. Steeling herself for a moment with her hand on the door handle, she fixed a smile on her face and opened the door. When she saw Erin standing on the other side, her smile widened instantly.

"Hey, honey," he said warmly.

"Hi, chicken. Come in." Kate took a step back and gestured for Erin to step inside. "To what do I owe this surprise?" she asked as she closed the door behind him.

"I was just on my way home and I thought I'd stop by. It's part of this whole grieving together thing."

"Well, I'm always happy for you to stop by like this."

"Good. I'm glad." Erin wrapped her in a hug. Kate sagged into his arms. "Are you okay?" he asked after several moments.

"What makes you think I'm not okay?" asked Kate, her voice slightly muffled as her head was pressed against Erin's shoulder.

"Hmmm, maybe because I know you," he said.

"Just a really weird day." Kate pulled away and sat down on the couch.

"Weird how?" asked Erin as he joined her.

"The short version? Well, I met with that cop just to hear her out. She believes I had a twin sister called Rowan. Well, that or I have a mysterious, magical doppelganger, but as we live in reality and not Narnia, I'm going with the first option. Then we got attacked by a giant fox, only to be saved by a wolf."

"That's...a lot to take in," said Erin slowly.

"Yes, well, if that wasn't enough," said Kate, "it turns out that this apartment belonged to my mysterious dead twin sister."

"Well, you've had quite the day."

"Thanks for the understatement of the century. I've kind of reached the point where I think I've shut down, at least temporarily."

"In the circumstances, I'm sure that's to be expected." Erin wrapped an arm around Kate's shoulders.

"Just promise me that we can go out for brunch and mimosas this weekend," said Kate as she snuggled into his chest.

"Your wish is my command." Erin dropped a kiss onto Kate's hair and rested his head on hers.

Nolan was sitting at his desk, reading through a document and making handwritten notations, when Eddie walked in. She dropped into the chair in front of his desk and drummed her fingers nervously against the armrest as she waited for Nolan to finish what he was doing.

"Are you going to say anything?" she asked.

"Are you okay?" asked Nolan.

"No, I'm not okay. Kate and I were just attacked by a large fox, only to be saved by a large wolf."

"But neither of you was injured?"

"No," said Eddie, "but thanks for the concern."

"There's no need for the sarcasm," said Nolan. "If it hadn't been for the intervention of that wolf, which I'm assuming you believe is some form of Fae, I'm sure things could have been a lot worse."

"I know." Eddie paused. "I was thinking about what you said."

"About?"

"About not being able to find a motive for a shape-shifter killing Rowan. But this attack on Kate suggests that the person responsible wants to kill both of Queen Titania's children."

"I take it you believe that Prince Cornelius was responsible?"

"Well, him or someone who wanted to gain favor with him. Who else has something to gain from killing the two legitimate heirs to the throne?"

"You may be right," said Nolan.

"So that means we should tell Kate everything, doesn't it?" asked Eddie. "About who she is? Who her parents are? Everything?"

The muscles in Nolan's face tightened. "No, I don't think so."

"What? Why not?" asked Eddie.

"All you have is a theory," said Nolan. "Don't you want something more concrete before you turn her entire world upside down? Do you want to be the one to tell her that everything she has ever known to be true is a lie and that she literally doesn't know who she is?"

"Not telling Rowan is what got her killed. I will not make the same mistake again," said Eddie firmly.

"And telling Katherine will get *her* killed."

"You don't know that."

Nolan steepled his fingers together slowly as he observed her. "No, but I know how she will feel if you tell her. Please trust me when I say that she will be far safer if we keep her completely in the dark. You will not tell her anything."

Eddie fidgeted, uncomfortable with the intensity of his gaze. Eventually, to break the silence, she asked, "What?"

"I'm just wondering when you will admit what this is really about."

"What is that supposed to mean?"

"You were in love with Rowan," said Nolan, sounding very matter-of-fact. "You never told her because you knew that she would never feel that way about you. But then she died, and now you're wondering whether Katherine is your second chance. You can't help but think that maybe she will love you the way you wanted Rowan to love you. You don't want to tell her to save her. You want to tell her because you want a reason to be close to her. You want a reason for her to depend on you." He leaned back in his chair. "Am I wrong?"

Eddie looked away from Nolan as she crossed her arms defensively in front of her. When her phone vibrated, she was saved from answering his troubling question. She looked at the screen to buy herself some more time to form a response or distraction. She had received a text message from Detective Lowell, including a picture of a blade and a short explanation that it had been found in the park near the bench where she was attacked. The blade was identical to the one found near Rowan's body.

"I don't think we have a choice anymore. We need to tell Kate," said Eddie.

"Why?" asked Nolan. "What can have possibly changed in the last few minutes?"

"There is evidence linking Rowan's death with today's attack on Kate." Eddie jutted out her chin. "That means that the shape-shifter that was paid to kill Rowan is now trying to kill her sister. That is something that Kate needs to know, and I'm going to tell her."

CHAPTER FOUR

After she left Nolan's Office, Eddie walked toward Pier 52, where the Washington State ferries departed regularly on their way to Bainbridge Island and Bremerton.

On many occasions when she was growing up in Seattle, Eddie had been drawn to the Pier when she was feeling overwhelmed and in need of clarity. She had found it while watching the ferries carry people around Puget Sound. They always had a way of relaxing her, and after her day so far, she was definitely in need of relaxation and clarity more than anything right now.

Eddie did not want to admit that there was some truth to what Nolan had said. Actually, a *lot* of truth.

Eddie had loved Rowan. Had always thought she was a proverbial ray of sunshine. She'd had this unique way of making Eddie feel warm simply by walking into the room. A smile from Rowan was enough to make even Eddie's worst day better.

But she had never told Rowan how she felt. She had known that Rowan would never feel the same way, and thought it was better to keep Rowan in her life in some way, even if it was not how she wanted. It was one of the reasons Eddie felt so responsible for her death. She had always thought she would do anything for Rowan, but when it really mattered, she hadn't been there for her. She did not want to make the same mistake with Kate.

Nolan was wrong, though. She did want to be close to Kate and protect her. But it was not because she felt like Kate was the twin that would love her the way she wanted. Eddie barely even knew Kate, so how could she feel like that was even a possibility?

No, Eddie wanted to protect Kate because she had not protected Rowan. She got the feeling that Kate's life had not been easy, and that the people in her life had damaged her. Eddie wanted to shield her from having to experience any more pain or loss or heartache.

Eddie also hoped, perhaps naively, that telling Kate the truth about who she was and where she came from would make up for the pain she had suffered. That telling her why her parents gave her up for adoption would help her understand that there were people who had loved her so much that they'd been willing to do anything they could to give her a better life. Eddie hoped that the truth could help heal the wounds that had clearly been left on Kate's heart, and bring her even the smallest amount of peace and solace. She appeared to need it desperately.

Eddie spent several more moments taking deep breaths of the fresh-smelling Elliott Bay air to clear her head before she pulled out her phone. She scrolled to Kate's number that she had placed in her contacts only hours earlier. She hesitated with her thumb raised over the screen. With another deep breath, Eddie dialed Kate's number and raised her phone to her ear.

"Hello, this is Kate."

"Hi, Kate, it's Detective Caulfield. How are you?"

"About the same as I was when you saw me last, Detective."

"Well, I suppose that's positive."

"Yes, it is," said Kate. "Was there a reason for your call?"

"Yes. Sorry. I was hoping you would be free to meet me."

"When?"

"Is now okay?" asked Eddie tentatively.

"Now is fine. Where would you like to meet?"

"I'm downtown at the moment. Did you want to meet at the north end of Waterfront Park near the fountain?"

"That sounds fine," said Kate. "I'll see you soon."

Hunter was sitting in his car a couple of doors down from the house that belonged to the woman calling herself Katherine Matthews, who had been with Detective Caulfield in the park earlier. Hunter had made sure he got the woman's address from the officer who took her statement after the incident. He needed to get to the bottom of who this woman was. He was sure that he would have at least one former employer on his doorstep demanding answers if he didn't do everything he could to get them.

If this woman was Detective Ashley, that would raise a lot of questions. He assumed that, if anyone had saved Ashley, it would be someone opposed to Prince Cornelius being on the throne. Only the rebels would have a reason to go to such lengths to protect Ashley. He knew from experience that such people would do anything to protect the person who gave their cause legitimacy.

In saying that, he could think of a million better ways to fake a death than renting the exact apartment she had previously lived in under a different name. She definitely would not win points for deceptiveness.

If his partner knew Detective Ashley had not been killed, it meant that Detective Caulfield was more closely aligned with the rebels than Hunter had initially surmised. He could use that to his advantage, though. He was always adept at playing the angles he needed, and it may be handy to have some leverage over Caulfield, just in case he needed it one day. Hunter would need to keep an eye on his partner and this woman.

Whether or not she was Detective Ashley, Hunter had been surprised when he came face to face with her at the park. There were some subtle differences, but the woman looked uncannily similar to the pictures he had seen of Ashley. It had surprised him that none of the officers at the scene had mistaken the woman for their former colleague. Though maybe that was to be expected. Over the centuries, Hunter had come to realize that humans tended to be far less observant than they believed themselves to be. He did not judge them for this, though, as it had always worked to his advantage. He had always found it easier to carry out his work when humans were too oblivious to ask questions or even remember the strangers that had been loitering around their homes.

Hunter rubbed two fingers against his temple as he imagined the can of worms that Katherine's presence in Seattle was threatening to open. But right now, it looked like whoever she was, she was going somewhere. Hunter watched the woman walk down her front steps and get into her car, then pull away from the curb. He turned on his car and followed.

It did not take Eddie long to walk along Seattle's waterfront to reach the park located between Pier 57 and Pier 59. Lamps, benches, and high, curving railings lined the park. It also had two viewing platforms from which there were excellent views of the city skyline, the waterfront, the ships in drydock, container cranes, the West Seattle Bridge, Magnolia Bluff, Blake Island, Bainbridge, and, on a clear day, the Olympic Mountains.

Eddie paused as she reached the coin-operated telescopes that dotted the sidewalk. She sighed, remembering the hours she had spent using those telescopes to look out across the Sound at places that seemed, at least then, to be so far away and filled with such mystery. On every occasion, she had promised herself that not only would she see all of those places up close, but she would also see every corner of the world. Unfortunately, that was before Nolan had sat her down when she was fifteen and explained that he had a very different plan for her life. Since that moment, she had never wanted to tempt herself with what might have been. Eddie gave the telescopes one last wistful look before continuing.

The north end of the park, where Eddie had suggested that Kate meet her, was close to the Seattle Aquarium. Scattered around it were benches, picnic tables, trees in planters, and the Waterfront Fountain, made of cast and welded bronze shaped in cubical structures.

As Eddie reached the fountain, she noticed Kate walking down the stairs that ran beside it. She waved, struggling to moderate her smile as Kate reached her. Logically, she knew that Kate and Rowan were different people. But she still seemed to have the same instinctual reaction to seeing Kate as she always had when she'd seen Rowan.

"Hi, Detective," said Kate.

"Ms. Matthews," said Eddie. "Thanks for coming."

"It sounded important," said Kate. "Plus, I kind of needed an excuse to get out of the house."

"Is everything okay?"

"Yes, it's fine. It's just been a weird day, and there's a lot going on in my head."

"Do you want to talk about it?" Eddie asked.

"No, it's okay. I'm not even sure I could right now, even if I wanted to," said Kate. "I'm not sure I have the words to explain it."

"Well, I'm here if you ever feel like talking when you've got everything sorted out inside," said Eddie.

"I'll keep that in mind," said Kate. "What did you want to talk about?"

Eddie rested a hand on the small of Kate's back and slowly guided her away from the fountain. "There are a few things I feel like I need to tell you. We didn't get the chance to talk about it earlier, but I wanted to start with the night that Rowan died."

Kate frowned. "What do you mean?"

Eddie opened her mouth, but the words died on her tongue as something heavy crashed into her back, knocking her down. She landed heavily, a burning pain stinging her hands and knees.

Eddie turned her head sharply as she heard Kate scream behind her, seeing Kate pressed against the concrete wall that divided the stairs from the fountain. In front of her stood a large fox. It looked identical to the one that had attacked them earlier.

Eddie turned over quickly, sitting on the ground with her legs outstretched to access the holstered service weapon on her hip. She reached for it as the fox advanced on Kate.

Eddie raised her weapon. The fox lunged toward Kate, who leapt out of the way of its sharp, snarling jaws. As she plunged into the fountain, the fox was left snapping at thin air.

Eddie pulled the trigger before the fox could follow Kate. The bullet hit the concrete wall just behind the fox's head. Distracted, it turned toward Eddie.

A flutter of movement behind it caught Eddie's attention. She watched Kate scramble out of the far side of the fountain, then turned back to the fox, panicking when she realized it had fixed its gaze on her and was advancing toward her. Eddie chastised herself for the momentary lapse in judgment. Sensing the danger she was in, she scrambled backward.

Before she could get too far away, she ran into something hard. She flinched as someone reached down to grab her and pull her to her feet. Eddie suddenly found herself face to face with a bedraggled, but somehow still stunning, Kate, who moved them away from the fox.

"Why didn't you run?" asked Eddie.

"You put yourself in danger to help me," said Kate as she pulled Eddie backward. "Like I wasn't going to do the same."

"Yes, well, you're so much more important than I am," said Eddie without thinking, her eyes still locked on Kate's face.

Kate snapped her gaze away from the fox and looked at Eddie. Her brow furrowed and her eyes narrowed. "Why would you say that?"

At that moment, they were so close Eddie could feel every part of her body that was pressed against Kate, could feel Kate's warm breath against her cheek. She flushed at the sensation before she realized that not only had they stopped moving backward, but they had both turned their attention away from the approaching fox.

Panicked, Eddie quickly turned back toward it, only to find it rapidly closing the gap between them.

The fox lunged. Eddie shoved Kate behind her, her warmth quickly disappearing. Confused and distracted, Eddie took one more step back, only to trip over Kate lying sprawled and slightly dazed beneath her. She must have fallen after Eddie shoved her backward. Unable to find her balance again, Eddie fell, and was only just able to shift her body weight in time to avoid landing on top of Kate.

The fox soared over the top of them and landed a few feet away. It scrambled to turn around, losing traction for a moment before it faced where Eddie and Kate were still on the ground. Eddie hauled herself up, pulling Kate up beside her in a similar position. The fox inched closer and snarled at them.

Eddie wrapped her arm around Kate and guided the other woman's head onto her shoulder. She could tell that Kate must still be a little dazed by how easily she acquiesced. Eddie tried to inch them back, but struggled to make much ground. The fox drew closer and closer until Eddie could feel its hot breath on her face.

She froze. She did not know what to do. In that moment, she felt like history was repeating itself. She hadn't saved Rowan. Now, she couldn't save Kate. She had let down her partner. She had let down her partner's sister.

"I'm so sorry," Eddie whispered as she pressed a light kiss into Kate's hair. "I'm so, so sorry. I wish I could've been better for you. I wish I could've saved you. Both of you."

Snarling and snapping shifted Eddie's attention back to the imminent danger. For a second, she wished the fox would just get it over with instead of playing with them and drawing out their fear. As if sensing her thoughts, it tensed suddenly as it prepared to lunge again.

Something sailed over Eddie's head just before the fox leapt. Whatever it was crashed into the fox and knocked it backward. Eddie now found herself looking at the back of a large wolf. It looked like the one that had protected her and Kate earlier in the day. The wolf quickly turned its head back toward the two women. It looked like it nodded in acknowledgment, then turned back to face the fox. The wolf started to advance, slowly forcing the fox away from them.

Without warning, it lunged forward, snapping at the other animal. The fox appeared to realize that it was outmatched. It turned and fled. The wolf remained in place until it was out of sight. Only then did it turn back to observe Eddie and Kate, looking at Kate almost with concern.

"She's okay," said Eddie. "You are okay, aren't you, Kate?"

Hearing her name, Kate looked up at Eddie, then turned to the wolf. Her eyes went comically wide as she looked into its face.

"Um," she said. "I'm not sure how to answer that question. Are you sure that isn't going to hurt us?"

Eddie regarded the wolf silently. She did not know why its presence felt comforting and reassuring, but she knew it would not let anything befall them. Unsure how to convey that to Kate, she simply said, "No, it won't hurt us."

"Okay." Kate started to shiver.

Eddie assumed it was partially due to her still-wet clothes and partially due to the adrenaline leaving her system. "Come on." She pulled Kate to her feet. "Let's get you home."

Kate turned around and leaned against her front door. Eddie hesitated, squaring her shoulders and tugging on the sleeves of her jacket before she took the final few steps up to the porch. She closed some of the distance between them, then stopped, smoothing down her still-drying hair.

"So, here we are again." Kate watched Eddie shift her weight nervously from one foot to the other.

"Are you still as okay as you can be in the circumstances?" asked Eddie. She finally settled on leaning her hip against the white banister that lined the edge of the porch, still several steps away from where Kate was standing.

Kate smiled. "That, or experiencing a terrible case of déjà vu."

"I suppose that's fair," said Eddie. "It probably hasn't been the best welcome to the city that you could have had."

"You are definitely right about that."

"I hope you don't let it discourage you, though. I feel like this could be good for you."

"You do, huh?" asked Kate, raising an eyebrow.

"Yes," said Eddie. "Sorry. Was that out of line?"

"No," said Kate. "It's good to know."

"Okay, I should go," said Eddie slowly. She pushed herself off the banister and smiled before she walked to the edge of the porch, then hesitated and turned around to face Kate again. "Sorry, I just have one more question."

"Okay."

"Are you going to stay?"

Kate tilted her head in confusion. "Stay?"

"In Seattle," said Eddie.

"Ask me tomorrow," said Kate.

Hunter entered the darkened, partially renovated office. The room was no more than a skeleton comprised of steel beams and prefabricated concrete slabs, lit only by the lights of surrounding buildings.

Hunter was flanked by two guards wearing cheap but durable dark suits. They pushed him to his knees when they reached the middle of the room and remained standing at ease behind him. In front of Hunter was a black leather wingback chair that in the dim light could have easily been mistaken for a throne.

"Thank you for coming," said the chair's occupant in a clear baritone voice. Despite Hunter narrowing his gaze, the speaker remained obscured from his view due to the shadows.

"It didn't really seem like I had a choice," said Hunter.

"You didn't." The chair's occupant leaned forward, and his face was bathed in light.

The man was tall and handsome with short coal-black hair, sapphire eyes, and a straight nose. He appeared to be in his forties, but Hunter knew he was far older than that. He also knew that the man was a confident, charismatic, strong-willed ruler.

"You assured me that my great-niece had been killed," continued the man. "Imagine my surprise when I am informed that she may still be wandering the streets of Seattle. If you cannot even get that right, what is the point in me paying you?"

"I have always done everything you have paid me to do, Prince Cornelius," said Hunter.

"Clearly, you and I have very different definitions of the word 'killed,'" said Prince Cornelius.

"Rowan was placed in the ground two months ago," said Hunter. "I don't know who the woman currently in Seattle is, but I am sure she is a different person."

"If she isn't Rowan ..." Prince Cornelius paused in thought. "The only remaining explanation is that Catriona has indeed come to Seattle."

"Catriona? Really? How many missing Faerie princesses do you have?"

Prince Cornelius smirked briefly in what Hunter assumed was amusement at the question. "My niece, Titania, had twin girls before her death. Their names were Rowan and Catriona. After the death of Titania and her husband, the safety of the twins was entrusted to the rebellious factions, which had rallied behind them during the civil war that followed my brother's death."

"If you want me to take care of this Catriona like I did her sister, I want you to double my regular fee," said Hunter.

"Any reason why?"

"I encountered some complications when I ran into her last time. When there is a greater risk to me, I require greater compensation."

"That can be arranged," said Prince Cornelius. "Tell me, though, what is your sense of Catriona? Is she likely to share her sister's sentimentality?"

"I didn't have the best opportunity to get a sense of her," said Hunter. "But she does seem to have a darker energy than Rowan. Like she lacks Rowan's idealism, pure intentions, and conventional human morality."

"You mean she may be more open to rational persuasion?"

"Perhaps. But if you truly want to eliminate the chance of the rebels using her against you, get to her first. I am sure you can find ways to ..." Hunter paused as he searched for the most appropriate word. "*Persuade* her of the virtues of your cause."

"That can be arranged. Can't it, my dear?"

A woman behind Prince Cornelius took a step forward. Hunter had not noticed her, as she had been standing in a darkened corner of the room. For the first time, he saw the long blonde hair and captivating blue eyes of Ainsley Cooper, the Prince Regent's most trusted adviser.

Ainsley only smiled in response.

Episode Two: Birch

Starting over can be challenging, but also it can be a great opportunity to do things differently.
—Catherine Pulsifer

CHAPTER ONE

Nolan crinkled his nose in disgust as he looked around the alleyway, inching his way past the nondescript concrete lined with trash can after trash can. Most were overflowing with garbage, reeking of rotting food and vomit. He was so glad that he had managed to talk the mayor into greenlighting a series of alleyway renovations. Hopefully, this one was next on someone's list for a much-needed facelift.

He was silently contemplating how much extra he would need to pay his dry cleaner to erase every trace of the stench from his expensive bespoke suit when darkness filled the alleyway. Nolan smiled wryly as the inky black tendrils slowly materialized into a somewhat humanoid shape.

"How very cloak and dagger of you," he said.

"You wanted discretion," said the figure in a voice that sounded neither male nor female. "It wouldn't have been very discreet if I came up to your office, now, would it?"

"I suppose that's fair," said Nolan. "What isn't fair, though, is that you promised results and failed to deliver. I paid for you to kill Katherine Matthews, and yet for some reason, she is still breathing."

"She seems to have a knack for choosing the people around her well," said the figure. "They appear willing to die to protect her."

"Yes, well, I have to say that I am disappointed. You promised me that you could get the job done quickly and quietly," said Nolan. "Instead, we are fielding questions from concerned citizens about why we're letting wild animals roam the streets, attacking residents."

"There were unforeseen complications," said the figure. "I assumed that you would keep your associates from intervening to protect her."

"Just get it done," said Nolan. "Quickly and quietly. No more foxes, though. Keep it simple and discreet. I do not want to draw any more attention to this, and I definitely do not want any of it to be traced back to me."

"And if anyone else interferes?" asked the figure.

"If there are obstacles," said Nolan, "eliminate them as well."

"Even that protégé of yours? Detective Caulfield?"

"Yes," said Nolan. "Even her."

"As you wish," said the figure as it dissipated.

As soon as the last swirling black tendrils had disappeared, Nolan turned on his heel and exited the alley, leaving behind only the pungent, revolting garbage. He doubted that there was any amount he could actually pay his dry cleaner to truly get the stench out of his clothing. Maybe, instead, he could buy himself a new tailored suit to celebrate the death of the second-last person standing between him and his throne.

In the months following Alex's death, Kate had felt something drawing her back to Seattle. At first, she had thought it was simply a need to be near the people and places that reminded her of Alex. But she dismissed this theory when she was not filled with the same longing to return to the places across New York and New Haven where they had spent time together. Instead, if she was being honest with herself, she actually wanted to put as much distance between herself and those places as physically possible.

Kate had wondered if the longing she felt was less about Seattle and more about needing to be around people like Erin and his father, who understood her loss. She hated the suffocating feeling that the people from her and Alex's life in New York had left her with. First, they'd been concerned that she was not grieving enough. It didn't seem to matter that at that point Kate was numb to what was happening around her. She had done everything she needed to do on autopilot right up to Alex's funeral. Then she broke. She remembered sitting on the hard and uncomfortable wooden pew in the church, looking up at her wife's coffin, when a dam inside of her split open, and suddenly she was sobbing.

After that, people thought she was grieving too much. They would look at her strangely as she burst into tears when a song or a story or a memory reminded her of Alex. Kate had thought that was the worst she could feel until people started asking when she would take off her wedding and engagement rings. But in the next breath, the same people would ask her when she would start dating again, as if it were the most normal thing in the world. She had even had one so-called friend offer to set up a Tinder profile for her. The same friend had suggested she would get a lot of sympathy dates if she mentioned she was a widow.

New York had been filled with so many people who Kate and Alex had only known peripherally. These acquaintances had not necessarily known of Alex's death when it happened. Consequently, afterward, they would ask Kate when they saw her about how Alex was. Kate had given them honest responses for the first few times. If it had not been so heartbreakingly difficult, she would have almost found it funny how quickly those same acquaintances backed away from her like she would go to pieces in front of them. She learned after that that it was best to deflect.

But Kate hated that she was the one who needed to be sensitive to the feelings of others. It became abundantly clear after Alex's death that a lot of people in her life only cared and were sympathetic because they felt like they had to be. They were far more comfortable when Kate started saying she was fine and moving forward, even if it was not true. If she were to heal, she needed to get away from the superficial, suffocating feeling that New York filled her with.

Even so, it still did not explain why she had felt so drawn to Seattle. While it had been comforting, familiar, and reassuring to have Erin, it still felt like there was something more at work. Whatever it was, it did not abate, even after she moved to Seattle. Instead, it plagued her dreams, and on waking it filled her with a desire to visit places that she had visited with Alex.

It was what pulled her out of bed at five o'clock one morning, calling her toward Pike Place Market.

On her trips to Seattle with Alex, she had sometimes struggled with the market. It was too loud, too crowded, too busy, and too overstimulating for Kate to truly feel comfortable. Admittedly, that was probably one of the reasons why Alex loved it so much and always insisted they visit. Not that she had deliberately placed Kate in situations where she was uncomfortable. But she'd been the kind of person who thrived on being in those crowded environments. She fed off the energy of other people.

Kate felt like this was an opportunity for her to make new memories of the same places without Alex. She only hoped that Pike Place Market would be less crowded at six o'clock in the morning than all the other times she had been.

"Give me your wallet."

The voice broke through Kate's thoughts just as she passed an alley. She looked up in surprise. A middle-aged woman with grubby, matted brown hair stepped out in front of her. It was difficult for Kate to tell the other woman's skin tone under all the grime, grease, and dirt. She could not help but think that she expected the woman to smell worse, given the tattered, filthy rags of her clothing.

"Give me your wallet," the woman repeated. She pulled one of her hands from behind her back.

The action drew Kate's attention to the sharp blade glittering in her hand.

The woman took another step closer to her before Kate could react. She drew the blade back, preparing to thrust it forward. But before either of the women could move any further, a hand grabbed Kate's shirt and pulled her backward.

In an instant, her back was pressed against the wall of the alley. A tall, well-dressed, attractive man with curled dirty-blonde hair and dark blue eyes stepped between her and the other woman. She felt like she should recognize the man from somewhere, but her brain was moving too slowly to place him.

The other woman stepped quickly to the side to get around the man and reach Kate. But the man saw this. He reacted almost preternaturally quickly, pulling a service weapon from the holster on his belt.

"Stop." He aimed the gun at the woman. "Seattle Police Department."

Right, thought Kate dimly as her brain fought to overcome the sluggish panic that was drowning out everything else. His name was Detective Hunter Lowell. Detective Caulfield had introduced them after the fox attacked them at Cal Anderson Park.

The other woman, however, was not fazed by Hunter's weapon. Instead, she lunged in Kate's direction.

As she moved past him, Hunter grabbed the hand that was grasping the blade, using her forward momentum to slam her wrist against the wall of the alley. The women's momentum continued to carry her forward, and her head hit the wall. She staggered away from Hunter and Kate, clearly dazed. Hunter quickly plucked the blade from her grip, disarming her. Sensing she was beaten, the woman fled, surprisingly fast considering her condition.

Hunter watched her disappear around the far corner of the other end of the alley. Once they were alone, he turned to Kate and asked, "Are you okay?"

Eddie pulled her car to a stop just before she reached the yellow crime scene tape. Fortunately, it was still early, and the scene was some distance from Pike Place Market, so at least the Police Department should be able to keep the attempted mugging under wraps.

She had initially been surprised when Hunter had called her so early in the morning. But that surprise had quickly faded to sheer terror tinged with relief and disappointment. She had been terrified to hear that Kate had been attacked. She had then been simultaneously relieved that Hunter had been there to intervene, and disappointed that she had not been the one to save Kate. Eddie knew that was selfish, but she wanted to find reasons to be close to Kate. She had spent most of her time over the last couple of days thinking about her, replaying the moment where Kate had been in her arms, pressed against her. It had filled Eddie with such warmth, and left her with an intense, almost constant craving to be closer to Kate.

Sighing as she stepped away from her car, Eddie looked up to see Kate sitting beside Hunter on the back step of a waiting ambulance. At that moment, she looked small, pale, and fragile, slightly slumped forward with her arms crossed in front of her like she was trying to take up as little room as possible. Hunter's jacket draped over her shoulders only seemed to emphasize her vulnerability.

Eddie shoved her hands into the pockets of her jeans as she pushed down the rising desire to wrap Kate up in a hug and not let go.

"Are you okay?" she asked as she stopped in front of where Kate and Hunter were sitting.

"Yes," said Kate, without looking up from her shoes. She was trembling slightly. "Thanks to Detective Lowell."

Eddie felt Hunter watching her as she squatted down in front of Kate in an attempt to meet the other woman's gaze.

"I was just doing my job, Ms. Matthews." Hunter looked between the two women. "I'll give you two a moment." He stood and walked toward a crime scene technician who was examining the scene.

"I'm glad you're okay," said Eddie, placing a hand on Kate's knee.

"Why does this keep happening?" asked Kate.

"What?" Eddie rubbed a thumb against the skin of her knee.

"I mean, do I have a colossal 'kick me' sign on my back?" Kate looked up at Eddie, meeting her gaze for the first time since she had arrived. "After everything that's happened this year, I didn't think my life could get any worse."

Eddie looked down, away from Kate's gaze. She wished she could say something to reassure the other woman. But after the attacks, she knew there was more going on that Kate needed her protection from. Maybe that meant Nolan was right. That the most important thing was ensuring that she was close enough to Kate to protect her. But telling Kate would only drive a wedge between them.

Until she found the person responsible for the attacks on Rowan and Kate, there was nothing that she could say that would make things any better. Nolan was right: the truth would hurt Kate more than it would help her right now.

"I don't think I have an answer for you," said Eddie eventually. She stood up and moved to sit beside Kate.

"I didn't think that you would," said Kate, her eyes narrowing as she followed Eddie's movements.

"Right. Another rhetorical question." Eddie scratched her nose. "Well, if I knew the answer, I'd tell you."

"Right. Well, um ..." Kate stood up and took a few steps away from Eddie. "Is it okay if I go?"

"Oh," said Eddie, surprised at the sudden change in her tone. "Yes. Sure. I'll let you know if we need anything."

Kate nodded, her mouth drawn tight. She shrugged off Hunter's jacket and placed it down next to Eddie, then turned and walked away, leaving Eddie wondering what had caused the sudden shift in the other woman's behavior. She had lied to Kate, but Kate would not have noticed that. Kate had said she was perceptive, but surely not *that* perceptive.

"Detective?" asked Hunter, interrupting Eddie's thoughts.

"Yes." Eddie shook her head slightly to clear it. "Did you have something?"

"Yes." Hunter held up a transparent plastic tube marked *EVIDENCE*.

The knife inside the tube was familiar. A double-edged blade. A handle with a triskelion and a nonagon etched into it.

"Another one of these knives. Whatever is going on, this mugging was perpetrated by the same person, or group of people, who killed your partner."

Eddie sighed. "Okay."

"Now, I know you don't know me," said Hunter, "but we are more likely to get to the bottom of this if we work together."

"Yes," said Eddie. "I agree. I think that's the best way for us to protect Kate."

"So, partners?" asked Hunter.

"Partners," Eddie agreed.

Agatha was sitting at the small round table in the living and dining room of the Eastlake apartment she shared with Ainsley. The apartment, which was on the Lake Union waterfront, had several large windows with a north-westerly outlook over Lake Union and Gas Works Park. It even had a view of the nearby marina where Ainsley had a boat slip.

Agatha sighed as she watched Ainsley cross from one side of the room to the other. She had been pacing anxiously since they had received Hunter's phone call earlier that morning. Agatha had initially tried to get her to calm down by reassuring her that Kate was fine, but the other woman had not listened. Instead, she had crossed her arms in front of her chest and started pacing. Agatha was beginning to worry that Ainsley was wearing holes in their carpet when the front door swung open and Hunter burst into the room.

Ainsley turned sharply toward him. "She was attacked?"

"Yes," said Hunter. He sat down at the table beside Agatha. "It was lucky that I just happened to be in the area."

"I thought you were supposed to be following her?" asked Agatha as she got up and walked through to the kitchen.

"That was what he meant. Right, Hunter?" asked Ainsley.

"Yes," said Hunter as Agatha placed a cup on the kitchen bench.

"Life would be simpler if people just said what they meant." Agatha poured coffee into the cup and returned to the living room, placing it in front of Hunter.

He nodded in appreciation. "I'd prefer if people actually did what they said."

"I'd like that too." Agatha returned to her seat beside him.

Ainsley sighed loudly in frustration, stalking over to the table. "Can we focus, please?" She sat down with a huff.

"I believe the attacks are linked," said Hunter. "We now have evidence that whoever killed Rowan has now made three attempts on Kate's life."

"Whoever is behind them is clearly persistent," said Agatha.

Ainsley drummed her fingers against the table. "Yes, well, let's hope they don't keep trying until they're successful."

"There is one more thing," said Hunter slowly. "My new partner and Rowan's former partner is Detective Edana Caulfield. I believe she is a Faerie. Or, at the very least, a member of the Lesser Fae."

"You said her name was Edana?" Ainsley stopped drumming her fingers and stroked her chin slowly, deep in thought.

"Yes," said Hunter.

"If she is who I think she is, then she most definitely is a Faerie."

CHAPTER TWO

Kate smoothed down her dark green, knee-length dress as she waited nervously for Ainsley Cooper to arrive. They had agreed to meet at the Broadway Coffee House. At the time, Kate had thought the familiar surroundings would be comforting and help her feel a little more at ease. But she still felt like a fish out of water.

Kate had grown to accept that she was naturally quiet and a bit withdrawn at times. But she was far from comfortable with how shy and socially awkward she could be. She could not help but wish, as she had on many occasions, that she could live her life without ever needing to meet anyone face-to-face. She didn't understand why she lost all ability to be articulate and eloquent when meeting someone for the first time. It was like she was compelled to make the absolute worst first impression, especially when she happened to find the person even remotely attractive. Fortunately for Kate, Alex had found her blushing and stammering adorable when they were first dating, but few people had been so understanding.

Kate looked up as a woman approached. While the woman appeared to be smiling at her, Kate had fallen victim too often to the awkward occurrence of smiling at a stranger in public to find that they were looking at someone behind her. She fought the urge to look over her shoulder.

The slim, tall woman ran her fingers over her collar before making her way through the coffee house. She tucked a strand of wavy blonde hair behind her ear, a smile lighting up her heart-shaped face. She looked to be in her early thirties.

"Hi." She stopped beside Kate and reached out her hand. Her captivating blue eyes were filled with warmth. "You must be Kate."

"Yes, I am." Kate took her hand; it was soft. A blush crept over her cheeks as the woman did not let go.

"I'm Ainsley Cooper. It's nice to meet you." Ainsley brushed her thumb across the back of Kate's hand, then straightened her navy blue sweater.

"It's nice to meet you too." Kate blushed again and silently cursed herself for hoping that this stunningly attractive woman had not been Ainsley Cooper when she'd first seen her.

"Do you want something?" asked Ainsley.

For a moment, Kate's brain short-circuited in response to the question. She was sure Ainsley hadn't meant to make it sound like an innuendo, but Kate's mind had jumped to the worst possible interpretation. Or at least, the worst possible interpretation when meeting someone to discuss a job offer.

"I'm sorry, what?" asked Kate eventually as she discreetly tried to fan her face. By this point, she was sure that her skin was a permanent shade of red.

"Did you want something to drink?" asked Ainsley as she gestured toward the counter.

"Oh, right. Yes." Kate rubbed the back of her neck and looked away, hiding that ever-present blush. "I was just going to get an iced chai."

"That sounds nice, and it's definitely the weather for it," said Ainsley. "How about I order and you take a seat?"

"Are you sure?"

"It's fine. It's on me."

"Oh, okay. Sure. Sounds good." Kate turned around and almost collided with a table. She blushed, hoping that Ainsley had missed her clumsiness. But the soft chuckle from behind her suggested that someone had definitely seen it.

Kate hung her head as she carefully walked toward a table at the back of the cafe. As she settled into a seat, she noticed that she had an unobstructed view of where Ainsley was standing in line to place their order.

The woman was absolutely stunning. Kate would have to be blind not to notice. Realistically, she knew that she may never see Ainsley after this coffee.

Perhaps Ainsley had only reached out as a favor to Greg. Maybe once she had fulfilled her obligations to her colleague, she may not want to see Kate again.

Or, thought Kate, she may not even be offered the position at the University of Washington, so there may be no reason to see Ainsley again. Not that she would take the job just to see her again. She had learned from experience that she should never make life decisions just to be near people she was attracted to.

Regardless, Kate had realized quite quickly that any relationship, whether friendship or romantic, that required her to compromise her core beliefs was not one worth having. Admittedly, there were points in her relationship with Alex when she had wondered how well she had learned those earlier lessons. Not that being with Alex had made her feel like she was compromising who she was. Alex had always made Kate feel safe enough, comfortable enough, and loved enough to be exactly who she was.

But Kate had regrets. Not about Alex herself. About the opportunities, experiences, and internships she had turned down because they would have involved being away from Alex. Admittedly, those were choices that Kate had made and choices she had to live with. But maybe Seattle and the University of Washington were offering an opportunity to address some of those old regrets. Maybe, as horrible as it sounded, this was a second chance to do things differently—and if Ainsley was a part of that, well, that would be nice. Not that Kate was necessarily ready to consider moving on. But she got the sense that Ainsley was going to be important in her life going forward. While they had only just met, she felt like she had always known her, like they were connected somehow. It left her with an incredible desire to get to know Ainsley better.

Kate blinked as Ainsley walked toward her, grinning. She bit her lip and ducked her head to hide how quickly and broadly she smiled in response as Ainsley slid into the chair across from her.

"I have heard a lot of really impressive things about you," said Ainsley warmly. "All of them have been about how talented you are, but you are also absolutely gorgeous."

"Uh, that is very kind of you to say," said Kate, her eyes still lowered and unable to meet Ainsley's.

"I only speak the truth. How are you liking Seattle?"

"It's, um …" Kate met Ainsley's gaze. Her posture relaxed as she offered a slight smile in acknowledgment of the deft change of topic. "Well, it's a nice change of pace."

"Very different to New York, I'm sure."

"Yes, but a good kind of different."

"And how are you? How are you feeling?" asked Ainsley. "Sorry, is it okay to ask that?"

A sudden wave of grief welled up inside her. She blinked rapidly. "Did Greg tell you?"

"It came up." Ainsley reached out to squeeze one of Kate's hands. "Not at first, but I was curious as to why Greg would be willing to let you go if you were as good as he said. I'm sorry, though, if me knowing makes you uncomfortable. I won't mention it again, if you would prefer?"

"No, it's fine," said Kate. "It's easier, in a way. But in answer to your question, it's okay to ask if I'm okay."

"I'm sure that's the only thing people have been asking you for the last five months," said Ainsley.

"Yes, it is," said Kate, "but people only seem to ask because they think it's what they should ask. They never really listen to the answer, or at least they don't want to hear an answer other than 'I'm fine, thanks.'"

"So, you just tell them what they want to hear?"

"Isn't that the social convention?"

"Perhaps," said Ainsley, "but that's not the reason I asked. I asked because I want you to know that you can talk to me. And that is going to continue, regardless of what decisions you make about your time here in Seattle."

"Why?"

"Greg isn't the first person I've heard from about you. Your reputation precedes you."

"Is that a good or a bad thing?"

"As far as you're concerned, it's a good thing. Hearing all of those people speak of you, I just knew you were someone I would really like to know better if I ever had the chance."

"That's very kind of you," said Kate again.

"It's the truth," said Ainsley. "And even if it wasn't, after what you've been through, I think you need someone to support you in what you're going through right now. Plus, just from experience, it's easier to tell people what you truly feel if they don't know you. I think there's some quote about that."

"'Man is least himself when he talks in his own person. Give him a mask, and he will tell you the truth,'" quoted Kate.

"That's the one."

"Oscar Wilde said that."

"Do you have an eidetic memory?" asked Ainsley.

"No, I don't," said Kate. "I just have good recall. I can remember a majority of what I hear, read, and see, particularly things that I read."

"How is that not an eidetic memory?"

"It's not like you see on TV. I don't remember absolutely everything, and it isn't like perfect flashes. I just remember a lot."

"Okay," said Ainsley, "but I think we will need to agree to disagree on that."

"I can live with that," said Kate.

"Good. But I just meant to say that I'm not going to judge. I'll just listen to anything you want to say about anything you want to tell me."

"Thanks," said Kate. "I appreciate that."

"You're most welcome," said Ainsley. "Now, let's talk about this role as an Associate Professor with the Department of Political Science."

"Are you going to tell me what you thought of her, or do I need to beg?" asked Agatha as she twisted the top off a bottle of cider and handed it to Ainsley.

The two women were sitting on the large balcony of their apartment. They had a stunning view of the sun setting as they looked out across Lake Union. Agatha had lost count of the number of times she had come home to find Ainsley standing on the balcony, looking out at that same view. She knew it was what had attracted Ainsley to the apartment. Ainsley said it made her feel calm and centered, as it reminded her that no matter how bad something got, all she needed to do was show up the next day.

"Who?" asked Ainsley, taking a sip of her drink.

Agatha opened another bottle of cider. "You know who."

"Voldemort? I can't say that we've ever been introduced."

"Funny," said Agatha, taking a sip.

Ainsley chuckled. "I thought so."

"I meant Kate."

Ainsley sighed as she looked out at the view. "It was weird. I've spent so much time watching her, but I guess when you're at such a distance you don't really see the truth of who someone is. Instead, you see the manufactured veneer that people choose to show the world. But underneath the polished and put-together exterior, she was not what I was expecting."

"In a good way or a bad way?" asked Agatha.

"Good, I think," said Ainsley. "I guess I was expecting someone more pretentious. Like your stereotypical conceited academic who's obsessed with her own self-importance and with always making sure you know that she's the smartest person in the room. I was expecting that I'd need to pretend to like her or get on with her. I guess I was expecting someone a lot more like her parents."

"I would say a lot of things about Titania and Oberon, but that wouldn't be how I would describe them."

"I meant her adoptive parents—Lillian and Edward."

"I didn't know that you met them," said Agatha.

"A couple of times. But I think the last time was just before you moved to Seattle," said Ainsley. "Maybe it was simple curiosity, or maybe it was something else, but when they were growing up, Cornelius wanted to be present at the important events in the twins' lives, like their high school and college graduations."

"What were they like then?" asked Agatha.

"The very definition of privileged, cold, and emotionally distant." Ainsley took another sip of her drink. "I'm sure they were different behind closed doors with Kate, but at least in public, they seemed superficial and guarded, only concerned about appearances."

"But Kate wasn't like that when you met her?"

"No." Ainsley picked at the label of the bottle. "She was warm. She comes across as so considerate, thoughtful, and conscientious. She makes you feel like she's really listening to what you have to say, and not just waiting for you to finish saying something so she can start talking again. She's quiet and reserved, but if you find the right topic of conversation, she is so articulate and passionate."

"While all of that sounds wonderful, was Hunter right?" asked Agatha. "Did she come across as less idealistic and moralistic than Rowan?"

"She's a pragmatist," said Ainsley. "As warm as she is, I got the sense that she's extremely intelligent and calculating. I would say she has a tendency to be quite rational and analytical, but I also think that is balanced with an incredible amount of empathy."

"She sounds special," said Agatha. She frowned slightly as she looked at the other woman staring almost wistfully out at the view.

"She is," said Ainsley. "She definitely is. And now we need to do everything we can to ingratiate ourselves with her."

"Dr. Griffiths shouldn't be too long, Ms. Matthews," said the assistant to the Chair of the Department of Political Science. "Please take a seat."

Kate looked around the reception area outside of Dr. Griffiths' office as she walked from the assistant's large, imposing walnut desk to a row of four leather chairs. Dressed in a black sheath dress with a square neck and cap sleeves under a pinstriped charcoal blazer, she didn't look out of place in the Chair's office, with its matching walnut bookcases lined with hardcover books—but she certainly felt out of place.

While she understood that interviews were a necessary part of any job application, she hated them. She found the entire concept to be forced and artificial. Kate remembered complaining about interviews to Alex once. It had been one of the many things they could never agree on. Alex hadn't understood Kate's reticence. She had even scoffed and said that Kate regularly stood up in front of groups of students and presented lectures, so how was that any different?

There were two things about that distinction that Kate had never been able to get Alex to understand. The first was that she always made sure that she knew a topic inside and out before she considered presenting or lecturing on it. It was the comfort of knowing everything she could, combined with her meticulous planning, that made any of it possible. That was the second thing: Kate planned every detail of her lectures. Not just her presentations and slides, but her notes and any additional information she may require to answer questions that may arise.

Interviews, though, were a completely different exercise. There were only so many questions she could anticipate and prepare responses to. There would always be those that she would not expect. And when that happened? Well, that was where she struggled. She hated being put on the spot. She needed time to process questions and consider her responses. She was not someone who could speak without thinking. Instead, she needed to carefully consider every single word before it left her mouth.

Kate sighed quietly to herself as she fidgeted in the deceptively hard leather chair. Logically, she knew it was important to talk herself up and emphasize her strengths during an interview. But that was something that had never come naturally. Maybe it was her inner perfectionist speaking, but it didn't matter that to most people, she had achieved so much already. In her mind, there was always room for improvement; there was always something she could have done better. Kate had unrealistically high expectations of herself. She judged herself harshly and was often harder on herself than anyone else.

Kate knew that she had internalized such thinking at a young age after her parents routinely treated her like she was insignificant. Her mother's constant criticism, no matter how well-intentioned, had left her with low self-esteem and crippling self-doubt as well as her inherent perfectionist and overachieving tendencies. She believed that she may never achieve enough to earn her parents' love.

That was a side of herself that she was reluctant to show people. Kate was sure that most would only see the damage left behind as something that needed to be fixed; however, to her, there was also an unexpected upside—she had incredible drive and motivation. She knew that she had only achieved everything she had because she'd been determined to prove her mother wrong. Maybe she had also been desperate to show her mother that she was deserving of her praise just as much as Robbie was. But that was an uncomfortable thought that she did not dwell on for too long.

Still, there were times when Kate could not help but struggle with why her mother had treated her the way she had. Kate was not her biological child, but that wasn't enough of an answer. She would never get any answers, though, as she would never ask her parents why. They were simply who they had been raised to be, not that that excused their behavior. Kate hoped that if she ever had children, she would not perpetuate the cycle of emotional neglect.

This much negative thinking before her interview was not productive or beneficial. But sometimes—most of the time—her mind was her worst enemy. She was the kind of person who overanalyzed everything. As soon as the interview ended, she would formulate two or three better responses to every question she'd been asked. Overthinking was her mind's routine form of torture.

"Ms. Matthews? I'm Martin Griffiths," said the Chair of the Department of Political Science. "Thank you for coming in."

Well, Kate thought, *once more unto the breach.* She forced a smile onto her face as she stood up and stretched out her hand. "Thank you for seeing me."

Martin shook her hand, then gestured to the door to his office. "Do you want to come on in?"

"Of course." Kate followed him in and sat down in the chair that Martin indicated.

"Now, Kate," said Martin, "Greg Spinda said that you are one of the most intelligent and promising minds in political science that he has ever seen."

Kate bit down on her tongue to prevent herself from squirming. "He is very kind. I would simply say that I've always benefited from a better-than-average memory and written communication skills."

She smiled at the slight sense of déjà vu as the words left her mouth. Alex had argued with her the first time she'd heard Kate say that. They had agreed to disagree, and Kate had made sure to never repeat the comment in Alex's presence. She still had the same critical view of herself, but just kept it from Alex as much as possible. She found it easier to talk about her weaknesses and how she could improve.

As Kate walked into the Broadway Coffee House, she noticed Erin sitting at a table across from a petite Asian woman. She smiled, but stopped herself from walking toward them. As much as she thought Erin would like to see her, she didn't want to intrude on whatever he was doing. But he would also not be happy if he found out she was here and did not go over. With a sigh, she decided to say hello, and if she felt like she was interrupting, she would excuse herself.

"Hey, you," said Kate as she reached the table.

"Hey," said Erin warmly. His eyes sparkled as he gestured for Kate to take a seat. "What are you doing here?"

"I just had an interview with the Political Science Department at the university." Her phone started ringing as she sat down between Erin and the woman. Kate looked down at the display. "Sorry, I should get this," she said. "Kate Matthews speaking."

"Kate, it's Martin Griffiths. I wanted to thank you again for your time this morning."

"No, thank you," said Kate. "I really appreciated the opportunity."

"I also wanted to say that I would like to offer you the position of Associate Professor that we discussed. I wanted to confirm whether you were still interested?"

"Yes, absolutely."

"Good," said Martin. "I'll send you a copy of an employment contract, and we'll go from there."

"That sounds great," said Kate. "Thank you again."

"I think you'll be a great addition to the Department," said Martin. "Please let me know if you have any questions."

Kate ended the call and released a sigh, putting her head down on the table beside her phone.

"You okay?" asked Erin as he placed a hand on Kate's shoulder.

"What?" Kate lifted her head. "Oh, yes. I was just offered a position at the university."

"That's great!" The skin around Erin's eyes and mouth crinkled as he smiled.

"Congratulations," said the woman at the table.

"Thanks." Kate looked at Erin and raised an eyebrow.

"Sorry," said Erin with a shrug. "This is Akiko. We work together. She's overly friendly and lacking in boundaries, but is generally harmless. Akiko, this is Kate, my sister-in-law."

"It's nice to finally meet you." Akiko sat up straighter and offered Kate an almost brittle smile.

"It's nice to meet you too." Uncomfortable with the intensity of the other woman's gaze, Kate picked up her phone and started to turn it over in her hands.

"Erin speaks very highly of you," said Akiko.

"Well, if given the opportunity, I'd speak highly of him too," said Kate. She blushed and looked away from Akiko's penetrating gaze.

"We should go out tonight," said Akiko.

"I'm sorry?" Kate frowned as she realized that Akiko had not stopped staring at her.

Akiko shrugged. "I just think we should celebrate."

"About the job?" Kate looked back down at the table. "It's not that big of a deal."

"It's a huge deal," said Erin. "It might be nice to celebrate it—and our big news, too. We've just received a substantial grant to continue our research into correcting or modifying genetic abnormalities in the tuberous sclerosis complex one or two genes. I finally feel like I'm getting somewhere with this."

Kate reached out to squeeze Erin's hand. "I'm not entirely sure what all of that means, but it definitely sounds like something worth celebrating."

"It is," said Akiko.

"Sorry," said Kate as her phone started ringing again. She smiled when she saw Ainsley's name on the display.

"Someone's popular," said Akiko.

"Not usually," said Kate before answering the call.

"Hi, Kate, it's Ainsley."

"Ainsley, hi." The sound of Ainsley's voice put her at ease. It was a feeling that took her by surprise, as it often took her longer to open up to people.

"Martin just mentioned that he offered you the job," said Ainsley. "I wanted to congratulate you."

"Thanks. I really appreciate it," said Kate. "I also want to thank you for reaching out in the first place. I wouldn't have been offered the job without you, and I hope you'll let me make it up to you sometime."

"You could invite her out tonight," Akiko interrupted in a loud whisper.

Kate looked up at her.

"Just invite her," repeated Akiko.

Kate turned to Erin, who nodded reassuringly.

"Sorry, Ainsley," said Kate, "but do you want to go out tonight? I'm going out with some friends. They got some good news about their work and want to celebrate."

"That sounds like a great idea," said Ainsley. "Where were you planning on going?"

"Um, I don't know." Kate looked toward Akiko and Erin. "Where are we going?"

"How about the Jade & Lace Bar?" asked Akiko. Erin nodded.

"The Jade & Lace Bar," Kate repeated to Ainsley.

"That works for me. When should I meet you?"

"Oh, um. I'll see you there at about ..." Kate paused as Akiko raised seven fingers. "Seven?"

"Okay," said Ainsley. "I'll see you there."

Kate ended the call and looked up at Erin and Akiko, who were watching her expectantly.

"So, who's Ainsley?" asked Erin.

Chapter Three

"I can't believe I let you talk me into this," said Kate. She was standing in her bedroom, looking through her wardrobe for something to wear.

"We're celebrating," said Erin, sitting behind her on her bed. "It's what normal people do for fun."

"Oh, really?" Kate pulled out two dresses and placed them on the beige linen bench seat at the foot of her bed.

"Yes, really." Erin shook his head and passed the dresses back to Kate.

"I can't imagine why these so-called normal people would consider going out to a club *fun*," said Kate as she returned the dresses to her wardrobe. "I mean, there's so much noise and far too many people."

"Sure, Grandma, but the Jade & Lace is not a club, it's a bar," said Erin as Kate continued to look through her wardrobe.

She pulled out a blouse to look at. "And the difference is?"

"A bar is a bar and a club is a club."

Kate returned the blouse and walked to her dresser. "Super helpful."

"I've been to the Jade & Lace before," said Erin. "It's more a place for socializing than dancing and hooking up. The music isn't too loud, so you can talk without having to shout. There also isn't really any kind of dance floor—unless you make your own again."

"That happened one time," said Kate as she shut the dresser drawers. "And I blame Alex."

"How exactly were any of the events of that night Alex's fault?" asked Erin. "She wasn't even there."

"That is exactly my point," said Kate as she started looking through her wardrobe again. "She had promised that she would be there, and I may have overcompensated in my attempts to appear happy and outgoing in her absence."

"Yes, well, as fun as that was, I'm hoping not to see a repeat of that night."

"I wasn't planning on it." Kate sighed in frustration. "I literally have nothing to wear."

"You have plenty to wear." Erin got up and joined her in front of her wardrobe. "Do you still have those black skinny jeans?"

Kate flicked through coat hangers to find the jeans. She pulled them out of her wardrobe and held them out to Erin.

"Good. Wear them with that teal silk blouse. You know, the one with the lace that goes up the back?"

"This one?"

"Yes, that one," said Erin with a nod as Kate pulled on the jeans. "If I wasn't completely committed to the other team, that blouse and those jeans would totally turn my head."

"I know you mean that as a compliment, but I'm not sure how I feel about gay men finding me attractive." Kate slipped on the blouse. "I don't think it actually sends the message that I want it to."

"Gay does not mean blind to objective truths, honey. No," said Erin as she started buttoning the blouse, "leave two buttons undone, not one. Good. Now, roll up those sleeves."

"Why?"

"Because you'll fidget with them all night if you don't do it right now."

Kate finished rolling and buttoning her sleeves. "Okay, done."

Erin gave her a final once-over. "Not quite."

Kate placed her hands on her hips. "What else is there?"

Erin gestured to her messy ponytail. "What are you planning on doing with your hair?"

"I was going to leave it up."

"Well, that does look nice, but I think you should leave it down. I think you look absolutely stunning with a loose, wavy curl. It just makes you look a bit softer, almost ethereally beautiful."

"Okay, fine," said Kate as she took the hairband from her hair. "Hair down."

"Good. All set?"

"Yep." Kate picked up a black clutch from her dresser. "Let's get this over with."

Erin ushered her out of her room and toward the front door. "That's a great attitude."

"Hey, I'm going," said Kate as she stepped into a pair of modest black heels. "You should take that as a win."

"Trust me when I say that I do," said Erin as he opened the door.

"First round is on me," said Kate as she entered the Jade & Lace with Erin and Akiko. "You two go sit down."

The space was bright and airy with a high ceiling. The chairs and bar were beautiful chocolate-brown wooden pieces that contrasted with the white walls and the white marble that topped the bar and tables. The black-and-white motif, which reminded Kate of Union Station in Washington D.C., contrasted with the splashes of greenery scattered throughout the bar. There was something about the laid-back atmosphere that made her want to curl up in the corner with a book.

"You truly are a goddess," said Erin. He wrapped an arm around Kate's shoulders and pulled her in for a hug. "A cider for me."

"Flattery will get you everywhere," said Kate as Erin pressed a kiss to her head. He nudged her playfully. "Will it get me a second round for free?"

Kate poked him in the side. "You haven't even started your first drink yet."

"But that isn't a no," said Erin with a wink.

"It isn't a yes, either." Still with a broad smile on her face, Kate turned to Akiko. "Akiko, what would you like?"

"Thanks, Kate. I'd love a gin and tonic," said Akiko, clearly amused. "If you two don't mind, I'm just going to touch up my lipstick in the bathroom. I'll be right back."

"I'll go get us a table, then." Erin sauntered off.

Kate shook her head, still smiling as she moved toward the bar. But before she could take more than a few steps, someone called her name.

Kate turned to see Detective Lowell and Detective Caulfield standing in front of her.

"Detectives," she said. "It's nice to see you."

"I can't imagine why that would be true," said Detective Lowell, "but it's nice to hear."

"Did you need something from me about the other day?" asked Kate.

"Oh, no," said Detective Caulfield. "We were just here for a drink."

"Let me buy you both a drink as a thank you, then," said Kate.

"I'll have a beer," said Detective Lowell.

"You don't have to do that," said Detective Caulfield.

"Please. I insist. My brother-in-law, Erin, is just over there. Why don't you take a seat and I'll bring everything over?"

"Let me help you with that," said Detective Caulfield.

"Sure." As Kate started toward the bar, she felt Detective Caulfield follow quickly behind her.

"So, you said you were here with your brother-in-law?" the detective asked as they stopped in front of the bar.

"Yes, I did," said Kate. She gestured to the bartender, who acknowledged her with a nod.

"Is he married to a sibling of yours?"

"No. I don't think Erin would make that kind of commitment. He's not the serial monogamist type."

"So, that means ...?" The detective cocked her head to the side as she watched Kate.

Kate brushed her hair back from her face. "I married his sister."

Detective Caulfield inhaled a sharp breath. "Oh."

"Yep," said Kate. Her shoulders tensed as she braced herself for the slew of questions she knew were to come.

"What can I get you?" asked the bartender abruptly.

"Can I get one beer, one cider, a gin and tonic, and a white wine?" asked Kate quickly.

"Sure. Anything else?"

"Detective?" asked Kate as she finally turned to face the woman beside her.

"Can we make it two ciders?" asked Detective Caulfield.

"Sure. We're just changing over the keg for the beer, but we'll get your order ready shortly, ladies," said the bartender with a nod before he turned away.

"Thanks." Detective Caulfield looked at Kate. "You can call me Eddie, by the way."

"Right. Okay," said Kate. She drummed her fingers against the bar as she tried to come up with something to distract the other woman from asking any further questions about Alex. "So, what was Rowan like?"

"She was loyal and good-hearted," said Eddie. "Quite possibly the most positive and friendly person you'd ever meet. She was just irresistibly nice. She could be a little goofy and overeager, but that was all part of her charm."

"So, basically the human equivalent of a Golden Retriever?" asked Kate.

"It was almost eerie sometimes how much she seemed like that," said Eddie. "But at least I was able to train her so she didn't drool all over crime scenes."

"I'm going to pretend you never said that last part," said Kate.

"That's probably for the best."

"What's for the best?" asked Ainsley as she stepped up to the bar beside Kate.

The woman next to Kate was only slightly taller than her, with a slim build. She had long, wavy blonde hair and bright blue eyes. Eddie guessed that she was in her early thirties.

She frowned slightly as she sized up the other woman. For some reason, the newcomer looked incredibly familiar, and Eddie was certain she had met her before, but she couldn't place her. Not that that was a surprise—Eddie was terrible with faces. It wasn't exactly the best trait for a police officer, but she brought other things to the metaphorical table.

Eddie's frown deepened and she narrowed her eyes as she watched the woman wrap an arm around Kate's shoulders and press a brief kiss to Kate's cheek. She felt an instant, intense dislike at how possessively this woman treated Kate, like she was some prize to be won.

She tried her best to ignore how Kate seemed to light up at the affectionate gestures the other woman was showering her with. Eddie didn't want to acknowledge that Kate seemed to be enjoying the treatment, or that Kate had never looked at her like that.

"Hey, you," said Kate warmly as she hugged the other woman. "I'm glad you could make it."

The woman smiled warmly at her. "I wouldn't miss this for anything."

Eddie wasn't sure how Kate had found time to become so enamored with someone in the short time she had been in Seattle. Plus, if Kate was going to be doting on anyone, it should be her.

Jealousy was not the most attractive trait—*but I did save Kate's life,* Eddie thought in defense of herself. Surely saving someone's life earned you some kind of brownie points. Instead, Kate acted so hot and cold with her. Like the other day at the Pike Place Market. One minute it had seemed like they were getting along fine, and the next it was like Kate couldn't wait to put some serious distance between the two of them. And it wasn't like Eddie had done anything. Well, she corrected herself, she had lied. But that was only a technicality, and it wasn't like Kate could tell.

Eddie realized it had been several moments now since anyone had said anything, and the other two women looked a little lost in each other's gazes. She cleared her throat to bring Kate's attention back to her.

"Sorry," she said, feigning remorse as both women turned to look at her. "Hi, I'm Detective Eddie Caulfield."

"It's nice to meet you, Detective," said the other woman. "I'm Ainsley Cooper."

Nope, thought Eddie, *that name doesn't sound familiar either.* Why did she look so familiar?

"How do you two know each other?" asked Eddie. She was curious as to whether the answer would shed any light on where she knew Ainsley from. If the question also helped her find out when this interloper had found time to ingratiate herself with Kate, well, she wasn't going to complain.

"Well," said Ainsley, "Kate here has just accepted a job offer to work with me at the University of Washington."

"You got a job?" asked Eddie. "I guess that means you're planning on staying in Seattle, then."

"Yes, that's the plan," said Kate. She fidgeted with the buttons of her rolled-up sleeve, then jerked her hand away abruptly.

"That's great news," said Eddie. She fixed Ainsley with a steely gaze.

"Yes, it is," said Ainsley as she inched even closer to Kate. She met Eddie's eyes steadily and without flinching.

Eddie crossed her arms in front of her. "Yep."

An awkward silence stretched between the three women. Eddie and Ainsley stared one another down while Kate continued to fidget nervously.

The sudden ringing of Eddie's phone broke the silence. When Eddie didn't answer, Kate asked, "Should you get that?"

Eddie looked at the display and saw Nolan's name. "Oh, um, yes. Sorry." She walked away and answered the call. "Do you know an Ainsley Cooper?" she asked in lieu of a greeting.

"No, I don't believe so," said Nolan. "Why?"

"I just met her, and she looks really familiar." Eddie stepped into the front corner of the bar and leaned back against the wall. She had a perfect view of where Kate and Ainsley were still standing at the bar. "I just can't place her."

"Where did you meet her?" asked Nolan.

"I'm at the Jade & Lace. It's a bar in Capitol Hill. It's a bit more upmarket than my usual, but my new partner wanted to come here for a drink," said Eddie. "But I also ran into Kate Matthews. She's here with the Ainsley Cooper I mentioned."

Eddie watched as Ainsley placed her hand over Kate's where it was resting on the bar, ducking her head in an attempt to meet Kate's gaze. Eventually, Kate looked up at her. Eddie couldn't see her face, but she hoped Kate was not falling for the other woman's overt advances. She narrowed her eyes as Ainsley started to stroke her thumb along the inside of Kate's wrist. Her hopes were dashed when Kate didn't pull away. Instead, she seemed to shift closer to Ainsley.

"Eddie?" asked Nolan, shattering her focus on the two women.

"Right. Sorry," said Eddie. She blinked and shifted her attention back to the conversation. "What were you saying?"

"I wasn't saying anything. You just stopped speaking."

"Sorry. I was distracted. It looks like Ainsley is doing everything she can to ingratiate herself with Kate."

"If you're that worried about this Ainsley Cooper person, then why not run her background?" said Nolan. "You are a police officer."

"That sounds like a great idea," said Eddie.

After Eddie left to answer her phone, Kate turned to face the bar as she waited for the bartender to bring over the drinks. It was only a matter of moments before Ainsley moved to stand shoulder-to-shoulder with her.

"For someone who only just moved here, you sure seem to know a lot of people." Ainsley bumped her shoulder lightly against Kate's.

Kate smiled at the affectionate gesture and turned her body toward Ainsley, placing an elbow against the bar. She rested her tilted head in her palm as she faced the other woman.

"She just worked with my sister," said Kate eventually. "They were partners together in the police force."

"You never mentioned you have a sister here," said Ainsley.

"Had a sister here." Kate dropped her arm to rest against the bar. "And it's not like we ever met."

"I'm not sure I understand."

"I was adopted," said Kate, dropping her gaze. "I never knew anything about my birth family, and to be honest, I still don't. But technically, she was still my sister."

"Are you okay?" Ainsley reached out to place her hand over Kate's.

"I guess so," said Kate without looking up.

"Are you sure?"

From the corner of her eye, Kate saw Ainsley ducking her head, trying to recapture her gaze.

"I'm sympathetic for Detective Caulfield's loss," said Kate as she finally looked back up, unable to keep her eyes off the other woman. "But I never knew her. It's hard to grieve someone you never knew existed."

"Particularly when you're grieving someone else who was such a big part of your life?" asked Ainsley. She started to stroke her thumb along the inside of Kate's wrist.

Despite the nature of the conversation, a warmth filled Kate. It had been a long time since she felt as understood by someone as she did at that moment. She had spent her life feeling like a perpetual outsider. At first, she'd thought it was just because she was adopted, an outsider within her own family—a feeling only exacerbated by her parents when she was growing up. But even when she'd started to build her own chosen family with Alex and their friends, she still felt like she faked being more like the people around her in the hope that they would accept her. The moments when she had truly felt comfortable in her own skin, being exactly who she was, had been rare. But there was something about Ainsley that made Kate feel like she could be herself completely, without judgment.

"I knew Alex for almost my entire adult life," said Kate. "Losing her feels like I've lost a part of myself."

"You have, though," said Ainsley. "You lost your wife. You lost your partner."

"She wasn't perfect, and our relationship wasn't perfect, but I loved her," said Kate. "More than I've loved anyone before. I don't know how to move on from that."

"I don't think you ever move on. You'll find a way to move through it, but she was a big part of your life," said Ainsley. "That will never change."

"You sound like my former therapist."

"I think it's important to cut yourself some slack."

"Now you *really* sound like my former therapist," said Kate. "Why should I, though?"

"You lost someone who was as much a part of you as one of your limbs. You'll be forever changed by your loss, and it will take time to adjust to what your life is now."

"Are you speaking from experience?" asked Kate.

Ainsley blinked and looked away. "My brother."

"I'm sorry." Kate pulled her hand out from under Ainsley's. "I didn't mean to pry."

"It's okay," said Ainsley as she turned back toward Kate. "Loss—like me losing my brother or you losing your wife—is like a crucible. It's the pain of that crucible that shows us the most about who we are and what we want. But the trick is not getting addicted to the pain while simultaneously not shutting yourself off from it, either. You need to find a way to survive it and grow stronger from the experience."

"I'll try to keep that in mind," said Kate. She realized how close the two of them had gotten when she noticed just how blue Ainsley's eyes were at that moment. Kate blushed, biting her lip.

Ainsley smiled warmly as she reached up to tuck a strand of Kate's hair behind her ear. She let her hand linger against Kate's cheek before she cupped her jaw.

"I promise to remind you if you ever need it." As her thumb started to stroke along Kate's cheekbone, Ainsley's eyes dropped to her lips, then back up to meet her gaze. Kate nodded slightly as her own gaze flitted down to Ainsley's mouth.

Just as Ainsley leaned toward her, a sudden shattering of glass broke the lingering look. Both women turned toward the sound.

A light bulb had exploded. Sparks rained down over the bar behind them. The combination of wood, sparks, and alcohol rapidly ignited a fire. It snaked down toward where the two women were standing. They moved away from the burning bar.

Suddenly, another two bulbs to Kate's left shattered, showering two tables with greedy sparks hungry for more fuel. On touching the surrounding chairs, they sparked into life, quickly spreading down to reach the wooden floor.

Kate and Ainsley continued to move backward as the fire slowly inched closer and closer. Kate came to a stop as her back hit the wall.

She and Ainsley were completely boxed in by the flames.

CHAPTER FOUR

"What are we watching?" asked Akiko as Erin observed a woman, whom he assumed to be Ainsley Cooper, stroking a thumb along Kate's cheekbone.

"We're watching someone hit on my sister," said Erin.

"And my partner is watching the two of them with irrational jealousy," said Hunter.

When Erin raised an eyebrow, Hunter inclined his head toward another woman leaning against a wall at the front of the bar.

"Oh, great," said Akiko as she leaned forward eagerly. "I love me some lesbian love triangle drama."

"I seriously can't take you anywhere, can I?" asked Erin.

"Nope." Akiko tilted her head to the side. "Well, actually, you can take me to a place twice."

"Why twice?"

"The second time is to apologize," said Akiko, just as the sound of shattering glass rang out.

The table's three occupants whipped their heads away from the bar as a shower of sparks rained down from a light socket. As soon as the sparks started to ignite the wooden bar, Hunter was out of his seat, pulling his phone out of his pocket. Before Erin could even react, he was calling the fire department and telling everyone to get out.

"Come on, Erin," said Akiko as Erin's brain finally caught up with what was happening.

He scrambled to his feet as another light bulb exploded across the room. Erin's eyes widened as he watched flames streak down the bar toward where Kate and Ainsley were standing.

"Hunter," yelled Erin as he ran toward them. He skidded to a halt as flames abruptly sprang up, separating him from the two women, who were now surrounded by fire. Kate met Erin's gaze as Hunter reached his side.

Erin stepped closer to the flames, only to have Hunter drag him backward again. "Maybe there's something we can do—"

"Yes," said Kate, appearing oddly calm. "You can leave now."

"Kate," said Erin through a tight throat.

"I need you to leave, Erin," she said. "I need to know that you're safe."

"No. I'm not leaving you." Erin stood his ground while his eyes burned. "I am not losing another sister."

"Detective," said Kate as she turned her gaze toward Hunter. "Get him out of here."

"No, Kate," said Erin as Hunter wrapped an arm around his waist.

"I mean it, Detective. Make sure he leaves," said Kate. "Detective. Hunter. Please."

"Come on, Erin." Hunter started to move.

"No!" Erin swallowed hard as tears streaked down his face. "No—Kate—"

He sobbed as he sagged into Hunter, who pulled him away from the flames.

"Okay," said Kate, her shoulders slumped as she looked at the flames slowly inching closer and closer. "I've filled my bravery quota for today, and I'll admit that I'm really scared."

"You'll be fine," said Ainsley as she pulled Kate back against the wall. "We'll both be fine."

Kate turned to look at her. "I wouldn't have picked you as an optimist in the face of insurmountable odds."

"Trust me," said Ainsley. She took one of Kate's hands between her own. "I'm not."

"Then how do you propose we get out of here? Because I don't see us being fine if we don't."

"Do you always talk this much in life-threatening situations?"

"Yes," said Kate. "Apparently."

"Okay," said Ainsley as she squeezed Kate's hand reassuringly. "Keep holding my hand and stay behind me."

"What? Why? I'm not letting you shield me."

"I need you to trust me," said Ainsley, "and trust that I can get us both out of here."

"How?"

"Kate," said Ainsley as she turned to face her. She cradled Kate's face in her hands and forced the other woman to look at her. "Do you trust me?"

Kate was not someone who trusted easily or quickly, but for some reason, she instinctively wanted to trust the woman in front of her.

"Yes," she said.

"Okay. Take my hand." Ainsley moved one hand away from Kate's face and offered it to her.

Kate took a deep breath. She bit down on her lip and placed her hand in Ainsley's.

"That's my girl," said Ainsley warmly, smiling at her. "Now, let's get out of here."

Ainsley turned back toward the flames. They had inched even closer. She took a small step forward and raised her free hand. Kate watched as she closed her eyes and breathed in and out deeply for several moments.

When it seemed like nothing was happening, she felt foolish for trusting Ainsley so quickly. Then she started to feel a slightly warm tingling in the hand clasped in Ainsley's. As the feeling spread rapidly across her body, the flames nearest to them started to bend slightly away. Kate frowned, assuming it was an optical illusion or smoke-induced delirium. But then the flames moved even further apart, leaving a space clear for the women to walk through in single file.

"How did you do that?" asked Kate, eyes wide in disbelief.

"Questions later," said Ainsley as she moved forward, pulling Kate behind her through the flames. "Survival now."

Kate could feel Ainsley's gaze on her as she opened her front door. Ainsley wordlessly followed her inside. It was not until she had settled on the couch beside Kate that she broke the silence that had settled over the women since they left the Jade & Lace Bar.

"You seem quiet," said Ainsley softly, turning to face Kate.

"I'm a quiet person." Kate raised her knees to her chest and leaned back against the arm of the couch. She rested her head on her knees and wrapped her arms around her legs as she met Ainsley's concerned gaze.

"I know," said Ainsley as she draped her arm along the top of the couch, "but you've seemed uncharacteristically quiet since we left the bar. Plus, you were the one who said you had questions."

"Well, in the last six months, I've been in a car accident, attacked by a giant fox twice, almost stabbed by a mugger, and almost killed in a fire, and most of those things have happened in the last month. I don't know why I've survived all of that and she couldn't survive a car accident."

"Alex?" asked Ainsley as she raised her other hand to squeeze Kate's.

"Yes." Kate laced her fingers with Ainsley's. "What you did back there. Was it magic?"

"It's not exactly what it's called, but I suppose that is a way to simplify it," said Ainsley. She started to draw small circles with her thumb against the back of Kate's hand.

"Are you a witch?" asked Kate.

"No, I'm not."

"Well, at least that explains the lack of a wand." In response to the eyebrow Ainsley arched, Kate continued, "What? I grew up with Harry Potter."

Ainsley chuckled softly.

"So, what are you exactly?" asked Kate.

"I'm a Faerie," said Ainsley. "And before you ask, I don't have the ability to bring anyone back from the dead or turn back time. Unfortunately, I don't know of anyone or anything that can. If there was some way, I would tell you."

"Why? I mean ..." Kate turned away. "I guess ... It's just that—" She looked back at Ainsley. "Well, I don't want to be disingenuous, but ..."

Clearly sensing that Kate wasn't going to finish her sentence, Ainsley asked, "Why would I bring Alex back if I could?"

"Yes."

She squeezed Kate's hand again. "Just because loss is a part of life doesn't mean it's fair. If I could take away your pain, I would."

"Thank you."

"You don't need to thank me. I did nothing."

Kate kept Ainsley's hand tight in hers. "You saved my life. That isn't nothing."

Hunter took one last look around the Jade & Lace Bar as the arson investigator from the Seattle Fire Department walked away, leaving him standing in the burnt-out shell.

The remaining tables and chairs were heaped together like piles of blackened matches. The formerly white walls were now covered in soot and scorch marks. The floor and bar were water-damaged and charred. It would take time and a lot of money to return the Jade & Lace to the condition it had been in, but

Hunter hoped that whoever the owner was, they would be willing to do what was necessary.

He sighed as he pulled out his phone and dialed Ainsley's number.

"Hi," she answered.

"Hi, Ainsley. How's Kate?"

"Physically, she's fine."

"And emotionally?" asked Hunter.

"I don't know," said Ainsley. "I think she's reaching the point where she is so overwhelmed that she isn't really processing anything."

"Information overload?"

"Exactly."

"So, what did you tell her?" asked Hunter.

"As little as possible," said Ainsley. "She needs to know more. She deserves to know everything about who she is and where she comes from."

"But you're worried she will shut down completely if you tell her everything?"

"Yes. There's only so much any of us can take all at once. I don't want to do more harm than good."

"Then what I'm about to tell you won't help."

"What is it?" asked Ainsley.

"I've just finished speaking to the arson investigator at the Jade & Lace," said Hunter. "It's not my jurisdiction, but I sweet-talked the investigator into doing me a professional courtesy as I was on the scene when it happened."

"Do they think it was arson?"

"It's too early to say definitively, but there are some things that don't add up."

"Like what?" asked Ainsley.

"The compact fluorescent bulbs used by the bar can explode. This usually happens in one of two circumstances," said Hunter. "The first is in the event of an electrical surge."

"But wouldn't there need to have been two surges for them to go at different times?"

"You'd think so. Plus, two surges like that should have taken out more than a couple of bulbs."

"What's the other way?" asked Ainsley.

"Faulty manufacturing causing the base to overheat," said Hunter.

"Were there signs of faulty manufacturing?"

"The bases looked melted, but the investigator said it looked like heat was applied to the outside of the socket as opposed to being generated by the electricity flowing through the bulbs."

"We would have noticed if someone was applying a blowtorch to the outside of the light sockets."

"That's what I thought, until I thought about the other attacks on Kate," said Hunter.

"You mean the mugging and the fox?"

"Yes. Think about it for a second. What comes to mind when you add fox, shape-shifter, and fire?"

"A Kitsune," said Ainsley.

EPISODE THREE: PINE

CHAPTER ONE

"A Kitsune makes so much sense," said Ainsley. She was pacing restlessly from one side of her living room to the other. "I don't know why we didn't think of it sooner."

"Well, I know I was more focused on the human women who are being murdered," said Hunter. He lifted a cushion and spun it around one hand before slamming his other fist into it. Then he threw it back on the couch and slumped down next to it.

Ainsley and Agatha exchanged a look of concern at Hunter's behavior before Agatha asked cautiously, "Everything okay?"

"It's just frustrating that four apparently unrelated women have all died in somewhat suspicious circumstances," said Hunter, "and the only lead we have is some German word that was found at all the crime scenes. I just don't understand why someone would target them."

"That seems to be going around, doesn't it?" asked Ainsley.

"Yes, it does," said Agatha. "But turning to the more pressing matter at hand, who would have paid a Kitsune to kill Kate and Rowan?"

"It would need to be someone connected to both of them," said Ainsley.

"You're thinking of Eddie?" asked Hunter.

"You said you thought she was a Faerie," said Ainsley.

"But if Eddie is a Faerie, why haven't any of us seen her use her powers to save herself or Kate?" asked Hunter. "Even the weakest Faeries can manage a magical barrier. That may not have stopped a Kitsune, but it would have slowed it down long enough to give them a chance to get away."

"Maybe it was part of the act," said Ainsley. "If she was attacked but survived, no one would suspect her."

"Or maybe we're wrong," said Agatha, "and she isn't a Faerie."

"She is," said Ainsley.

"And?" asked Hunter.

"And what?"

"This is the second time that you've implied you know who Eddie is," said Agatha.

"I don't know her exactly," said Ainsley, "but I believe I know who her parents were."

"Who?" asked Agatha and Hunter simultaneously.

"Edan Verity and his wife, Aine."

"Well, that explains a lot," said Agatha.

"Not to me, it doesn't," said Hunter.

"The Verity family were a very old and well-respected Faerie family," said Agatha. "Their lineage is as old as any of the Faerie royal families and probably better respected than at least half of them. They held positions as magistrates, lawmakers, and members of the constabulary. Instead of having the traditional magical gifts of Faeries, they had the ability to see things invisible to the normal eye. They couldn't use Faerie magic, but they could tell whether someone was lying or if someone was using magical gifts, among other things."

"I remember Edan and Aine having a young daughter at the time of the civil war," said Ainsley. "Plus, Eddie bears a strong resemblance to Aine."

"You would remember something like that," said Agatha with a raised eyebrow.

"We don't need to go about rehashing that part of the story," said Ainsley. "At least, not right now."

"Okay, I have no idea what either of you are talking about, but why would Edan and Aine align themselves with the rebels?" asked Hunter.

"I don't believe that they did," said Ainsley. "They supported Titania as the rightful heir. But they also believed that Cornelius was telling the truth about the death of his brother, King Regulus."

"Then what happened?" asked Hunter.

"Someone assassinated them," said Agatha.

"That has an oddly familiar ring to it, don't you think?" asked Hunter.

"It was a civil war," said Ainsley. "There was a lot of senseless death and violence."

"You know I would be the last one to disagree with you about that," said Agatha, "because there were a lot of people, including your brother, who died needlessly. But it was family against family, with Faeries doing anything they could to garner favor. However, you and I also know that the deaths of the Verity family were an outlier. They never made sense."

"Do you know who killed them?" asked Hunter.

"No," said Ainsley. "But I don't believe that either Titania or Cornelius would have done something as foolish as encouraging or soliciting the death of the Veritys."

"But that doesn't exactly leave anyone else, though, does it?" asked Hunter. "No third person was vying for the throne, were they?"

"Maybe they were," said Ainsley.

"What do you mean?" asked Agatha.

"Maybe the same person who orchestrated the deaths of Edan and Aine is also behind Rowan's death and the attacks on Kate," said Ainsley.

"That's one seriously long end game," said Agatha. "Who would be that patient and that motivated?"

"Better yet," added Hunter, "who would have something to gain from all of that?"

Kate saw Ainsley waiting patiently at a table as soon as she walked into the Broadway Coffee House.

She had only taken a few steps toward the other woman when Ainsley noticed her and smiled broadly. Kate smiled reflexively in response. She instantly felt self-conscious at her actions, sure that Ainsley must think she was a dork. Kate blushed and ducked her head to hide her embarrassment. She smoothed down her dark green sheath dress as she walked across to the table, only glancing back up to Ainsley when the woman stood to greet her.

"Hello," said Ainsley as she stepped closer to press a brief kiss to Kate's cheek. "You look lovely. Green is definitely your color. It brings out your eyes."

"Thank you. You look great too," said Kate, gesturing awkwardly at the color-blocked white-and-blue sweater that Ainsley had paired with dark blue jeans.

"Thanks," said Ainsley warmly. She gestured for Kate to take a seat. "I ordered you an iced chai, if that's okay?"

"That sounds great," said Kate as she sat down. "How did you know that was my drink of choice?"

"I remember you ordering it when we were last here, so I thought it was a safe bet," said Ainsley. "You said that you wanted to talk about something?"

Kate didn't hesitate. "You said it isn't magic that you have. So what would you say it is?"

"Everything in this world shares energy or a life force flowing through it," said Ainsley. "Faeries can channel that innate power from within themselves in several ways. It can be used for nearly every purpose, but not all Faeries' powers are of the same strength. There are certain Faerie families, such as our royal families, whose powers are particularly potent."

"So, besides varying levels of strength, are the powers of each Faerie the same?" asked Kate.

"Most have one or two areas where they are especially talented or adept."

"Such as?"

"Some Faeries have a natural affinity for healing others," said Ainsley. "Some have a particular talent for communicating with animals and other creatures unable to communicate with humans. Others can channel their power to make people see things that aren't there or to hide things that are."

"And you?" asked Kate.

"I have a bit of an affinity with the forces of nature, weather, and the Earth, including various types of elemental currents," said Ainsley. "I can only generate fire or water in times of extreme emotion, but I can control most aspects of the weather—rain, hail, lightning—and I can manipulate the wind."

"And flames," said Kate.

"Yes, and flames."

"So most Faeries have a particular affinity for one thing?"

"It depends on the individual and the strength of their powers," said Ainsley. "I can sometimes hear things that the wind does. But that's far less useful than it seems. I know that some Faeries who can communicate with animals can also heal them. But they can't heal other beings."

"Okay," said Kate.

"I know it's a lot to process."

"I think that may be in the running for understatement of the year. I mean, if I hadn't seen what you did, I'm not sure I would be willing to believe any of this. I just ..." Kate paused, searching for the right words. "I mean, it's a lot to get my head around, and I'll need some time to ... I don't even know."

"I know," said Ainsley. "I know, and you can take as much time as you need to process all of this, because it is a lot. To be honest, I think I'd be more worried if you weren't struggling to get your head around it."

"Why?"

"I'm not so ignorant as to assume that everyone processes things in the same way that I do," said Ainsley. "I've seen enough introverts in my life to know that they need time to not just process information, but soak it in and consider the best response. I've always found that the deeper thinkers often provide responses that are the culmination of all their knowledge and understanding if you give them the time to think things through. So I'm not going to push, and I'm not going to put you on the spot. You'll work through everything in your own time, and when you're ready to talk, we can talk."

"Okay," said Kate hesitantly. She looked down at her hands resting on the table in front of her.

"Are you sure?" Ainsley reached out and placed her hand over Kate's, ducking her head slightly to recapture Kate's gaze.

"I'm not really used to people understanding that sometimes I need time to get my head around things." Kate eventually looked back up to meet the other woman's eyes. "I'm more used to people just being baffled or frustrated or annoyed that I can't give them the answers they want then and there."

"Well, I promise to always give you the time you need to process everything that's going on inside that head of yours," said Ainsley. She squeezed Kate's hands reassuringly.

"Thanks." Kate turned away from her warm, comforting gaze again as she was overwhelmed with gratitude.

Too often, the people in her life, whether they were friends, family, or colleagues, had tried to put her on the spot and force her to provide answers. Kate had always found it incredibly frustrating that no matter how many times she asked for time and space, it was always her fault that she couldn't give them an instantaneous response about how she was feeling and why she felt that way. Whether or not they intended it, people had always made her feel like there was something wrong with her because of that. She was unsure how to respond when someone not only understood, but was willing to give her the time she needed.

Kate looked back at Ainsley to see the other woman watching her intently. "You okay?" asked Ainsley with a frown.

Kate nodded. Just as she was about to say something to assuage Ainsley's concern, she noticed a barista she had seen on a number of her visits approaching the table with their drinks.

"Now, here's your chai, Kate," said the barista as she placed Kate's iced chai in front of her. "That means this must be yours." She set a drink in front of Ainsley.

"Oh, and I have your change." She reached into the pocket of her apron and placed several notes on the table.

"Was there something wrong?" asked Ainsley as she reached over to the money.

"No," said the barista brightly, "I had just promised Kate a free drink the next time she came in, so once I saw this was for her, I thought I'd give you a refund."

"Seriously, you didn't have to do that," said Kate.

"I wanted to," said the barista.

"But—"

"Well," the barista cut her off, "if you won't take the extra change, how about I get you a muffin?"

"That sounds great," said Ainsley.

"Fantastic. I'll be right back."

Ainsley watched the barista walk back toward the counter before she turned back to Kate and asked, "Why do you do that?"

"Do what?" asked Kate.

"I saw you turn down free drinks the other day. Now, you're turning down free coffee."

"I'm really more of a tea drinker," said Kate jokingly before she looked up to see the seriousness etched on Ainsley's face. "I'm just not interested."

"In free drinks?"

"In the names, numbers, and polite conversations that come with free drinks."

"Why not?" asked Ainsley. Her eyes darted toward the barista. "She's super cute."

The barista's brown apron complemented her hazel eyes framed by thick, dark lashes. She flashed her perfect white teeth in a grin, giving a small wave when she noticed the two women watching her.

Kate returned her smile before quickly looking away, heat flushing her cheeks. "She definitely is."

"So, what's the problem?"

"I'm not ready for another relationship."

"You're the only one saying *relationship*." Ainsley took a napkin and used it to wipe a non-existent stain off her sweater. "I'm definitely not."

Kate gulped a deep breath of the balmy coffee house air. "It just feels too soon."

"If you were to ask anyone, they would tell you that there's no timeline on grief. It comes and goes in waves," said Ainsley. "In saying that, I don't think it's healthy to just put your life on hold while you wallow. That doesn't mean you need to get over Alex today and dive straight into a relationship. That wouldn't be fair on you, or your memories of Alex, or whoever you may start seeing."

"So," said Kate, drawing out the word, "what exactly are you suggesting?"

"I'm suggesting you indulge in some sexual sorbet," said Ainsley.

"What?"

"You need some uncomplicated sex with someone. Anyone. You need a palate cleanser before you can move on."

"So, I'm just supposed to ask some random person if they'll have sex with me without strings or complications?" asked Kate.

"Yes," said Ainsley. "Exactly."

"That is so weird."

"It really isn't. When was the last time you slept with someone who wasn't Alex?"

"Almost five years ago," said Kate hesitantly, trying her best to avoid squirming awkwardly in her seat. She wasn't uncomfortable with the question itself. She was uncomfortable with her answer. She hoped that Ainsley didn't know or think to ask when she had first started dating Alex. Not that Kate had ever been unfaithful, but while their relationship had spanned over nine years, they had not been together for that entire time.

"So," said Ainsley, "do you want the first person you sleep with after Alex to be someone you really care about? Isn't that putting a lot of pressure on both you and whoever that may be?"

"Okay, point taken," said Kate, "but who on Earth would agree to that?"

"I would," said Ainsley.

"Really?" asked Kate.

"I like sex. That's not a crime, and it never should be. I will happily have uncomplicated string-free sex with you for however long you need."

"That is the least romantic thing I've ever heard."

"That's kind of the point," said Ainsley. "No romance. No strings. No complications. Just you, me, and some healthy sex."

Kate bit her lip and frowned. Some people enjoyed casual flings, one-night stands, and friends-with-benefits arrangements. But she was not the type of person who felt comfortable engaging in those kinds of casual relationships. She had always craved a greater level of intimacy and moved from one long-term serious relationship to the next as a result. Even the idea of casual dating made her hesitate—partly because it could take her a while to open up to someone, and sometimes it just felt like too much effort if she knew the other person had no intention of sticking around. The other part was that she longed to have someone by her side to share the highs and lows of her life as she navigated the world.

"Where are you at with the Harrigan, Manson, and Tidbury cases?" asked Captain Montoya as he flicked open a case file. He looked up at Hunter and Eddie, who were seated in front of his desk.

"We are now at four suspicious deaths in as many weeks," said Hunter. "All women in their late twenties and early thirties."

"Other than the way they died, do they have anything else in common?" the captain asked.

"Not that we've been able to find," said Eddie. "One lived in Belltown, two in South Lake Union, and the last was in Ballard."

"All of them had different jobs, too," said Hunter. "There was a teacher, a lawyer, a nurse, and one who worked in IT. Three were born in Seattle and one in Portland. One went to college here and the other three went to college interstate."

"And what makes you sure that the four deaths are related and suspicious?" asked Captain Montoya. "It sounds like the coroner is still on the fence about it."

"Well, the people closest to the four women all gave us exactly the same story," said Eddie. "They all changed pretty dramatically in the week before their deaths. First, they were reporting distressing nightmares, exhaustion, and irritability, then feelings of guilt, misery, and depression."

"Plus, there are these." Hunter leaned forward to hand Captain Montoya several photos.

"What are these?" asked the captain as he looked through them. They had all been taken at the various crime scenes near where each woman had died. They all featured the word *Schuld*.

"Every crime scene had this written somewhere," said Eddie. "It was found either near or on the bodies at the time of their deaths."

"What does it mean?" asked Captain Montoya.

"Well, it's a German word that roughly translates to *debt* or *guilt*," said Hunter.

"And I take it that none of the women spoke German?"

"No," said Eddie. "And we don't know what it means to these women, or to the person who may have orchestrated their deaths."

"Well," said Captain Montoya, "find out."

Understanding the dismissal, Eddie and Hunter got to their feet and walked back to their desks. As Hunter slumped into his chair, he watched his partner drop her files on her desk, shove her pen into the penholder, and drop heavily into her seat. Eddie then opened the drawer of her desk, only to slam it shut. Hunter barely had a chance to react to the loud bang before Eddie had wrenched open the drawer and slammed it shut again.

"You good?" he asked as his partner reached for the drawer once more.

"Just peachy," said Eddie. She sighed and rubbed her temples. "I'm just frustrated with our complete and utter lack of progress."

"I'm right there with you," said Hunter, "but we aren't going to get anywhere feeling that way. So, how about we both head home, get some rest, and hit the ground running tomorrow morning?"

CHAPTER TWO

Kate looked around at the Broadway Coffee House. Despite all the people, it was like someone had pressed mute on every noise. There was no whistling, clanging, or clinking as the baristas made coffee after coffee, and no sound as the customers ate, drank, and engaged in conversation.

As the sudden crash of something being dropped on the table echoed in the quiet room, Kate whipped her gaze away from the baristas to Ainsley sitting in front of her. Between the two women on the table was a Monopoly board complete with dice, pieces, and plastic houses and hotels. The game's two dice were in the outstretched hand Ainsley was offering to Kate.

"It's your turn," she said as she dropped the dice into Kate's hand.

Kate shook the dice and released them. They jumped and spun across the board before they landed on a number three and a number five. She picked up the Scottie Dog piece from Virginia Avenue and moved it forward eight spaces until it came to a rest on the space that read *Chance*. Kate reached out and pulled the top card from the waiting deck. It read *Go to Jail, Go Directly to Jail*.

Kate looked down. She was wearing a black-and-white striped shirt with matching pants, just like a stereotypical old-fashioned prisoner costume. Her hands were handcuffed in front of her.

She was suddenly seated in a car. Kate looked to her left and saw Alex sitting beside her, wearing the same thing she had been wearing during the accident: a white button-down and denim jeans under a tan wool-blend coat. She even wore her wedding ring.

"Alex?" asked Kate softly, staring with wide eyes and raised eyebrows.

"We had an agreement," said Alex. "When you finished your postdoctoral appointment at Princeton, you would take a position at either Columbia or NYU."

"Now is not the time to be having this conversation again," said Kate. She looked around and noticed how close they were to the street where their accident had happened. "You need to slow down and be careful. There's ice everywhere."

"Princeton is not in New York," said Alex. "How can we have a relationship if we aren't even in the same place? Would you work at the University of Washington, if they offered it?"

"You need to pull over—"

"Washington is on the other side of the country," said Alex, just as the car hit an icy patch and fishtailed out of control.

"Alex!" screamed Kate. The loud screeching of tires filled the air and a blinding white light filled Kate's vision.

As the light faded, she looked around. She was suddenly sitting in a courtroom. At the front was a throne where the judge would normally sit.

The woman sitting on the throne wore a glamorous red velvet dress with an attached white stand-up collar and black sleeves. The center of the dress was a white layered net with red sequined hearts on top. A golden tiara sat on top of her chestnut hair. Her face was not visible from where Kate was seated; she was looking toward where Erin was standing on the other side of the room.

Erin was wearing a black formal coat over a red vest with a single yellow button on the front, a white short-sleeved button shirt with a yellow tie on the collar, khaki pants, and yellow shoes with blue soles. He also wore a light blue formal hat with a gold lining. He was carrying a red umbrella with white-gloved hands.

"And then, five months after you died, she was using your death as a way to pick up women for sex," said Erin. He bowed and stepped backward.

The woman on the throne looked in Kate's direction. It was Alex.

"How could you?" she asked harshly as she met Kate's gaze. "Using me like that? Well, off with your head."

"What?"

"She said off with your head," said a voice from beside Kate.

Kate turned as Detective Caulfield grabbed her arm.

"That's right," said Detective Lowell as he took Kate's other arm. "She said off with your head."

"And the queen gets what she wants," said Ainsley as she stepped in front of Kate and placed a hood over her head. As the hood blocked out the light, the crowd picked up the chant of *"Off with her head"* until it faded into a droning buzz of noise.

Kate blinked open her eyes and groggily rolled over to silence her phone's chiming alarm.

Okay, she thought as she rolled onto her back and stared up at her bedroom ceiling, which looked gray in the early morning light. She understood the message her subconscious was trying to give her, loud and clear. She got it. Clearly, she should not be thinking about moving on from Alex. It was far too soon, and she would just need to tell Ainsley that she wasn't ready.

But, asked the traitorous and cynical part of Kate that sounded suspiciously like her mother, *what if that's all that Ainsley wants? What if she only wants to get into your pants?*

Eddie looked around at the darkened front porch of Kate's apartment, then turned suddenly toward the road when she heard Kate's voice coming toward her. Kate was talking into her phone as she walked up the steps.

"I just got home," she said as she reached her front door. "I needed to grab a change of clothes before I head back."

As Kate placed her key in the lock, Eddie saw a shadow separate itself from the others at the edge of the porch.

"Yes," said Kate as she turned the key. "She has three broken ribs, a punctured lung, a lacerated spleen, and a severe concussion. They were taking her into surgery when I left."

Eddie frowned in confusion as Kate turned the doorknob. Without warning, the stray shadow came up behind Kate and slammed her head into the doorjamb.

"Kate," screamed Eddie as Kate dropped her phone and keys in surprise and fell to her knees.

Kate fumbled for the weapon in the holster on her hip as the shadow stabbed her in the back twice.

She suddenly looked directly at Eddie. "I saved you. Why couldn't you save me?"

"Wait," said Eddie as she took a step toward the other woman. "Rowan?"

"You forgot about me so quickly, partner?"

"No, of course not."

"I thought you loved me," said Rowan.

"I do," said Eddie. "I did."

"So, why was it so easy to forget about me?" asked Rowan as she slumped forward against the front door.

"It wasn't." Eddie ran toward Rowan and cradled the other woman against her. "I'm sorry. I'm so sorry. Please come back. Please don't leave me. I'm sorry. I need you."

Eddie looked up as the stray shadow moved back toward her. She screamed, then awoke with a start.

I'm a horrible person, thought Eddie as she rolled over and sobbed into her pillow. How could she have forgotten about Rowan so quickly?

The chants of *"Off with her head"* from her dream echoed in Kate's mind. It was like her brain enjoyed torturing her. Not that it needed any help. Far too often, it was her own worst enemy. She sighed as she glared darkly down into her coffee cup.

She knew it was borderline illogical how often she had picked herself apart and criticized every little detail of herself. That was the part of Kate that made her feel weird, awkward, and out of place every time she talked, and often when she didn't even open her mouth. It was the part of her that forced her to focus on her faults, as numerous as they were, and held her back from the things that she really wanted. But no matter how much she attempted to drown out that part of her brain and tell herself that she was being insecure and needy, the louder that part seemed to get, and the more it seemed to drown out everything else.

It was like she could not switch off the thoughts in her head. Like she found herself on a downward spiral that she was unable to stop until she hit rock bottom. Alex had always been adept at picking up on when Kate was in this headspace, and even more adept at snapping her out of it before she got too far deep. It was just one of the many things Kate had relied on her wife for. She knew she shouldn't need someone else to make her feel better, but while Alex may not have always understood her, her wife had always been there when she'd needed her.

Then again, though, she often questioned what Alex—or anyone else, for that matter—had seen in her, in light of all her neuroses. She had never fully understood what exactly about her kept Alex interested. Not that she had ever asked Alex about it. Kate had never wanted to put her on the spot like that, or for Alex, or anyone else, to think she was that needy and insecure. She knew her own opinion of herself was warped, but she had always hoped that over time, she and Alex could work together to break down the walls she had built to protect herself. But losing Alex had meant the walls had gone back up, higher, wider, and stronger than ever before.

Now, Kate wondered whether anyone else would want to know her and see who she really was underneath the neurotic insecurities and social anxiety. She hoped she would find someone who could understand her—perhaps better than she understood herself. Someone who accepted her and loved her for who she was, no matter how similar or different they were. Whoever that was, she also hoped they would let Kate love them back. But she was not sure she was ready for that day to be any day soon.

She could not help another heavy sigh escaping her mouth as she picked up her cup.

"Sounds like you've had a rough day," said a woman who had moved to stand near her table at the Broadway Coffee House.

Kate looked up quickly. Her frustration dissipated the instant her gaze met Ainsley's warm blue eyes and even warmer smile.

"Hi," said Ainsley as she sat down.

"Hey," said Kate, exhaling in a whoosh as her shoulders slumped forward.

"How are you?"

"I'm fine, thanks. You?"

Ainsley crinkled her nose in disbelief. "Are you sure you're fine?"

"Yep," said Kate.

"You just seem a little flat."

"I'm just tired." Kate sighed and rubbed her forehead. "I didn't sleep well last night."

"Anything in particular that's bothering you?" asked Ainsley.

"Nope," said Kate shortly.

Ainsley frowned slightly. "Have I done something wrong?"

"No, why?"

"It's just that you've never been this monosyllabic with me before."

"No. I swear it's not you. Things in here"—Kate gestured toward her head—"are just on overdrive at the moment."

"Because of what I said yesterday?" asked Ainsley. "You know, about you, me, and Alex?"

"Yes," said Kate. "No. Maybe."

"You don't know?" asked Ainsley. "Do you want me to repeat the question?"

"Funny."

"I thought so. But in all seriousness, if this is about yesterday, I'm sorry if I overstepped or offended you."

"No, you didn't," said Kate. "There's nothing wrong with you saying what you said. It's just me. I have this tendency to overthink and overanalyze everything. It can make my head feel a little crowded sometimes."

"Okay," said Ainsley slowly. "Would you tell me if I had done something to upset you?"

"I don't know," said Kate with a shrug. "I mean, I'd want to."

"But you aren't sure whether you feel comfortable enough with me yet?"

"I'm sorry. I want to be comfortable to tell you things, and I want to trust you, but sometimes it just takes me a while to open up."

"You don't have to apologize for being who you are," said Ainsley. She reached out to place a hand over one of Kate's. "I want you to know that whatever is going on in that head of yours is something you can tell me. You never have to feel uncomfortable. You never have to feel like I'll judge you."

Eddie drummed her fingers on her desk as she paged through the background check she had run on Ainsley Cooper. It had come back surprisingly clean. Despite this, Eddie still felt like there was something suspicious about Ainsley and her interest in Kate Matthews.

She looked up as Hunter opened and closed the drawer of his desk. "Got some inspiration?" he asked.

"What?"

"You seem to be on a roll with something." Hunter inclined his head in the direction of the file Eddie had open on her desk. "I just assumed you'd had some kind of breakthrough on the Harrigan, Manson, and Tidbury case."

"No, it's for another case," said Eddie. "Just like yesterday, I have nothing on that one."

"Okay then. Do you want to run through it again?"

"Sure," said Eddie, "because there's totally something we're going to see now that we missed the first ten times."

"Do you have a better idea?"

"Nope."

"Right," said Hunter. "You okay?"

"Just peachy," said Eddie.

"How about trying that once more with feeling?"

Eddie sighed. "I'm just stressed. I want to solve this case and get it out of my head."

"Everything okay?" asked Hunter.

"Just having nightmares," said Eddie. "I'll be fine once we get this one closed."

"Hi, you two," said Kate as she dropped into the chair across from Erin and Akiko at the Broadway Coffee House.

"Hey, chicken," said Erin warmly.

"Hi, Kate." Akiko closed the notebook open on the table in front of her.

"I'm not interrupting anything, am I?" asked Kate as Akiko closed her laptop and put it into her bag.

"I wouldn't have asked you to join me if you were going to be interrupting," said Erin.

"Sorry," said Kate.

"It's nothing to be sorry about," said Akiko. "I had to head off anyway. At least this way Erin isn't left on his lonesome."

"Are you sure?" asked Kate.

"Absolutely." Akiko stood up and gathered her things. "It was nice seeing you again, Kate. Erin, I'll see you later."

"See you tomorrow."

"Bye, Akiko," said Kate as Akiko walked away.

Erin turned to look at her. "No offence, but you look like hell."

"Why would I ever think of taking offence to that?"

"You okay?" he asked.

"Just tired. I haven't been sleeping well." Kate rested her head on her palm, propping her elbow on the table. "Just a lot of really vivid dreams at the moment."

"Anything I can do?"

"I'm sure I'll be fine."

"That wasn't what I asked," said Erin. "Is there anything I can do?"

"Don't worry about it," said Kate.

"Kate ..." Erin paused. "How about I come over tonight? You, me, and as many movies as we can watch before the sun comes up."

"You don't have to do that."

"I know I don't, but I want to. Plus, isn't that what's always helped when you've had problems sleeping before?"

"Yes," said Kate. "This is the problem with knowing people for as long as we've known one another."

"Yep," said Erin. "So, you, me, and movies. It's a plan."

The graveyard that Ainsley found herself standing in was neat, with rows and rows of tombstones rising from the manicured lawn. Some were weathered and crumbling with age while others were smooth, polished marble with new black writing. The silence was oppressive, not even a bird chirping or the sound of the wind rustling through the trees.

Ainsley looked down at the tombstone in front of her. It looked new, with several bouquets of flowers in front of it. The epitaph read: *In loving memory of Alexandra Emma Quinn (1985–2018) and Katherine Eleanor Matthews (1990–2018)—Never say goodbye. Always say so long ... until we meet again.*

"No," said Ainsley as her eyes began to well up. "That didn't happen. Kate didn't die."

"But it could've happened," said a voice to her left.

Ainsley turned to see herself standing beside her, watching her.

"But it didn't," she said.

"Okay then," said the other Ainsley. "But you couldn't save Alex."

"I tried."

"Did you?"

"Of course I did," said Ainsley. "Why would you suggest otherwise?"

"Well," said the other Ainsley, "in one fell swoop, you eliminated your competition and ensured that Kate would be indebted to you for saving her life."

"That's not what I did."

"Good luck convincing Kate of that when you can't even convince yourself. Would we be having this conversation if you believed it? You seem to have forgotten, or at least not realized, that I'm you. I know what you think and feel. I know that you want her. You have for years, and now, not only is she within your grasp, but Cornelius has permitted you to throw yourself at her. And, let's face it, Alex is not the first person who stood between you and Kate who has died because of your actions—or should we say inaction?"

"My brother's death was not my fault," said Ainsley.

"And yet you knew exactly who I was referring to," said the other Ainsley. "What do they say? Once is an accident, twice is a coincidence, three times is a pattern? So, I wonder who will be lucky number three? Eddie? Maybe Agatha? Or, who knows, maybe Hunter is also her type?"

"Get out of my head."

"Aww, come on. I'm sure you can admit, just between the two of us, that losing Kate is your greatest fear."

"So what if it is?" asked Ainsley. "It hasn't happened. I was able to save her that day."

"But you couldn't save Alex," said the other Ainsley.

"And I have to feel the guilt for that for the rest of my life."

Chapter Three

"Guilt," said Ainsley as soon as Hunter answered the phone. She slowly pulled her car out of the lot. "It's all about guilt."

"I would say you've lost me, but that kind of infers that I know where we started," said Hunter. His voice sounded a little staticky through Ainsley's car speakers.

"The nightmares," said Ainsley. "I just had a nightmare about guilt. Kate has been having them as well, and I would wager that those women you've been investigating were too."

"That would explain everything, but what would cause so many women—human and Faerie—to have nightmares about guilt?" asked Hunter.

"An Alp," said Ainsley.

"A mountain?"

"No, not that kind of Alp. Alps are a type of Lesser Fae. They feed on their victims while they sleep. The victims experience vivid, distorted nightmares and are left with feelings of exhaustion and guilt."

"It fits, but how are we supposed to find it?" asked Hunter.

"I think it requires contact with the victims each time it wants to feed, so it will need continued contact with either Kate or me."

"Or Eddie."

"What?" asked Ainsley.

"She mentioned that she was having nightmares," said Hunter. "She said it was just due to the stress of the case, but considering the circumstances, it could be more than that."

"Okay," said Ainsley. "You stay with Eddie and stop her from going to sleep. I'll do the same with Kate."

"Sounds like a plan, but what do we do if it shows up?" asked Hunter.

"That I have no idea about, but I'll call Agatha and ask her to look into it. I'll let you know if she finds anything."

"Good, you're still awake," said Ainsley as Kate opened her front door.

"Um," said Kate. She self-consciously smoothed down her beige silk-and-cashmere sweater. "Hi to you, too."

"Sorry. Hi, baby. How are you?" asked Ainsley as she pulled Kate in for a hug.

"I'm fine, thanks," said Kate. They reluctantly pulled away from each other and she ushered Ainsley into her home.

Kate couldn't help but smile at Ainsley's words. They filled her with so much warmth. But it was more than that. There was something about Ainsley that made Kate feel safe, like she could trust the other woman. She was not someone who usually felt instantly comfortable with people, but with Ainsley, she was comfortable being herself.

Kate had even once said to Alex that if everyone she knew was gathered in a room, they would collectively only know about seventy-five per cent of what had happened in her life, as well as what she felt about those situations. There was a lot she did not share. Maybe that was because she had trust issues a mile wide. She'd had too many people in her life disappoint her or abandon her. But it was like Ainsley had effortlessly waltzed past all the walls and barriers Kate had spent the better part of three decades erecting, just as easily as she walked across Kate's living room now. And Kate was willing to let her do it, even though it was terrifying.

"She lies," said Erin from his seat on the floor in front of the couch.

"I'm not lying," said Kate. As Erin raised his eyebrows, she reiterated, "I'm not."

"Okay, so what would you call it, then?" he asked as the two women settled onto the couch.

"I know this one," said Ainsley. "Let me guess: the social convention?"

"Clearly, I can't win with either of you," said Kate. As much as she wished she could be mad at the two of them, she loved watching Ainsley connect with Erin. "I haven't been sleeping well," she added, "so Erin suggested that we have a movie marathon. That way I'll either not sleep or be too exhausted not to."

She could have said more to Ainsley about her nightmares, and she was sure that a lot of other people would not have hesitated to spill what exactly had been bothering them. But Kate was not like a lot of people. As much as she wanted to connect with Ainsley, she was still private and reserved. She hoped Ainsley would be willing to give her the time and space to enable her to open up, be vulnerable, and show the other woman her most authentic self. Kate wanted to show Ainsley the real her, and she hoped that Ainsley would respect that person. She wanted Ainsley to know that she could offer a lot—deep and philosophical conversation, a sense of humor, encouragement, friendship, and her whole heart. But to offer that, Kate needed to know that she would be accepted despite her quirkiness, her awkwardness, and her slight off-centeredness.

"Kate?" asked Ainsley, breaking through her internal monologue.

Kate blinked and looked between Ainsley and Erin, who were both watching her.

"Are you okay with Ainsley joining us?" asked Erin.

"Yes, please," said Kate. "I mean, if you want to. You don't have to, though, if you have somewhere else you'd rather be."

"There is nowhere I'd rather be," said Ainsley. "So, what are we watching?"

Eddie sighed as she stood up from her desk. She picked up her messenger bag and slung it over her shoulder. "I'm off."

"I was thinking," said Hunter as he scrambled to his feet. "Do you want to go out and grab a drink?"

"Given our last night out," said Eddie, "I'd rather not have as much excitement tonight."

"I promise no excitement. Just a quiet night with a couple of drinks."

"Sorry, I'm not feeling up to it. How about a rain check?"

"We could also do beers and takeout at mine?" asked Hunter. "Or yours, if you'd prefer that?"

"Honestly," said Eddie, "I just want to sleep."

"Are you sure I can't convince you to change your mind?"

"Oh—um..." Eddie stopped short at Hunter's insistence. "Are you asking me out?"

"No. No. Sorry. No. I just, um—"

"Just spit it out."

"Your nightmares," said Hunter.

Eddie crossed her arms. "I didn't say I was having nightmares."

"Well, you said you were having vivid stress dreams, and you've been irritable and mopey since," said Hunter. "Plus, the friends and family of those women we were investigating all mentioned that they had been talking about guilt before their deaths."

"And?"

"I think it's an Alp."

"A what?"

"Long story," said Hunter. "But the short version is that it's a form of Lesser Fae."

Eddie's eyebrows shot up toward her hairline. "A Lesser Fae?"

"Yes," said Hunter. "And I hope I'm not wrong about you knowing exactly what that means."

"You aren't wrong," said Eddie cautiously. She definitely had not expected her new partner to know anything about her world, but maybe, just maybe, she had found herself an unexpected ally. Just knowing about the Fae didn't mean that he could be trusted, though. She watched Hunter closely, searching for any signs of deception. When she saw none, she continued, "So, what exactly is an Alp?"

"It feeds on women while they're sleeping, causing them to have vivid nightmares and feelings of guilt and remorse," answered Hunter.

"So, don't go to sleep?"

"Yep."

"Okay," said Eddie. "Drinks and Chinese takeout at mine, then?"

Kate cast a brief glance at the woman beside her on the couch. Erin had long since slumped down on the floor. Kate picked up the remote and switched off the TV, looking over her shoulder at Ainsley as she placed the remote back on the coffee table.

Ainsley raised an eyebrow. "What if I was watching that?"

"Please," said Kate. "You stopped paying attention about five minutes before I did, so I thought we could talk or something instead."

"Is there something in mind that you want to talk about tonight?" asked Ainsley. She leaned back on the arm of the couch and pulled her legs up underneath her so she was facing Kate.

"Well ..." Kate mirrored Ainsley's position on the opposite end of the couch. She chewed on her lip for a moment before she continued hesitantly, "I feel like we often spend a lot of time talking about me, so I was thinking that we could play twenty-one questions, if you want to?" She cringed at how hopeful and awkward the words sounded.

"As a way to get to know one another?" asked Ainsley.

"Yes." Kate hoped Ainsley didn't think her idea was juvenile. She often found it easier to answer questions instead of offering up the same information without prompting. "But we don't have to, if you think it's a silly idea," she said in a rush, filling the silence that had stretched between them.

"I think it sounds fun," said Ainsley. "But how about instead of taking turns to ask each other a question, we both answer the question."

"So, we would just alternate who thinks of the question?"

"Exactly."

"I like the sound of that," said Kate. A mischievous smile spread across her face. "I want to go first."

"Okay," said Ainsley softly.

Kate dropped her gaze to her wine glass as she gathered her thoughts. "Who is your celebrity crush? Or crushes, if you have more than one?"

Ainsley chuckled warmly. "Okay, but I have one point of clarification. How are we defining celebrity? Are we just talking about athletes, singers, and actors?"

"Now, that in itself has me curious," said Kate. "So, let's go broad. For the present purposes, a celebrity is someone who has achieved some kind of fame or has become well-known for something. That can include actors, writers, musicians, athletes, politicians, philosophers, or anything else you can think of."

"Okay," said Ainsley slowly. "So at the top of the list would be Katie McGrath and Lucy Lawless."

"Who else is on your list, though?" asked Kate as she placed her glass down and scooted toward the middle of the couch. "I don't think you would clarify what I meant by celebrity if it were just those two—they fit any definition of the word."

"I guess something about Eleanor Roosevelt has always intrigued me," said Ainsley as she placed her glass down as well.

"Now that is an interesting answer."

"That's good to know," said Ainsley. "Your turn."

"There are a few on the list," said Kate. "Cate Blanchett, Gillian Anderson, and Zoie Palmer."

"A thing for accents, huh? And blondes."

"Maybe."

"Also, Cate Blanchett?" asked Ainsley. "When you picture her in *Thor: Ragnarök*—well, suddenly your attraction to Alex makes so much sense."

"Hush, you," said Kate, returning Ainsley's smile.

"Is there anyone else on that list you want to share?"

Kate's gaze dropped from the other woman's eyes to her lips. She quickly looked back up, and Ainsley's gaze suddenly felt darker and more intense. Kate swallowed hard. She wasn't sure what prompted the next word out of her mouth, but she couldn't stop herself from answering Ainsley's question.

"You."

Kate blushed instantly at her own candor and looked away, cursing her unexpected forwardness. She leaned back against the arm of the couch in an effort to reestablish some distance.

"Sorry. I shouldn't have said it."

"I'm glad you did," said Ainsley.

Kate looked up quickly as Ainsley moved toward her side of the couch. For a moment that felt simultaneously infinitesimal and achingly long, Ainsley hovered hesitantly over her.

Kate lay back against the arm of the couch. She looked up at Ainsley, aware that the other woman wanted her to set the pace.

"Please," she whispered softly into the air between them.

Ainsley moved forward, placing her knees on either side of Kate's hips. One of her hands landed beside Kate's head. Ainsley paused for another moment before she reached up to cup Kate's jaw. Her hand shifted from Kate's cheek to the back of her neck.

Kate drew in a ragged breath as she looked up into the heated gaze of the woman above her. As she did, the echo of *"Off with her head"* sounded through her mind like a ringing indictment of her actions.

Before Ainsley could close the distance between them, Kate suddenly pulled away. In an instant, she had slipped out from under Ainsley and off the couch. She snagged both wine glasses off of the table. Before she could move further away, Ainsley's hand encircled her wrist.

"Is everything okay?"

"Yes," said Kate without turning around. "I just ..." She felt unable to look at the other woman; not because of Ainsley's actions, but her own. "I'm sorry."

"It's okay," said Ainsley as she squeezed Kate's hand reassuringly. "It's too soon. I get it."

Eddie ushered Hunter into her studio apartment in Seattle's Lower Queen Anne district. It had twelve-foot ceilings, with oak hardwood floors that contrasted with its exposed historic brick and large west-facing windows that provided a lot of natural light.

Eddie pointed Hunter toward a window seat. As he sat down, she placed the takeout boxes on the table and opened the fridge to grab two beers. Eddie sat down beside Hunter and opened one of the takeout boxes wordlessly. She felt Hunter watching her for several moments before he twisted the cap off his beer and opened his box of food.

The tense silence between the two partners stretched for several moments as they both ate slowly. Ultimately, it grew too tense for Eddie, and she placed her chopsticks on the table and turned toward Hunter.

"So," she said.

Hunter placed his chopsticks down. "So?"

"You know about the Lesser Fae?"

"Direct and to the point it is, then," said Hunter. "Yes, I do. As do you."

"Was that a statement or a question?"

"A bit of both."

"Yes, I do," said Eddie. "Does that mean you know about Faeries too?"

"Yes."

"Okay. So, what exactly does that make your role in all of this?"

Hunter sighed before he said, "I'm a shape-shifter."

Ainsley looked down at Kate as the other woman's eyes fluttered closed. "I thought you were supposed to be staying awake," she said.

She had reassured Kate that she was not hurt by what had happened between them. She had been confused initially, for sure, but not hurt. If it had been anyone else, she would be questioning the mixed signals, but Kate had a reason to be so skittish. If Ainsley hadn't been so caught up in the intensity of the moment, she would have stopped it before things got as far as they did. She knew Kate was not ready to move on from her wife.

Eventually, Ainsley had coaxed Kate to lie down on the couch with her head on top of the pillow on Ainsley's lap. She had also turned the TV back on with the volume down low so as not to wake up Erin.

The soft light from the TV screen accentuated Kate's cheekbones. Her body sagged limply into the couch. There was something so comforting about that. It filled Ainsley with warmth to have Kate so close, looking so soft and peaceful. She could not help but imagine Kate looking just like this in her bedroom one morning—or, hopefully, many mornings.

"Hmm?" asked Kate softly as Ainsley brushed strands of her hair behind her ear.

"I said I thought you were supposed to be staying awake." Ainsley moved her hand away from Kate's cheek and ran her fingers up and down Kate's arm.

"I'm awake."

"You don't sound like it."

"I just feel all nice and warm," said Kate. "Plus that thing you're doing feels really good."

"Do you want me to stop?" asked Ainsley; her fingers stilled for a moment.

"No," said Kate.

"Okay." Ainsley started moving her hand again. "Stay awake, Kate. Talk to me."

"'Bout what?"

"I don't know. We already played twenty-one questions." Ainsley thought through ways of both keeping the other woman awake and encouraging her to open up. "Okay, I know. How about we play two truths and lie?"

"'Kay," said Kate.

"You go first."

"I ... don't like balloons, the city I loved visiting the most is a tie between Edinburgh and Salzburg, and I've watched every episode of *Game of Thrones*."

"Balloons," said Ainsley. "Who doesn't like balloons?"

"Well, me."

"Really? Why?"

"I've just never liked them. I think I associate them with clowns," said Kate. "But even the sound of people making those balloon animals puts me on edge and makes me a bit anxious."

"So, what was the lie?" asked Ainsley.

"I haven't seen every episode of *Game of Thrones*," said Kate. "I've never seen a single episode and I've never read any of the books either."

"Seriously?"

"Yep."

"You and I are going to have a conversation about that."

"Aren't we already?"

"Another one when you aren't looking all soft and adorable, I promise," said Ainsley.

"I like the sound of that," said Kate.

"Good. Okay, my turn. I've never dyed my hair, I've been to more than one Olympic Games, and I've never been to Disneyland," said Ainsley. After several moments of silence, she looked down at Kate, waiting for her response. Kate's eyes were closed. "Kate? Come on, baby. Talk to me. Come on, Kate. Wake up."

She was just about to shake Kate when she saw a cloud of mist seeping into the apartment through the gaps in the windows and doors.

"That is never a good sign," said Ainsley. The mist edged closer and closer. "Okay, Kate, now is the time to wake up. Come on, baby."

Ainsley looked up again as the mist seemed to form a humanoid-shaped mass. It slowly solidified into a tall, well-built man with blonde hair, a full beard, and blue eyes, wearing lederhosen, a checked shirt, and a brown felt alpine hat.

"Okay, I'm so sorry in advance," said Ainsley, pushing Kate off her lap and getting to her feet.

CHAPTER FOUR

Kate was jolted awake by her head suddenly hitting the side of her couch. She sat up, rubbing her head.

"What on Earth is going on?"

As she heard scuffling, Kate looked toward her front door. Ainsley was there, pinned to the ground by a tall, well-built man.

Startled, Kate sat bolt upright as a surge of fear and adrenaline cleared away any remaining cobwebs of sleep. She stood, but tumbled back onto the couch again when her feet landed on something softer and with more give than her floor. In her haste, she had accidentally stood on Erin, who had still been asleep in front of the couch.

"Ow. Kate, what are you doing?" Erin sat up. Kate met his gaze for a moment before she turned back in stunned silence to Ainsley and the tall, blonde man. Erin followed the direction of her gaze. "Am I dreaming?"

"Not unless we're having the same dream," said Kate.

"A little help here, guys?" said Ainsley as the man's grip tightened around her throat.

"Oh, right." Kate got to her feet again, more mindful of Erin this time. She looked around the room to find something to help, but drew a blank until her gaze landed on the heavy wooden grazing board on the coffee table. "I hope this works."

She grasped the handle and ran toward Ainsley and the man grappling on the floor. Kate hesitated, then raised the board and swung it at the back of the man's head. She stumbled forward slightly when her blow did not meet the resistance she was expecting. Instead of connecting with the man's head, she had only succeeded in knocking off his hat. As it hit the floor, the man's arms buckled slightly.

Ainsley looked quickly at the hat, then over the man's shoulder to meet Kate's gaze.

"Kate, get the hat."

"What?"

"I said get the hat!"

"Right." Kate dropped the board and quickly grabbed the hat from the floor. "Okay, now what?"

The man turned and looked at Kate over his shoulder. "Give it back."

Ainsley used his moment of distraction to push up and flip the man onto his back, landing on top of him. Erin jumped in to help Ainsley hold him down.

"Should we call the police?" asked Erin, looking between Kate and Ainsley.

"Right," said Kate. "Just let me get my phone—"

"No, Kate," said Ainsley quickly. "Wait. This isn't something the police can help with."

"Um, a strange intruder in someone's home is definitely within their job description," said Erin.

"Not this intruder," said Ainsley.

Kate frowned. "Oh, he's like you?"

"No," said Ainsley. "Well, yes. Kind of."

"Can someone please explain to me what is going on?" asked Erin.

"Later," said Ainsley.

"So, what exactly are we supposed to do about this besides pinning him to my living room floor?" asked Kate. "Because I do not see that as a long-term solution."

"Tell him to leave, Kate," said Ainsley.

"What?"

"He will do anything you ask if you promise to give him back the hat."

"Seriously?" asked Kate.

"Hey, I don't make the rules," said Ainsley, "I just follow them."

"Right. So, hey, you, guy … person—if you want your hat, you, um …" Kate paused. "How dangerous is he?"

"What?" asked Ainsley.

"If I tell him to leave, will that send him after someone else or not?" asked Kate. "I just need some parameters to work within here."

"Tell him to leave Seattle and not come back," said Ainsley. "It should be enough."

"Okay, great." Kate turned to look at the man. "So, you, if you want this hat back, then you need to agree to leave Seattle and not come back."

"Fine," grunted the man. "Just give me back my hat."

"With the German get-up, I was not expecting him to speak English," said Erin.

"Stupid American," grumbled the man.

"Okay, now I feel insulted," said Erin.

"Well, a large percentage of the world's population does speak English," said Ainsley.

"Plus," said Kate, "he came here as a traveler. I feel like you should show some respect for local cultures when you travel by at least learning the language to engage in basic conversation."

"Kate, honey," said Ainsley. "Now is not the time."

"Right. Sorry." She turned back to the man. "If I give this back, do you promise to leave Seattle immediately and not come back?"

"Yes," he said.

"Okay, Erin and Ainsley, let him up." Kate waited for her friends to release the man before she offered him the hat. "Okay. Well, here you go."

The man grunted once in acknowledgment as he grasped the hat. In an instant, he disappeared in a mist that quickly dissipated, leaving Ainsley and Erin sitting on the floor.

"I have no idea what that just was, but I wish I could make an exit like that," said Erin as he got to his feet and dusted off his jeans.

"Do you think that's the last we'll see of him?" asked Kate. She reached out to help Ainsley to her feet.

Ainsley kept her hand entwined with Kate's, stroking her thumb against the inside of Kate's wrist. "I think so. He will be true to his word. He won't be back."

"So," said Erin. "Is someone going to explain what on Earth just happened?"

"Is there anything else you wanted to ask?" asked Hunter.

"There are a million things that I want to ask," admitted Eddie slowly. She didn't want to admit that she had been overjoyed when Hunter had mentioned the Fae. That she'd thought she had finally found an ally to help her find Rowan's killer and protect Kate.

"Why don't you, then?" asked Hunter.

Eddie shrugged. "Because I'm not sure you'll tell me the truth."

"And the truth is important to you?"

"I don't enjoy being lied to, and I don't enjoy knowing when I'm being lied to."

Hunter rolled his eyes and sighed in exasperation.

"What?"

"I don't know," said Hunter. "It just sounds like you're so used to people hiding things from you that you expect everyone to lie to you."

"Not everyone," said Eddie.

"But you expect me to lie, even though I've never lied to you before. Why do you assume the worst of me?"

"I just don't trust you," said Eddie automatically. That hope about Hunter being an ally had been extinguished the minute he had told her he was a shifter. A shifter was responsible for Rowan's death and the attacks on Kate. It was unlikely that there would be another shifter in Seattle, which left only Hunter as the most likely culprit.

"Right, but you trusted me just fine until about an hour ago," he said.

"Yes, of course I did."

"Watch it, partner, your prejudice is showing."

"I'm not prejudiced," said Eddie.

"Really?" asked Hunter. "You automatically assume that I'm lying because of who I am. That is the very definition of prejudice."

"It's not like that."

"Seriously? Are you really that naïve? Have you lived your whole life inside a pretty pink bubble?"

"What is that supposed to mean?" asked Eddie.

"Imagine if the shoe was on the other foot. How would you feel if I immediately distrusted you because of something about you that you can't change? How would that make you feel?" asked Hunter. "This world is filled with people different to you. Try not to write them all off based on those differences."

"I didn't mean it like that," said Eddie.

"Regardless of what you'll admit, you did, actually," said Hunter. Before he could say anything further, his phone chimed with an incoming message. Hunter read it, then looked up at Eddie. "Looks like the Alp has been neutralized. Guess that means I can leave."

"Hunter, wait," she said as he got to his feet and strode toward the front door.

"I'll see you at work," said Hunter before he opened the door and walked out.

"Are you sure you don't want me to stay?" asked Ainsley as she and Kate stepped out onto the landing.

"No, it's okay." Kate closed the door behind them and leaned back against it.

Ainsley stepped closer to her. "I can help explain to Erin what that was."

"I'm not sure there's any way that I could explain, even if you were here." Kate looked down at her feet and crossed her arms across her chest. "I mean, I'm still getting my head around the whole Faerie thing, and now there's ... whatever that was."

"It was an Alp."

"A what?"

"An Alp," Ainsley repeated. "It's one of the Lesser Fae. As it feeds on its sleeping victims, they experience vivid, distorted nightmares. The victims are then left with feelings of exhaustion and guilt."

"So, the dreams I had …" Kate looked up at Ainsley as a sudden warmth filled her chest, a spark of hope flaring to life. "They were just because of that Alp thing?"

"Possibly." Ainsley reached out to cup Kate's cheek. "Your dreams, though—are they what's been eating at you?"

"What makes you think that something's been eating at me?"

Ainsley raised an eyebrow. "You weren't yourself when I saw you at the coffee house."

"Okay," admitted Kate. "Fine. I had a nightmare. Or a stress dream. I have very vivid dreams when I'm stressed."

"And you thought it had something to do with what we talked about?" Ainsley stroked her thumb against Kate's cheek.

"I'm sorry," said Kate. She looked away from Ainsley and over the other woman's shoulder.

"Hey," said Ainsley as she shifted to meet Kate's gaze again. "You don't need to apologize for anything. You don't have to worry about upsetting me or offending me. You have a right to your feelings, and I would have understood if you had told me. You can trust me."

"I want to. Trust you, that is. I just don't trust people easily or quickly. I'm sorry," said Kate again. She reached out to entangle her hand with Ainsley's free one. "But it's just hard for me to open up as much as I may want to."

"Once again," said Ainsley, "you don't have to apologize. I mean it. I'm never going to judge you for being who you are."

"I'm trying to believe you," said Kate sincerely as she looked up at Ainsley.

"That's good enough for me."

"An Alp? Really? It's good that it's been handled. Thanks for letting me know." Nolan hung up the phone and turned toward Akiko, who was sitting on the other side of his desk. "Now we have Alps roaming the city."

"My understanding was that it was just one Alp," she said.

"Does that make it any better?"

"Yes. The fewer Alps the better, unless you want a whole pack terrorizing Seattle."

"My question is, why was one terrorizing the city in the first place?" asked Nolan. "I've never heard of one traveling this far from continental Europe before."

"I suppose the Alp would be here for the same reason as the other Lesser Fae that have been flooding into the city," said Akiko.

"And that is?"

"The power expelled by your first Faerie princess when she saved her partner's life by healing her—well, that kind of power leaves a trace," said Akiko. "A residue of sorts that members of the Lesser Fae can sense. As I said, a number of Lesser Fae have already come to the city, and I wouldn't be surprised if more will be drawn here for the same reason. They sense the power and they are looking for it."

"And all Lesser Fae can sense the residue of Faerie powers?" asked Nolan.

"Not all Lesser Fae, and not all usage of Faerie powers," said Akiko. "Most residues are barely perceptible above the existing baseline from the power that flows through everyone and everything. But an untrained Faerie bringing someone back from that close to death's door—that leaves a trace. To be honest, even if she had training, it would have left a residue."

"So, why would they be looking for it?" asked Nolan.

"It's more instinctual than anything," said Akiko. "They crave the potency of the power denied to them."

"Maybe we can use that to our advantage. We can use the Lesser Fae to orchestrate the deaths of Kate and Cornelius."

"And then?"

"Then the throne that was my birthright will finally be mine," said Nolan. "And no one will be able to trace any of this bloodshed back to me."

Kate kicked off the comforter draped over her in frustration. She had been lying in bed, trying to drift off, for almost an hour. One would think that after a couple of nights of nightmare-plagued tossing and turning, she would have found it easy. But she could not seem to turn her brain off. Admittedly, this was not the first time that she had struggled with falling asleep. But she had always had Alex to distract her before.

Kate picked up her phone from her bedside table as she thought about calling Erin instead. She sighed, remembering how tired he had been when he'd left. It was likely that he would already be at home and well on his way to being fast asleep. Kate reached out to place her phone back down when another name popped into her head.

Her text to Ainsley had already been sent before she questioned whether she was being selfish, bothering Ainsley or waking her up.

She was also a little unsure about where exactly she stood with the other woman. Ainsley had said that she understood, but Kate could not help but wonder whether she would see her again. She had given Ainsley mixed signals, but she was unsure what she wanted their relationship to be. There was a strong connection between them. There was something about Ainsley that she was drawn to. But what did it mean?

Ainsley seemed willing to start a physical relationship, but her reasons weren't clear. It may have simply been a continuation of her suggestion to have some meaningless fun to help Kate move forward. That was not the kind of thing that interested Kate, but she wasn't sure where that left them.

She nearly dropped her phone in surprise when it suddenly vibrated in her hand, startling her from her thoughts. She smiled at Ainsley's name on the screen.

Kate answered the call. "Hi."

"Hey," said Ainsley as she stifled a yawn. "I saw your message. Is everything okay?"

"I'm sorry for waking you up. You should go back to sleep."

"You didn't wake me up."

"Really?" asked Kate incredulously.

"Yes, really," said Ainsley, voice half soft and half exasperated. "I was just getting into bed when I saw your message. Now, what is going on?"

"I couldn't sleep," said Kate, her voice sounding small and quiet even to herself.

"I think that's pretty understandable given the night you've had. So, how can I help?"

Kate closed her eyes as that warm feeling filled her chest again at Ainsley's words. As much as she hated feeling so vulnerable and needy, she loved how willing Ainsley was to help her, again. It also helped to silence her earlier doubts about Ainsley distancing herself after Kate's rejection earlier that evening.

"How about you tell me about your day?" asked Kate. "Or at least, the parts of it that I wasn't there for."

She let Ainsley's words wash over her as she focused on the other woman's voice. It did not take long for Kate to drift off to sleep.

EPISODE FOUR: HAWTHORN

But seduction isn't making someone do what they don't want to do; seduction is enticing someone into doing what they secretly want to do already.
—Steven Dublanica

CHAPTER ONE

Grief, thought Kate as she looked away from her laptop toward the window of her office, comes in waves. Some days it feels like you're okay and you're through the worst of it. It was easy to think that she was ready to move on when she had a lot of those types of days together. There were even times during those periods where she thought that she was ready to start rebuilding her life again, like building castles on the sand. But then, without warning, another wave of grief would come crashing in and the sandcastle she had built would come crumbling down.

She had become so accustomed to the waves of grief, no matter how unexpected they may be, that she had stopped making her castles in the sand. Had stopped trying to move forward. Instead, she continued to stand on the shore, paralyzed and unsure.

Yet somehow, that was not the worst of it. No, the worst of it was the people she was holding on the beach with her. What if Erin was moving forward? What if he had learned to build his castles further from the shore? Was she the one who kept throwing a bucket of water on his castle every time she brought up Alex? What if Erin was only saying he was willing to talk because he believed it was the right thing to do? What if he was only humoring her? Was Kate forcing him to shoulder her grief as well as his own?

And what about Detective Caulfield? She was grieving the loss of her partner—a woman who had looked identical to Kate. Kate could not help but wonder whether her presence was bringing up ghosts the detective had put to rest. Was she a constant reminder of what the other woman had lost?

Then there was Ainsley. Was Kate leading her on? She'd been sending mixed signals, particularly the other night on her couch. Was Ainsley going to grow tired of the backward and forward, of them coming together and Kate pulling away? Was Ainsley even going to want to be in Kate's life when she realized how much of a mess she was, how broken she was?

Kate questioned whether any of them would stick around if they ever saw who she truly was beneath the facade. If they saw that she was barely holding it together, barely making it through the day. Would it be better if she walked away and left them to their lives? Would they be happier? Would their lives be better if Kate was not in them as a constant reminder of the people they'd lost, the people they could not have?

She could walk away. She could disappear and rebuild her life on the other side of the world. She could let them live their lives without her as the albatross around their necks constantly pulling them down. She could, she should—but she wasn't sure that she was really that selfless.

"Knock, knock," said Ainsley, interrupting Kate's darkening thoughts.

She turned away from the window to see Ainsley leaning against the door frame of her new office at the University of Washington. Kate hesitated for a moment before meeting Ainsley's gaze. The warmth in her eyes felt like someone lighting a candle in a darkened room to chase away the shadows. Kate was helpless to stop the soft smile that spread across her face.

"Hey," she said. "How are you?"

"I'm well, thanks." Ainsley entered and sat down on the other side of Kate's desk. "How are you?"

"Tired," said Kate. "It's been a long day. Is it wrong to say that this whole working thing is a little overrated?"

"No, but it is reassuring."

"Why is that?"

"You've just seemed remarkably calm, nonchalant, and put-together through all of this," said Ainsley. "I honestly wasn't expecting that."

"What were you expecting?" asked Kate.

"I guess a bit more organized chaos," said Ainsley. "Well, that or a complete and utter meltdown."

"Have you ever seen a duck before?" asked Kate.

"That was an abrupt change of conversation," said Ainsley. "Yes, I've seen a duck before."

"Have you seen one on a lake or pond?"

"Yes, I think so," said Ainsley with a frown.

"They tend to look very calm. Just floating along. Barely leaving a ripple. What you don't see is that under the water, they're paddling furiously."

"Are you saying you're a duck?"

"I'm saying that just because things appear one way, it doesn't make it true," said Kate. "There's often a lot more going on below the surface than is visible to the naked eye."

"Like an iceberg?" asked Ainsley. "I've heard that over ninety per cent of an iceberg's volume is below the waterline."

"I'm pretty sure that was the entire issue with the *Titanic*," said Kate.

"Never seen the movie," said Ainsley. "I always figured I knew how it would end."

"Isn't that a tad pessimistic? Plus, it's a love story. A tragic one, but a love story all the same."

"It figures you'd say something like that."

"And why is that?" asked Kate.

"You're one of the few people I know who have the perfect blend of optimism, idealism, and realism," said Ainsley. "Not to mention being kind, compassionate, intelligent, and incredibly eloquent."

"Flattery will get you everywhere," said Kate, looking down to hide the blush spreading across her cheeks.

"Not flattery," said Ainsley, "honesty. However, if it truly can get you anywhere, how about a drink?"

"Unfortunately, I still have some work to do before I can leave," said Kate.

"Well, fortunately for me," said Ainsley as she got up and walked back to the door, where she had left a bottle of wine on the floor, "you don't have to go anywhere for us to have a drink."

"Okay, then." Kate got up to grab some water glasses from the sideboard. "I must warn you, I don't exactly keep wine glasses in my office."

Ainsley laughed. "I think I can manage."

"Good," said Kate. "So, what are we toasting to?"

"Well, how about the fact that you've made it through your first month in Seattle in one piece?"

"See, when you say things like that, I can't tell whether you're joking," said Kate. "I mean, should we really be celebrating the fact that I haven't suffered some kind of bodily harm?"

"I don't think anyone would view what you've been put through as a positive."

"Ah, so sarcasm is your second language, then."

"Sorry," came another voice. Kate looked up to see Erin standing in the doorway beside Akiko. "Are we interrupting?"

"Hi, you two," said Kate. "What brings you by?"

"Well, I was thinking we could go to this," said Akiko. She stepped forward and passed a flyer to Kate.

"A Halloween masquerade party?" asked Kate incredulously. She handed the flyer to Ainsley. "Isn't this for students?"

"It's for anyone who wants to go, and I think it sounds like a good idea," said Erin. "Please come with us, Kate."

"You know that's really not my kind of thing," said Kate.

"I know, but it's Halloween," said Erin pleadingly.

Kate shook her head. In response, Erin widened his eyes and pouted almost comically. Kate narrowed her gaze and furrowed her brow. Erin smiled broadly back. Ainsley laughed at the exchange until both Kate and Erin turned toward her, each with an eyebrow raised in question.

"Don't think you're getting out of this one," said Erin.

"I'll go if Kate goes," said Ainsley with a shrug. Erin grinned victoriously.

"Traitor," said Kate with a look at Ainsley. She sighed. "Fine. Sure. I'll go, but only if you come over, Erin, and help me find something to wear."

"Deal," said Erin. "I'll even protect you from any stray clowns we come across."

"Clowns? You're afraid of clowns?" asked Ainsley as Kate shivered slightly.

"No, I'm not afraid of clowns. I'm just very uncomfortable with them. I had a phobia when I was a kid, but I grew out of that. Same thing with the balloons and face painting."

"You almost had a panic attack last year at that fair we went to, when the person making balloon animals for kids popped one," said Erin.

"Hush, you."

When Erin raised an eyebrow in response, Kate poked her tongue out. Erin shook his head, laughing.

"Well, I'll protect you from any dentists then," she said defensively.

"A fear of dentists is completely rational," said Erin.

"No, it isn't."

"Yes, it is. One literally tried to kill me."

"Children, please," said Ainsley.

"Sorry," said Kate.

"So, what are we drinking to?" asked Akiko as she poured herself a glass of wine. Without waiting for a response, she walked toward the shelves in Kate's office to examine the books Kate had placed there.

"I'm up for some wine," said Erin. He poured a glass and dropped into the seat next to Ainsley.

"Sorry," said Kate as she looked up at Ainsley.

"It's okay, baby." Ainsley reached out to squeeze Kate's hand, smiling softly before she slowly levered herself out of her chair. "I should go and let you catch up with your friends."

"Are you sure?" asked Kate as she got to her feet. She picked up the bottle of wine and passed it back to Ainsley.

"Please don't leave on our account," said Erin.

"No, it's fine," said Ainsley. "We'll do this again sometime soon."

"That sounds great," said Kate as the two women walked toward the door.

Ainsley smiled and reached out to squeeze Kate's hand. "I'll call you."

Kate noticed Erin watching her as she took a seat back at her desk.

"Baby?" asked Erin.

"It's not like that," said Kate.

"But do you want it to be?"

"It doesn't matter."

"Alex would want you to move on," said Erin.

"I'm not having this conversation here." Kate gestured in Akiko's direction.

"But you'll have it later?" asked Erin. "Great. Drinks at yours tonight, then."

"So, what was that?" asked Erin as he settled onto the couch in Kate's apartment with a glass of wine.

"What was what?" Kate played coy as she moved to mirror Erin's position at the opposite end of the couch, wanting to delay the conversation as long as possible.

"You and Ainsley just seem to be getting very ..." He paused, seemingly searching for the most appropriate word. "Chummy."

"We're friends," said Kate. "Well, we're friendly at least, and working toward friends. Maybe friend-adjacent."

"Just friends?" asked Erin with a raised eyebrow.

"Yes," said Kate, "just friends. It's just too soon after Alex for me to consider anything more than that."

"Does Ainsley know that?"

"She knows that we're friends. She's only ever offered to be a friend. Well, she may have offered a friendship with benefits, but that's beside the point."

"I'm pretty sure that is exactly the point," said Erin.

"She just wants to be friends, and to be honest, I need more friends," said Kate. "Between losing Alex and moving here, there aren't many people I can talk to about how things are going at the moment."

"You can always talk to me."

"I know. And I appreciate it."

"Okay," said Erin. "Now, I don't want you to take what I'm about to say the wrong way."

"That is never a good opening line," said Kate.

"Well, compared to what I'm about to say, I'm sure you'll think that was practically cheery."

"Even less comforting, but please continue."

"It was clear how much you and my sister loved one another," said Erin. "Anyone who saw you together could see how in love you were."

"Why do I feel like the next word you're about to say is 'but'?" asked Kate.

"But," said Erin, "the two of you never made sense long term. I just didn't see you staying together without one of you making some serious compromises."

"Relationships do involve compromises."

"I know that. At least in theory, if not from experience. But it always seemed like you were the one making the compromises. Like you were the one trying to change all the time. She seemed to make decisions about her life and you changed to accommodate them. It was her taking and you giving."

"Okay, so Alex and I were imperfect people. Who isn't?" said Kate defensively.

"That isn't what I meant."

"Things between us weren't always easy. Sometimes they were even downright hard, but you know what? It was worth it, because I loved her and she loved me. I didn't need anything more than that. She didn't need to do anything more than that."

"Please don't misunderstand me. I'm not saying either of you did anything wrong," said Erin. "I loved my sister, and I miss her every day, but she was set in her ways. She could be rigid and inflexible."

"She was actually flexible," said Kate, breaking the tension with a mischievous grin.

"That was more information than I needed to hear," said Erin with a shake of his head. "I feel like I need to bleach my brain or something to remove that visual."

"Sorry," said Kate, still smiling.

"You don't look sorry," retorted Erin.

"On the inside." She patted a hand against her chest. "So, why are you telling me all of this?"

"Because I want to see you happy," said Erin. "And I think Alex would have wanted you to find a way to move on."

"Okay?"

"And I think Ainsley could be good for you," Erin added. "She comes across as everything Alex wasn't."

"Okay, firstly, you've only met her, like, three times," said Kate. "Secondly, it has only been a few months, and once again, I'm not sure I'm ready."

"As you said, maybe all she wants is to be your friend with some really fun benefits," said Erin. "It doesn't need to be more than that if you don't want it to be. You don't always need to be thinking about relationships and commitment and forever. You can just try to enjoy yourself. You're in a new city with a new job and a new home, so have fun, have a fling, have hot sex."

"Thanks for meeting with me," said Ainsley as she sat down across from Hunter at the Broadway Coffee House. She placed a short Americano in front of Hunter and took a sip of her caramel macchiato.

"It's what you pay me for," said Hunter.

"Seriously?"

"You do make life interesting." Hunter offered her a wry grin.

"Thanks ever so much," said Ainsley dryly.

"I try," said Hunter with a shrug. The grin dropped from his face and he gave Ainsley a calculating look. "Okay, so what can I do for you?"

"There's a party on campus tonight."

"Wouldn't have picked you for the kegger type."

"I'm far too old to enjoy going to a kegger." Ainsley took another sip of her coffee. "It's a masquerade party."

"And?" asked Hunter.

"And Kate is going."

"So, you're going to this party because she wants to go?" asked Hunter.

"Well," said Ainsley, "I think her brother-in-law is making her go, but all things considered, she'll be safer if I'm there, and it will give me more time to get closer to her."

"And you want me there as a backup?"

"Yes."

"Then there I will be," said Hunter.

"Thank you," said Ainsley. "I appreciate it."

"Hey, partner," said Eddie as she suddenly appeared at the table. "Fancy seeing you here."

"Detective," said Hunter. He closed his eyes and exhaled heavily. After a moment, he opened his eyes and reluctantly looked up at his partner. "Hello," he said tightly.

Sensing his discomfort, Ainsley asked, "Detective Caulfield, right?"

"Right," said Eddie.

"I'm Ainsley. We met at the Jade & Lace Bar the other night with Kate."

"Right."

"I just ran into your partner and I was asking if he knew anything about the fire," said Ainsley.

"Okay," said Eddie with a frown as she looked between Hunter and Ainsley.

"Right," said Hunter. "So, I'll see you at the station later?"

"Yep." Eddie turned and walked quickly away from the table.

"Is it just me," asked Ainsley, "or was that whole thing really weird and awkward and uncomfortable for everyone involved?"

Eddie looked over her shoulder through the window of the Broadway Coffee House. Hunter was still sitting with Ainsley Cooper. Eddie waited until she crossed to the other side of the street before she pulled out her phone and dialed Nolan.

She didn't give him a chance to get a word in before she said, "Hunter killed Rowan."

"Eddie?" asked Nolan. "Is everything all right?"

"Yes, it's me, but what sounds all right about that sentence?"

"I'm just not sure I understand."

"Hunter is a shifter," said Eddie. "He told me the other night. And we know a shifter killed Rowan, so it must have been him. And now I just saw him with Ainsley."

"Ainsley?"

"Yes. Ainsley Cooper. Remember, I was telling you about her and how familiar she seemed, and you told me to do a background check on her?"

"Okay," said Nolan slowly. "Was there something that came up?"

"Of course there wasn't." Eddie glanced toward the window of the coffee house. "She was completely clean, but no one is that clean. We aren't just talking about no parking tickets or speeding fines or criminal records of any kind, but perfect grades and absolutely no gaps in her employment history, even when leaving college. There's just something too neat about her records. There can't be that many people whose history looks like that. Nothing organic looks like that. She has got to be in league with Cornelius."

"Don't you think that's a leap?" asked Nolan.

"No, it isn't. But that isn't the worst part. If Ainsley is in league with Hunter, then it means that Hunter is in league with Cornelius. So, Cornelius must have had Hunter kill Rowan."

"Well," said Nolan, "if you're so sure of his guilt, then follow him."

"What?" Eddie looked at the coffee house again. As she did, she saw Hunter and Ainsley walking toward the door.

"If you believe that Hunter will lead you to Cornelius and Rowan's killer, follow him."

"Okay, then. Gotta go." Eddie hung up and took a deep, steeling breath before she did as Nolan said.

CHAPTER TWO

Kate nervously ran her hands down her dress. It was teal with cap sleeves, a scoop neckline, a full skirt, and a sash, giving a wide band across the back and a soft tie at the front.

She felt awkward and out of place as she stood beside Erin and Akiko. She tried to pretend that she was listening as they chattered enthusiastically about how the large courtyard was beautifully decorated. The trio was standing at one of several small, high tables around the edge of the dance floor. The tables were covered with heavy white tablecloths, with centerpieces of three candles inside glass cylinders. The candles added to the soft glow from the small paper lanterns that crisscrossed in rows overhead.

Kate tensed slightly as she suddenly felt a warm presence at her back. She relaxed instantly when a familiar voice whispered in her ear, "You look absolutely stunning."

She bit her lip as she turned around to face Ainsley, who was wearing a cobalt floral lace midi dress. "So do you," she said softly, smiling warmly at the other woman. Ainsley smiled back, leaning forward to press a brief kiss to Kate's cheek.

"Look who's finally here," said Erin.

"Great," said Akiko. "Can we go dance now?"

"Why don't you guys go?" suggested Kate without looking back at Erin and Akiko.

"Are you sure?" asked Erin.

"Yes." Kate offered him a slight indulgent smile.

"Okay," said Erin as he raised an eyebrow in response. "We'll see you in a bit." He waved regally for a moment before Akiko quickly dragged him in the direction of the dance floor.

Kate laughed at the pair as Ainsley stepped up to the table next to her. Her cheeks flushed as Ainsley draped an arm around her back, then placed her hand on the table, effectively trapping Kate between the table and her body.

"Not a fan?" asked Ainsley.

Kate turned, unsure of the meaning of her question. Ainsley gestured with her other hand toward the dance floor.

"Oh, um ..." She shrugged in response.

Ainsley butted her shoulder softly against Kate's. Kate sensed that she was offering silent gestures of encouragement to ensure that Kate could share whatever she felt comfortable sharing. She bit her lip and looked away from Ainsley's warm, encouraging smile.

Kate was not sure how to tell her that while she enjoyed dancing, she was usually far too self-conscious to feel comfortable doing it in front of other people. She shivered as she remembered Alex practically dragging her out onto the dance floor more than once. She had stood there, stiff and tense in Alex's arms, feeling like everyone was watching her and judging her.

Kate shook herself to chase away the melancholy, which had settled like the suffocating weight of a heavy coat across her shoulders. She turned back toward Ainsley to find the other woman looking at her, still with such warmth.

"Did you want to dance?" asked Kate earnestly, chiding herself for not considering what Ainsley wanted before.

"I wouldn't mind dancing," said Ainsley, "but we don't have to do anything you don't feel comfortable doing."

As clichéd as the words may have sounded, there was something about the intent and genuine concern behind them that warmed Kate. It was irrational and illogical given the short amount of time she had known Ainsley, but she felt like no matter what she did, Ainsley would always keep her safe.

Kate took a deep breath and downed the rest of her wine, then entangled her hand with Ainsley's where it rested on the table. She only had to tug slightly for Ainsley to get the hint and draw Kate with her onto the dance floor.

After they found a space, it appeared to Kate that Ainsley was concentrating on respecting her boundaries as she kept distance between the two of them. Despite this, it also seemed like Ainsley wanted to ensure it was clear to anyone watching the two of them that they were dancing together. It was surprising that she achieved this without coming across as overly possessive and without touching any more of Kate than the one hand that remained entangled with hers.

Kate lost track of how long they danced like that without ever coming any closer together until someone bumped into her from behind. The sudden and unexpected movement propelled Kate forward into Ainsley. Ainsley placed her hands on Kate's hips to steady her. Kate blushed instantly as the heat from Ainsley's hands warmed her skin despite the barrier of her clothes.

"Sorry," said Ainsley as she slowly withdrew her hands after Kate had regained her balance.

"It's fine," said Kate, biting down on her lip. Part of her was screaming that it was too soon for anything to happen. But she decided to throw caution to the wind as she stepped closer. She watched the other woman for several moments before she looped her arms around Ainsley's neck. "Is this okay?"

Ainsley smiled as she nodded. Kate took a deep breath as Ainsley leaned closer. Her lips brushed against Kate's ear as she whispered, "It's more than okay."

Kate was helpless to stifle the shiver that ran down her spine at the feeling of Ainsley's warm breath against her ear. Her eyes fluttered closed as she heaved in another deep breath.

"Are you okay?" asked Ainsley.

Kate opened her eyes. Ainsley had pulled back slightly, watching the reaction she had elicited.

"Yes," said Kate, voice breathy and face flushed.

Thickening tension built between them. Kate watched Ainsley's face intently as the other woman raised her hand to cup Kate's cheek, stroking a thumb along her cheekbone. Ainsley moved closer to press a lingering kiss to Kate's other cheek.

"Talk to me, Kate," she said.

Kate pulled back slightly to look away. "What do you want me to say?"

She knew it seemed like she was being guarded, but she honestly did not know. Well, it was more that she didn't know how to say what she wanted to say. Even if she could work out what she wanted to say, which was not always a given, she preferred to keep her thoughts to herself. She always felt uncomfortable burdening the people around her with her thoughts, concerns, and problems.

"I want you to tell me what is going on in that beautiful head of yours," said Ainsley as she ducked to recapture Kate's gaze.

Kate let a breath out as she steeled herself. As difficult and unnatural for her as it was, she desperately wanted to open up. Maybe she needed to stop overanalyzing and take a leap of faith.

"I want you," said Kate quietly, blushing and looking down at the ground. "I want you so much that it feels like every nerve in my body is on fire when I'm with you."

"But?" prompted Ainsley.

"But I'm just not ready, and I don't want to say or do the wrong thing." Kate blinked at the sudden burning in her eyes. "I don't want to lead you on or frustrate you or scare you away, because even though we've just met, you feel like you're going to be important. And after everything, I can't lose that. I can't lose you."

"You won't lose me."

Ainsley gathered Kate in her arms. Kate rested her head against Ainsley's collarbone.

Ainsley pressed a kiss to her hair. "There is nothing that you can do or say that will scare me away. You're stuck with me."

She raised her head to look up at Ainsley. "Really?"

"Really," promised Ainsley as she held Kate's gaze. "You take all the time you need, because I will be right here waiting for you when you're ready."

"Okay," said Kate softly.

"Okay," echoed Ainsley. "How about we get more drinks?"

Kate let Ainsley lead her away from the dance floor and back toward their table. They didn't comment on the fact that neither let go of the other's hand.

Ainsley smiled warmly up at Kate as she stroked her thumb against Kate's hand. She found the woman before her breathtakingly beautiful, but her attraction to Kate was far more than superficial. She was attracted to Kate's intelligence, determination, compassion, and heart.

She would have been content to have continued to watch Kate's life from afar, though. More than anything else, Ainsley wanted Kate to live the life she wanted and be happy doing so. As conflicted as she'd been when Cornelius had decided it was best that the twins stay with their adoptive parents instead of being brought back to their home, she'd understood that it was the best chance they had at not becoming pawns in someone else's war. She had spent twenty-eight years trying to ensure that they made their own choices and forged their own paths. Ainsley had never wanted Kate to be drawn into the conflict that had cost the lives of her parents and so many others, but she knew that when given the opportunity, Kate would make the right decision about her allegiances.

Part of her was guilt-ridden about how much Kate's life had changed since she had come to Seattle and faced the things she'd faced. But another part was grateful that she finally had an opportunity to know Kate up close and not just from a distance.

"Are you having a good time?" asked Ainsley. "Did you need another drink?"

"I'm okay," said Kate. "You don't have to worry about me."

"Yes, I do. I have always worried about you and looked out for you. Your happiness matters to me."

"I'm not sure happy is a word I'd use to describe my life this year," said Kate, "but right now, I'm the closest I've been to happy in a while. But do you know what would make me happier?"

"What's that?"

Kate smiled warmly. "Another drink. Did you want anything?"

"No, I'm good."

"Okay. I'll be right back."

Ainsley watched her walk to the bar, filled with an overwhelming sense of pride, warmth, and affection. For many years, her pride had simply been for how much Kate had achieved. Kate was remarkably down to Earth and humble, almost to the point of self-deprecating, but that did not lessen the significance of those achievements.

However, that pride had become something else over the last couple of weeks. Seeing who Kate was as a person, what she had overcome, her strength of character, filled Ainsley with a warmth and affection that had grown the closer she had gotten to Kate. The more of her beautiful heart and soul that she had shared despite the walls she had built to protect herself, the more Ainsley felt drawn to her.

Ainsley knew she should stop what appeared to be growing between them. She was not worthy of someone like Kate, but she couldn't stay away, couldn't keep her distance. While she was sure that some would question whether she was simply trying to prove Titania wrong, she was drawn to Kate in a way she had never been drawn to her mother. As much as she had cared for Titania deeply, those feelings paled in comparison to what she felt for Kate.

Ainsley glanced toward where the band had just started playing. Erin and Akiko were dancing together in front of the makeshift stage.

Ainsley frowned as she noticed part of a tattoo on Akiko's shoulder, under the strap of her dress. It looked like the same triskelion within a nonagon that Hunter had on his arm. Ainsley was sure Hunter had mentioned that it was a marking common to the nine shifter clans. But if Akiko had the marking, that would mean she was a shifter—quite possibly the shifter responsible for Rowan's death.

Without thinking, Ainsley took a step closer to Akiko. As she did so, her gaze met that of the lead singer of the band. He was a stocky Latino man with captivating green eyes, wearing a large wide-brimmed hat that almost seemed comical, mismatched to the rest of his clothing—worn but expensive dark jeans and a black button-down. The hat curved over his brow, stopping just above his eyes. It only seemed to make the green of his eyes glow that much more, and Ainsley found it difficult to look away.

She was not sure how long it took to wrench her gaze from him, but when she did, she looked over toward where she had last seen Kate.

Kate was not at the bar. Instead, she was at the far corner of the dance floor. But she was not just standing there. She was dancing with a very attractive, well-built Latino man with dark hair, wearing a hat similar to that of the band's lead singer. Once again, it seemed at odds with his attire, dark slacks and a vest over a white shirt.

As Ainsley watched the man dance closer and closer to Kate, the pair turned so that Kate's back was to her and she was looking into the face of the stranger, meeting his vivid, captivating emerald eyes.

Ainsley's mind swam as if she were standing on a ship rolling between swells. As her head reeled, the sounds of the party reverberated in her ears and the colors dazzled her eyes.

She stumbled as someone bumped into her from behind. Before she fell, strong arms grabbed her and held her upright. She looked up into Erin's face. His cheeks were flushed, eyes bright and smile wide as he raised an eyebrow.

"You okay there?" he asked. "Have one too many?"

"No, I'm fine." Ainsley blushed and took a step back once she'd regained her balance. "Thanks for that."

"It's no problem."

Ainsley glanced back at where she'd last seen Kate. The space was suddenly empty.

"Kate?" She looked around, trying to spot her.

"Ainsley?" asked Erin. "Is everything okay?"

"I can't see Kate."

"I'm sure she's around here somewhere," said Akiko, stepping closer to Erin and Ainsley.

"Where? Can either of you see her?"

"No," said Erin. "Where was the last place you saw her?"

"Um ..." Ainsley tried to think back to even a few moments ago. It felt like trying to wade through honey. She wasn't even sure why she thought Kate had been on the dance floor when she was so sure that they had spoken about getting drinks. "I'm not sure. I can't remember."

"Thank you for meeting with me," said Cornelius as Agatha sat down across from him.

"I do as my liege commands."

"You do not need to be so formal. Your ongoing fealty has well and truly earned my respect and admiration," said Cornelius. "Now, I wanted to get an indication of your views on matters involving my niece."

Agatha's eyes widened slightly. "Kate? Was there anything specific? I only ask as I'm sure that Ainsley would have been keeping you up to date on her developing relationship with Kate, and I wouldn't want to cover things she has already addressed."

Cornelius frowned. "Do you believe that Ainsley is getting too close to Kate? Is she losing her objectivity?"

Agatha paused for a moment as she wondered just how frank she should be with Cornelius. She owed him her fealty. She also owed loyalty to Ainsley, and she wanted to believe that Ainsley would make the right decisions when it came to Kate Matthews. But Agatha still harbored a growing suspicion that, if given a choice between Cornelius and Kate, Ainsley would choose Kate over her uncle.

"Your honesty and frankness on this issue would be appreciated," said Cornelius.

"I'm not sure whether Ainsley has ever been truly objective when it comes to Kate," said Agatha slowly. "I feel that they share a bond far deeper than either of them—or anyone else, for that matter—realizes. Is that an issue, though? Ainsley always said that you loved the twins."

"I do. Just like I loved their mother. But I also watched their mother tear our people apart. I am not going to let history repeat itself when it comes to her children, because our people will not survive that. If I need to sacrifice Kate to ensure that, I will."

"There is something else, though, isn't there?" asked Agatha.

"We have all heard the stories about Faerie twins," said Cornelius. "One personifies light and the other dark. They are opposites."

"So, why not act now?"

"It is not something I will do lightly. I will give her every opportunity to prove herself, and I will protect her however I can. But I will always put our people first."

"Does Ainsley know about that part of the plan?" asked Agatha.

"While I hope that Ainsley knows where her loyalty ought to lie, her devotion to Titania's children is useful," said Cornelius. "There is no need to question that unless absolutely necessary."

"And Ainsley's lack of objectivity is something you can use."

"How so?"

"I say this with the utmost respect, but you are far from blameless when it comes to the events that resulted in the death of your brother," said Ainsley. "We both know that his death caused both the civil war and the deaths of many others, including Kate's parents."

"I am aware," said Cornelius.

"So, the risk you face from the rebel faction, which remains loyal to Titania and her husband, is one of them using that to persuade Kate that you usurped the throne that rightfully belonged to her mother."

"Go on."

"Well, it's as you said to both Hunter and Ainsley," said Agatha. "You need to persuade Kate that your actions and decisions were justified. You need to inoculate her, in a manner of speaking—persuade her that, ultimately, you will be on the right side of history."

"History is written by the victors," said Cornelius.

"Yes," said Agatha. "And the way you win this war is by winning over Kate. By winning her heart and mind, you will be the victor, and Ainsley is just the person who can achieve that outcome for you. So, use Ainsley and her bond with Kate to shape the image that portrays you in the best possible light."

"You want me to use propaganda against my niece?"

"Propaganda has more negative connotations than I feel are appropriate to the current circumstances," said Agatha. "All you need to do is show Kate that you are and have always been the loving uncle who wants the best for her. Encourage Ainsley to tell her about how you have watched over her and protected her. She has spent the better part of her life wanting to know who her family is, so give that to her. Someone who has craved a connection with her biological family her whole life will not be able to turn her back on that easily."

"You are far more calculating than I have given you credit for," said Cornelius.

"Well, the true beauty of it all is that none of it has to be a lie. If you or Ainsley tell her about what really happened to Alex, that will probably be enough."

"Speaking of Kate's wife, I wanted to know whether you have been able to come up with any ideas as to why my niece decided to move to Seattle."

"I've been giving it some thought," said Agatha. "Faerie twins have always had a special connection. It's possible that the power Rowan expended on the night she died created some kind of beacon that drew Kate here."

"I suppose it's possible," said Cornelius. "There is a reason why Faerie twins are rare. Two halves of one whole forever destined to be separate from one another. Perhaps it stands to reason that the loss of one half leaves the other craving what is missing."

"Have you ever wondered just which one Kate is, though?" asked Agatha. "I know both Hunter and Ainsley have suggested that she is the darker of the two, but is Kate the Holly or the Oak?"

Before Cornelius could respond, Agatha's phone chimed.

"Sorry," she said as she pulled it out. She frowned as she read the message.

"Is something wrong?" asked Cornelius.

"Kate's missing."

CHAPTER THREE

"Where is she?" asked Ainsley, as much to herself as to Erin and Akiko. She knew she was panicking without a lot of justification, but with everything that had occurred since Kate had come to Seattle, she was only coming up with all of the terrible things that could have happened while she wasn't paying attention.

"I don't know," said Akiko with a shrug.

"You said she would show up," said Ainsley. "We've now checked the entire party twice and Kate is nowhere to be seen."

"I'm sure there's a completely rational explanation," said Erin.

"Like what?"

"Maybe she went to the bathroom or something like that?" suggested Akiko.

"For fifteen minutes?" asked Ainsley.

Akiko gave another shrug. "Maybe."

Ainsley could only grit her teeth at Akiko's nonchalant attitude. Akiko knew Kate the least of the three of them, but surely even a degree of concern would have been appropriate in the circumstances. Ainsley hoped it was just paranoia, but something inside of her was screaming that Akiko did not care if something happened to Kate.

"It's not like her to leave without saying anything," said Erin.

"Okay, then," said Akiko. "What exactly are we supposed to do?"

"I called an acquaintance who's a detective," said Ainsley. "He should be here soon to help."

"You rang," said Hunter as he materialized out of the surrounding crowd at Ainsley's side.

"Funny," said Ainsley.

"I thought some humor may lighten the mood." When Ainsley only glared at him, he continued, "But I stand corrected. What happened?"

"Kate has disappeared."

"I knew that from your message," said Hunter. "What I want to know is: what is the last thing you three remember? Where did you last see her? What was she doing?"

"Um ..." Ainsley struggled to sort through her memories from the evening. When she failed to come up with anything, she looked over at Akiko and Erin for assistance.

"Well ..." Akiko shrugged and looked at Erin.

"She ..." Erin stopped and looked at Hunter.

Hunter frowned. "Have the three of you had anything to drink tonight?"

"No more than a couple, I think," said Erin.

"Okay, folks, I just need to speak to Ainsley real quick." Hunter grasped Ainsley's elbow and gently led her away. When they were safely out of earshot, he asked, "What is going on?"

"I'm not sure." Ainsley rubbed her forehead. "It's like there's a weird blank spot in my memory. She was here one second and then she was just gone. Plus, I know something important happened that I need to tell you about, but no matter how hard I try to figure out what it was, I keep coming up empty."

"That's not normal," said Hunter.

"I know that."

Before she could say anything further, Akiko drifted toward where they were standing.

"Maybe, and this is just a suggestion," said Akiko as she reached them, "Kate found someone else she wanted to talk to, or even leave the party with."

"Kate isn't the kind of person who would do something like that," said Erin as he joined them. "She wouldn't leave without saying something. I'm worried that something has happened."

"Me too," said Ainsley as she reached out to squeeze Erin's shoulder. "Okay, so let's go back to looking around outside the party. Maybe she went out to get some air."

"We are outside," said Hunter.

"You know what I meant."

"Nope, kind of a head-scratcher."

"Just go look," said Ainsley as she brushed past him.

"Have you told Agatha?" asked Hunter as he stopped her with a hand on her wrist.

"Yes, I messaged her after I called you," said Ainsley. "She should be on her way."

Kate kept trying to tell herself that she should look away, that she *needed* to look away from the man's eyes. But every time she attempted it, his gaze seemed to move to capture hers again. It seemed hopeless as she struggled to find a way to break the hold he had on her. The only possible option for escape was letting her heavy eyelids slip shut. That would block out his eyes, she thought, but she knew that would be a very bad idea. That would only be admitting defeat.

But would that really be a bad thing? questioned a traitorous part of her mind. It whispered that she could just give in. No one would blame her. They would assume that she'd tried, but there was nothing she could do. They might even thank her for it one day. She would be giving them the chance to move on. All she had to do was give in.

The contrast between the moonlight and the shadows cast by the man's hat seemed to make his eyes seem larger and more luminous than they should be. All Kate could think was that they looked like warm, glowing emeralds. But emeralds didn't really glow in the way the man's eyes did. Maybe they were more like the green of a leafy rainforest, bathed in sunlight.

Kate knew that a face framed those eyes. She remembered seeing it when he'd started speaking to her at the bar. But it now seemed far less important. Nothing seemed important when compared to those eyes and their never-ending tunnel of green. Kate did not understand how the man's gaze never broke.

She was only vaguely aware that her body was moving without any conscious direction from her. It felt heavy, like she was walking through a pool of honey. Her face felt expressionless, a reflection of the emptiness that filled her mind. There was nothing she could do to shake the man's hold on her as his eyes held her gaze like magnets.

Ainsley would be able to save me, thought Kate suddenly, as the other woman's long blonde hair and warm blue eyes suddenly appeared in her thoughts. She fought to keep Ainsley's face fixed in her mind as a single thought to which she could anchor herself to keep from drowning in the endless green.

But those captivating eyes seemed to crowd out everything else, including Ainsley's face. It just seemed so important that she keep watching his eyes and letting them draw her in, just like they had when she'd first seen them.

She vaguely remembered the man speaking. The memory of his voice was far too hazy to leave anything other than an impression that it carried a lilting, musical quality. By comparison, his eyes spoke volumes. It felt to Kate that their image would be forever burned into her mind. It was like a siren's song, beckoning her to lose herself.

The further she sank, the more difficult it became for her to look away. She could not even summon the strength to move a muscle without his permission. She was surprised that she could even remain standing. Her mouth was hanging open slightly. His eyes were just so beautiful, and fighting them seemed so hard. It was simply inevitable that she would drop deeper and deeper into his gaze, allowing it to empty out every last thought, leaving nothing behind.

His eyes had seemed darker when his gaze first caught hers as she walked across the party toward the bar. But now, they just seemed to glow. Even trying to remember that moment was a bad idea. It only seemed to deepen the intensity of her surrender. It was like she found herself trapped in an endless loop, and the bliss that spread through her just continued to amplify her desire to give in.

Soon all Kate could remember was falling into those eyes and sinking deeper and deeper into bottomless darkness.

Eddie ducked down behind a large wine barrel that had been converted into a planter box just as Ainsley, Hunter, and two people she remembered from the Jade & Lace passed by. She had been surprised when she had followed Hunter back to the university, but whatever was going on clearly involved Kate.

"Kate has disappeared," said Ainsley.

Eddie's head shot up over the edge of the planter box. If Kate was in danger, she didn't care if Hunter found out she was following him.

"I knew that from your message," said Hunter. "What I want to know is: what is the last thing you three remember? Where did you last see her? What was she doing?"

"Um ..." Ainsley stopped and looked over at the man and woman beside her. Eddie frowned as she tried to remember whether Kate had told her about them. Yes, she had. The man was her brother-in-law, Erin.

"Well ..." said the other woman before she shrugged and turned to Erin.

"She ..." Erin stopped and looked at Hunter.

Hunter frowned. "Have the three of you had anything to drink tonight?"

"No more than a couple, I think," said Erin.

"Okay, folks, I just need to speak to Ainsley real quick." Hunter led Ainsley away from Erin and the woman.

Ainsley and Hunter spoke too quietly Eddie for her to hear what they were saying, but she could tell from their body language that they were concerned about Kate's disappearance. That was concerning to Eddie, as it meant that whatever had happened to Kate had nothing to do with them and Cornelius. It also meant that Kate could be in some serious trouble. Not that being kidnapped by her uncle would not represent serious trouble, but the devil you know is always better than the one you don't.

Eddie looked up again just as the other woman drifted closer to Ainsley and Hunter with Erin in tow. She watched as the group conversed for a moment before deciding to search for Kate outside the party.

"Just go look," said Ainsley as Eddie inched away from the barrel. She did not need to be told twice.

"Come on, Ainsley, pick up, pick up, pick up," said Agatha as she held her phone to her ear. She was walking quickly across the park toward the party. Agatha sighed as the call went to voicemail. She was placing her phone in her back pocket when she bumped into someone walking past her in the opposite direction.

"Sorry, Kate," said Agatha automatically as she looked up. "Wait, Kate?"

Agatha frowned as Kate stopped in the middle of the path without acknowledging her. Kate's gaze was blank, unfocused, and glazed over. It was then that Agatha noticed a man standing beside Kate. He was very attractive, well-built with dark hair. He wore a large, wide-brimmed hat, and his emerald eyes appeared to glow in the dark.

"Kate, what's going on?" asked Agatha as she stepped closer. "Kate, talk to me."

"Don't listen to her, Kate," said the man as he nudged her forward slightly. "Just listen to me. Follow me."

"Kate, please," said Agatha as she watched Kate follow the man obediently. Agatha moved to step in front of them. "I'm your friend."

"She's not your friend, Kate," said the man.

"Okay, yes, technically that's true. We have only met that one time, but I knew your sister. When she was in college, we were friends, and although you're really nothing alike, you look the same—so that counts, right?"

The man only looked at Agatha with a smug smile and a raised eyebrow before he continued to usher Kate away, in the direction of Lake Union.

"No," said Agatha. "Okay, I'm going to find someone better equipped for this conversation. Just stay here, or at least don't go too far." She shook her head in frustration. "Great. Trying to reason with the woman in a trance and the person controlling her. That sounds like a winning strategy, Agatha."

As Kate and the man reached the water's edge, he said, "I am from a city far more beautiful than you have ever seen. It is a glowing metropolis far below the surface of the ocean. It is so beautiful that few who have the opportunity to look upon it ever want to leave. Would you like to see it, my dear?"

"Yes." Kate nodded, staring helplessly into his eyes. The part of her agreeing, though, was oddly detached from the part that was screaming that she should not be there, that she should not have left the party, that she should have let Agatha help her.

But that part was drowning in the sea of green. It was like nothing mattered other than staring into his eyes and agreeing to anything and everything he said. As long as she did so, there was nothing to be concerned or alarmed about. She could simply experience the moment without any of the thoughts that so often overwhelmed her. She could finally be free of the guilt, insecurities, and grief that crippled her.

"Good girl," said the man. "You will love coming with me to visit my home."

Ainsley was jogging through the park, looking for Kate, when she stumbled and collided with the lead singer from the band that had been playing at the party. She stumbled, but prevented herself from falling. The singer, however, was knocked to the ground, dislodging his hat.

"I'm so sorry about that," said Ainsley as she reached out to offer him her hand. She stopped short when she noticed a bald spot on the top of his head, surrounding what looked like a blowhole. It looked a bit like what she had seen on a dolphin. Ainsley frowned instinctively before she realized what that meant.

"You're a shifter—an Encantado. You took her, didn't you? Where is she? Where is Kate?"

"Kate?" asked the singer as he placed his hat on his head and regained his feet. "Is that your friend's name? Well, I suppose it won't really matter what her name is when she drowns in the lake."

"I won't let you hurt her," said Ainsley.

"You think stopping me is going to save her? She will be gone before you can even find her," said the singer. "A pity you won't ever be able to remember the last moments you shared with her. They seemed special, intimate, leading to something. Though I guess you won't get a chance to find out what exactly that something is or was or could have been."

CHAPTER FOUR

"We will need someone to help us reach my home," said the stranger to Kate.

She looked around expectantly, waiting for a boat of some kind to appear. Instead, the stranger turned and took a step closer to the edge of the water. He uttered a series of rapid, high-pitched clicking sounds that reminded Kate of dolphins in an aquarium.

She frowned. She did not understand how that would help them.

"It is nothing to worry about," the stranger explained. "I am only calling for my brother to help us. He will me bring you to my city."

As the singer took a step away from Ainsley, she inched closer to him. "I told you I will not let you hurt her."

The singer smiled smugly and arched an eyebrow. "And how exactly do you plan to stop me?"

"Like this." Ainsley stretched out her hand and a wall of fire shot up in a tight circle around him.

"Clever." He hunched in on himself to keep a safe distance away from the ring of fire. "But, as I said, you keeping me here won't save your precious girlfriend."

"No, it probably won't," said Ainsley. "But you will be my leverage. Your life for hers."

The singer laughed. "Pity they won't believe you. I don't even believe that you would harm me just to get to her."

"That's because you don't know me." Ainsley clenched her fist and the wall of fire inched closer to him. "I won't hesitate to singe you to prove that I am serious."

"You wouldn't dare," snarled the singer.

Ainsley smirked. Despite his bravado, he had paled visibly in response to her threat.

"Oh, but I would," she said as she stepped closer. She closed her fist again, signaling the gap between the fire and the singer to shrink further. "Because I will do everything within my power to make sure Kate makes it home tonight, and killing you to make that happen is a small price to pay. Do you understand me?"

"Yes," said the singer.

"Good. Now, you get Kate here now."

The singer regarded her coldly for several moments before his gaze shifted over her shoulder. Concerned that another Encantado was sneaking up behind her, Ainsley turned away. As she did so, someone barreled into her side. She hit the ground. Her concentration shattered and the wall of fire was extinguished.

"Them's the breaks, honey," said the singer before he turned and dashed off toward the shore of the lake.

Ainsley surged to her feet. She looked down to size up the figure that had run into her, and sighed in frustration as she recognized Agatha.

"I'm so sorry about that. My clumsiness picks the worst possible moments to rear its ugly head," said Agatha as Ainsley reached down to help her to her feet. "But I'm gathering levity is not the right thing right now, so let's just jump to it. I was just coming to get you, and I saw Kate."

"Where is she?" asked Ainsley.

"She was near the lake. But she was in some kind of trance. I couldn't get through to her."

"Another Encantado must have her under his thrall," said Ainsley as the two women started jogging toward the lake.

"Encantados? What are they doing this far north?" asked Agatha. Ainsley glared at her. "Sorry. Now is not the time for that."

"Right," agreed Ainsley. "Can we just grab Kate and keep her on the shore? Will that be enough?"

"No," said Agatha with a shake of her head. "Simply stopping her from following them will not be enough. We need to actually break the Encantados' hold over her."

"How are we supposed to do that?"

"Leave that to me." Agatha opened her bag and started pulling out packets of herbs. "You just make sure that Kate does not leave the bank."

Ainsley stepped out from under the tree line and onto the bank. At the same time, the singer leapt from the shore toward the lake. In midair, he transformed into a pink dolphin. Encantados were known to shift into something resembling the pink river dolphins called botos commonly found in the Amazon. But this boto was far larger than any Ainsley had ever seen, and its pink color was much more intense. It glowed with an eerie luminescence. Ainsley stopped in her tracks, but then she saw another man with his hands resting on Kate's hips. He looked like he was about to lift her onto the back of the boto.

Ainsley punched out in frustration, fire streaming from her fist and cutting off the man on the bank from the boto. He looked up in surprise.

"Any time now, Agatha," Ainsley called out.

The man pushed Kate behind him.

"Just give me a second," answered Agatha.

Ainsley sent another stream of fire in the man's direction. He moved out of its path, his step taking him away from the bank.

"We don't exactly have a second," said Ainsley as she advanced. She used more bursts of flames to force the man further from the edge of the water.

"Well, keep doing what you're doing," said Agatha. "It's going fine."

"No, it isn't."

The man ducked under her next burst of fire and stepped closer to the water. "Get her out of here," he said to the boto as he pushed Kate toward the lake.

"Need you now, Agatha," said Ainsley, reaching out to grab Kate's wrist and pull her back.

"All right, all right." Agatha stepped out from the tree line and threw some powder in the direction of the two Encantados.

As soon as it touched their skin, both let out high-pitched yelps. At the same time, Kate blinked and staggered slightly. Ainsley reached out to steady her. The man on the bank transformed into a boto and joined the other in the water. They swam away from the shore, leaving only a faint trail of phosphorescence on the surface of the lake.

"Are you okay?" asked Ainsley. She moved her hands away from Kate, but remained close.

Kate opened her mouth to respond, but coughed as she inhaled some of the powder that remained floating in the air. Ainsley reached out to steady her again.

Kate looked up, eyes watering slightly. "Not that I'm not appreciative, but what on Earth is in that stuff?"

"Manioc flour and dried, crushed chili peppers," said Agatha. "It's supposed to be very effective against Encantados."

"Against what?"

"I'll explain," said Ainsley as she placed a hand on the small of Kate's back and steered her away from the water. "But first, let's get you home."

Kate approached her front door with Ainsley and Erin trailing behind her like baby ducklings. Kate herself was more the baby duckling in need of protection than the mother duck providing it. But all things considered, maybe they'd be safer if they weren't trailing after her anymore.

"Thank you both for making sure I got home," she said.

Erin stepped toward her. "I'm not leaving you here alone tonight, Kate."

"I'll be fine," said Kate. She was the furthest thing from fine. But it was better if they believed she was. If they didn't know how much she needed them, even if the thought of being alone tonight was terrifying.

"Maybe," said Erin, "but I'd like you to humor me just this once."

Her shoulders slumped in reluctant defeat. "Okay."

"Okay." He reached out to squeeze her shoulder.

Kate offered him a small, brief smile before he walked past her and into her apartment. As the door closed behind them, she flicked her gaze up to meet Ainsley's. The other woman had remained silent during her exchange with Erin.

"Are you sure you're okay?" asked Ainsley softly as she stepped closer.

Kate sighed, looking away briefly. "It just feels like too much, and I don't know how to deal with all of this."

"No one, least of all me, is going to judge you for being overwhelmed, because it has been a lot," said Ainsley. "Anyone in your situation would have found everything that has happened to you since coming to Seattle to be too much, and that's without even taking Alex into account."

"So, what do I do?" asked Kate.

"You just keep doing what you've done every day before this one. You take things one day at a time, and you lean on the people around you whenever you need it."

"I'm not particularly good at that."

"I've noticed," said Ainsley, "but no matter what happens, I'm going to keep showing up for you. I will be here every day, every time that you need me."

"Promise?" asked Kate, part question and part desperate plea.

"I promise," said Ainsley as she pulled Kate close.

Kate rested her head on Ainsley's shoulder as she wrapped her arms around Ainsley's waist. Ainsley smiled, resting her chin against Kate's head.

The two women remained in a tight embrace until eventually Ainsley asked, "Are you sure you don't want me to stay?"

Kate shook her head, pressing her face into Ainsley's neck.

"Do you want me to go?" asked Ainsley. Kate shook her head again. Ainsley rubbed a hand up and down her back. "I think it has to be one or the other."

"Why?" asked Kate as she pulled back slightly to meet Ainsley's warm gaze. "Why can't we stay just like this?"

Ainsley smiled and raised one of her hands to cup Kate's cheek. Kate's eyes fluttered closed. The skin along her cheekbone tingled in the wake of Ainsley's thumb as it moved across it. "I'd love nothing more, but Erin is waiting for you."

"Right." Kate slowly disentangled her arms from around Ainsley.

"How about I stop by tomorrow evening?" asked Ainsley quickly as she moved her other hand to Kate's hip to prevent her from moving too far away. "We can talk about how things went, or anything that you want to talk about."

Kate smiled. "I'd like that."

"You get Kate home okay?" asked Agatha as Ainsley walked into the kitchen of their apartment. She poured Ainsley a glass of white wine and handed it to her.

"Yes." Ainsley took a sip. "Her brother-in-law, Erin, is going to stay with her tonight." She placed her glass down, bracing her arms on the bench and leaning heavily against it, then sighed and dropped her head, studying the bench's surface.

"Are you okay?" asked Agatha.

"What do you think?" asked Ainsley without lifting her head.

"I'm sensing the answer is a clear no, but I'm not exactly sure why."

Ainsley finally looked up. "Kate was nearly kidnapped."

"I know. I was there." Agatha paused. "She wasn't, though. She's safe and sound at home. That's the best possible outcome."

"It shouldn't have come to that," said Ainsley. "I should have been paying better attention. I shouldn't have taken my eyes off her."

Agatha took a sip of wine, steeling herself before she repeated Cornelius' question from earlier in the evening. "Do you think you're getting too involved with Kate?"

"What is that supposed to mean?"

"It's supposed to mean that it sounds like you care for her more than you should," said Agatha, "and that you're letting your past relationship with her mother cloud your judgment."

"So?" asked Ainsley.

"I'm just worried that if the time comes to choose between Cornelius and Kate," said Agatha, "you won't pick Cornelius."

"I know what I'm doing." Ainsley picked up her glass of wine and stormed off to her bedroom, slamming the door.

Agatha flinched. It didn't seem like Ainsley knew what she was doing.

EPISODE FIVE: HEATHER

With a secret like that, at some point the secret itself becomes irrelevant. The fact that you kept it does not.
—Sara Gruen, *Water for Elephants*

CHAPTER ONE

K ate took a deep, steeling breath and walked across the restaurant to the table where her parents were seated.

Her mother, Lillian Matthews, was taller than Kate and slim. She had green eyes, fair skin, and brown hair cut to her ears in a simple but elegant bob. Kate's father, Edward Matthews, was several inches taller than Lillian, with light brown hair, dark brown eyes, and a mole above his left eye. Both stood to greet Kate as she reached the table.

"Hello, Katherine," said Lillian. Edward only smiled perfunctorily before he returned to his seat.

"Hi, Mother. Hi, Dad," said Kate as she sat down across from her mother.

"I thought you were bringing your brother with you," said Lillian. "Is he still coming?"

"Yes, he should be here soon. He said he had a class that was running a bit late."

"I suppose that is what happens when you decide to pursue such a stable career as medicine," said Lillian.

"What exactly is that supposed to mean, Mother?"

"Well, majoring in political science and economics is not exactly the most secure of career paths," said Lillian. "However, if you want to consider going to law school after you finish your undergraduate degree, your father and grandfather could find you something relatively quickly. You could probably even start interning this summer."

"I am happy studying what I'm studying, Mother," said Kate. "And I don't want to be a lawyer."

"I just think you could be doing something so much more rewarding with your life. You have the education, training, and connections to make a difference. You know I think you're wasting your talent doing the work that you're doing."

"Lillian, how about we have this conversation another time?" asked Edward.

"No," said Lillian. "I believe it is important to address this behavior before it becomes irreversible."

"I think I'm just going to check where Robbie is," said Kate. She quickly rose from the table before either of her parents could argue.

She walked in the direction of the bar, looking for a secluded spot as she pulled her phone out of her clutch and called her brother.

"Hey," said Robbie. "Is everything okay?"

"I'm having dinner with our mother," said Kate. "Nothing about that is okay."

"Mom isn't that bad."

"Robbie, your relationship with her is very different to mine," said Kate. "I've been here less than five minutes and I've already been told that I am wasting my talent in studying what I am."

"I'm sorry, Kate."

"I can't sit there and keep being attacked. She seems less inclined to do that when you're here, so I just wanted to check how far away you are."

"I'm just leaving school now."

"What do you mean? You were supposed to be here ten minutes ago, and school is at least thirty minutes away."

"I just got caught up chatting with the T.A."

"And you didn't think to let me know?"

"Well, I'm on my way now."

"Don't bother."

"Come on, Kate. Don't be like that."

"Sorry," said Kate. "I just needed you here now. You know what Mom is like. You know what our relationship is like. I needed you to be a buffer for me."

"I know, Kate. I'll be there in about thirty minutes, and Grandpa has got to be close. You've just got to hold out a little longer."

"Okay," said Kate. "I'll talk to you later."

With a heavy sigh, she moved to the bar and ordered a glass of sparkling water. She couldn't help another heavy sigh as she picked up her drink.

"That sigh sounds like you've had a rough day," said the woman sitting beside her at the bar.

Kate turned to face her. The woman was a few inches taller than her, with raven-black hair, pale skin, and blue eyes.

Kate smiled. "More like a rough night. I'm having dinner with my parents."

"Ah," said the woman. "I'm guessing you don't have a good relationship with them."

"My mother and I have a difficult relationship," said Kate as the two drifted to one of the tall tables scattered around the bar.

"Do you mind if I ask why?"

"Nothing I do is ever good enough." Kate slowly tilted her head to the side and frowned as she looked at the woman.

"What is it?" asked the woman.

"Nothing." Kate bit her lip quickly. "You just seem familiar."

The woman laughed warmly. "Now that you mention it, so do you. Do you go to Columbia?"

"Right, of course," said Kate. "You're the T.A. in my Intermediate Macroeconomics class. It's Alex, right?"

"Yes. Alex Quinn."

"It's nice to meet you." Kate reached out to shake Alex's hand, which was warm and soft in hers. She couldn't help feeling a pang of loss when Alex let go. Kate let her hand drop to rest on the table in front of her.

"And you are?" asked Alex as she reached out and ran a finger along the length of Kate's hand.

Kate blushed. "I'm Kate. Kate Matthews."

"Ah, yes. How could I forget the name that goes with such a gorgeous face?" Alex smiled as Kate ducked her head.

Before Kate could respond, she heard someone behind her call her name. She turned to see her grandfather walking up to the table. He was tall, with hazel eyes, weathered skin, and white hair he parted at the left and combed over. Alex's hand slipped away from hers as he reached them.

"Hello, darling," said Neil, pressing a brief kiss to her cheek. "Are we waiting for your parents? I thought they would be here."

"They are here. They're sitting at the table," said Kate. "I was just getting a drink."

Neil smiled in understanding. "Okay, then. I'll see you there."

"I'll be right there." Kate turned back to Alex. "I should probably go. It was nice to meet you. I mean, meet you outside of class."

"It was nice to meet you, too," said Alex softly. She offered Kate another smile. Kate held her gaze as the other woman slowly backed away from the table.

She closed her eyes and took one last fortifying breath before returning to her parents.

When Kate opened her eyes again, she found that she was no longer in the restaurant in New York, reliving the night she had met Alex. Instead, she was lying on her bed in her apartment in Seattle, looking up at the ceiling.

She sighed as the last vestiges of warmth that the memory had filled her with fled, as quickly as darkness does when someone turns on a light. She was not in New York, and Alex was not there with her.

"Thank you for agreeing to see me," said Eddie as she entered Nolan's office.

"It sounded urgent, Detective."

Eddie closed the door and approached his desk. "It is." She took a seat. "I followed Hunter last night. He went to an area near the University of Washington."

"Is that significant?" asked Nolan.

"In itself, no," said Eddie. "But while he was there, I overheard him saying that a pair of Encantados had almost kidnapped Kate."

"Encantados? Really? That would be rare this far north."

"That's kind of irrelevant. What is relevant is that they were here and they tried to abduct Kate."

"Okay, but you've already indicated that they were unsuccessful," said Nolan. "It sounds like any potential crisis was averted."

"That's not the point, though," said Eddie. "Hunter continues to be present when these attempts happen, just like he was at the Jade & Lace. While I'm not sure that Cornelius was directly involved in this one, I do believe that he was behind Rowan's death and every attempt on Kate's life. It means that Kate isn't safe as long as she stays in Seattle."

"Well ..." Nolan paused. "I will look into a way to keep Kate away from Cornelius. Meanwhile, you continue to follow Hunter to see if you can figure out what his and Cornelius' next moves are. It's important that we know where he is at all times."

"Agreed."

As Kate approached the bar at the New Yorkers for Children Annual Fall Fête, she smiled warmly as she noticed a very familiar woman standing at a table. She moved to stand beside Alex. "Hey, you."

Alex turned quickly at the sound of Kate's voice, a grin of recognition breaking across her face. Her gaze traced Kate's body before settling on her face. "Hey, fancy seeing you here. To be honest, I kind of had you pegged as the girl who would rather spend her night at home watching baseball than come to something like this."

"I'm not sure whether or not that was a compliment," said Kate, "but my family supports the Fête. I've been coming every year for as long as I can remember. But it's not how I usually prefer to spend my time."

"I didn't mean what I said negatively. I like people who appreciate the simpler things in life," said Alex. "So, are you a Yankees or Mets supporter? No, wait, let me guess—you have got to be a Yankees fan."

"Well, to be honest, I don't really have a baseball team that I support."

"What New York native doesn't have a favorite baseball team?" asked Alex, half jokingly, half in disbelief.

"Well, I'm not actually a New York native," said Kate.

"Really? Sorry, that must seem very rude of me. I guess I just assumed you were—it sounded like you've lived in New York for a long time."

"It's okay," said Kate as she reached out to squeeze Alex's hand in reassurance. "It's an easy assumption to make. I was actually adopted, so I'm not entirely sure where I'm from. Plus, between summers in the Hamptons and boarding school in Andover, I didn't spend a huge amount of time in New York when I was growing up."

"I could tell you were well educated and articulate, which clearly suggests some kind of elite prep school," said Alex as she held Kate's hand loosely in hers, "but the other parts I didn't know."

"All things considered, it's an easy assumption to make."

"I'm a little surprised to hear that you didn't even go to prep school in New York. I would have had you pegged as either a Brearley or a Dalton girl."

"My brother went to Browning, but I studied at Speyer Legacy School before going to Andover."

"So you're one very smart cookie, then." Alex paused. "Okay, I have another slightly rude question."

Kate gave her a reassuring smile. "Go ahead."

"Why study at Speyer and Andover over Brearley or Dalton?" asked Alex. "Andover is a brilliant school, but with your parents, I would have thought New York was a more logical choice than boarding school."

"People have always had a lot of expectations for me, particularly my parents," said Kate. "They always had, and still have, a view of how they want my life to go. If I'd let them, they'd have me interning at some law firm in the city each summer before going to some law school and then to work for the District Attorney or U.S. Attorney's office, before eventually transitioning into some kind of political or judicial career. But that plan isn't me, so the more they said that that was what I should do, the less I wanted to do it. I've always tried to live my own life."

"I think I'm beginning to understand why you said you had a difficult relationship with your parents," said Alex. "But I'm curious about the reluctance for a career in politics. Political science, even without a law degree, does lend itself well to working for a politician."

"It does, but it's not what I intend to do with my career. My grandfather has been the only one who's really supported me in that."

"I'm sorry. That must have been difficult."

"It has been," replied Kate. "To be honest, it still is."

"So, why did you want to study political science and economics?"

"It was one of those things that happened a little unintentionally. Don't get me wrong, I enjoy what I'm studying, and I think I'm doing okay with it, but it wasn't something I planned on doing."

"I think from all accounts you're a lot more than just okay," said Alex. "But why do you say that it wasn't planned?"

"The summer before my senior year, I was involved in a student leadership program. While I was there, I met this female Senator who represented the State of New York. She was just so inspirational, you know? Well, the following summer, she was looking for assistance in her re-election campaign. I had no other plans, so I thought I wouldn't mind helping out. The campaign was the first time that I had really engaged in politics, and while this is kind of dorky to say, I found it fascinating, so I just decided to learn more at college. Admittedly, when I first told my parents about that, they automatically assumed I was finally agreeing to adhere to their plan for my life. They were less enthusiastic when I said I was more interested in the theoretical than the practical, though."

"Why decide to add in economics, then?" asked Alex. "If you were certain about studying political science, why not just leave it at that?"

"At my core, I'm a pragmatist, and I need a practical fallback option when a degree in political science doesn't prepare me for much."

"I guess things have a way of working out for the best, then," said Alex. Her thumb slowly brushed backward and forward over the pulse point in Kate's wrist.

"I guess so," replied Kate quietly.

Alex held her gaze until someone called Kate's name. Kate turned to see her mother walking over. Before Lillian reached them, Alex turned to Kate and quietly asked, "Someone you know?"

Kate smiled tightly. "My mother."

"Your grandfather wanted to talk to you about something," said Lillian as she approached.

Kate frowned. She turned to Alex and said, "Sorry, I should go."

"It was good to see you again," said Alex. She squeezed Kate's shoulder quickly.

"Likewise." When Kate had followed her mother some distance from the bar where Alex was standing, she asked, "Where's Grandpa?"

"He doesn't need to see you," said Lillian, taking Kate's hand and leading her toward the back of the ballroom.

Kate stopped short and pulled her hand out of Lillian's. "But you just said that he wanted to talk to me."

"Well, I lied," said Lillian. "Now, come on. I've organized rooms for everyone in the hotel upstairs for the night, and I need your help setting everything up."

"Why did you lie?" asked Kate.

Lillian sighed and stopped her attempts to maneuver Kate out of the room. "I didn't like the way she was looking at you," she said. "You know she must be—"

Kate cut her mother off. "A lesbian? So what? She's a T.A. at school and a good contact to have."

"I know," said Lillian, "but now is not an appropriate time or place to make those kinds of contacts."

"And this isn't the way to go about making such a statement," retorted Kate.

"Katherine, please, can we just go somewhere quiet to talk about this?" said Lillian, once again taking Kate's hand to lead her away.

"No. I just need some space."

Kate walked away from her mother and out of the room, tears threatening to fall down her face.

She felt a hand on her shoulder. "I said I needed space, Mother."

"It's not your mother. It's Alex."

She guided Kate away from the ballroom and into a more secluded area.

"It looks like you need somewhere private, and I don't feel like the bathroom is the right place. I have a room upstairs. Do you want to go there? I can give you my key."

"Can you actually come with me?" asked Kate quietly.

"Of course. Whatever you need," said Alex. "Do you need me to get your things?"

"No. I'll text my brother and ask him to bring them out."

"Are you okay to wait here?"

"Yes, I think so."

"It kind of looks like you need a drink or a hug—or both," said Alex.

"Both would be nice," said Kate, "but I'm happy to wait until we go upstairs. How much did you see?"

"Not much," replied Alex. "But I know that you look like you need a friend."

"I could definitely use one of those right now."

"Then you've got one for as long as you need."

"Are you okay?" asked Erin as Kate slumped down into the seat across from him at the Broadway Coffee House.

"I'm fine." Kate propped one of her elbows on the table and leaned her head on her hand.

Erin raised an eyebrow. "How about we try that once more with feeling?"

"Please don't start singing 'The Mustard Song.'"

"Don't mock 'The Mustard Song.' It's still my favorite ringtone."

"I wouldn't think of it."

"So, what's going on?" asked Erin.

"I don't know. I'm just in a bit of a weird headspace," said Kate. "Although, I do have a question for you. What are the signs of a nervous breakdown?"

"Oh, Kate." Erin reached out to wrap a hand around her elbow.

"I'm just having all these memories of Alex lately. And they're just so vivid that it feels like I'm back there reliving it all over again."

"Maybe it's just grief."

"Maybe," said Kate, "but I'm also at an age where schizophrenia, bipolar disorder, and other mental disorders start manifesting."

"True."

"And it's not exactly like I know my family history of those kinds of things."

"I know in the past you've said that finding out anything about your parents was going to raise questions you didn't want to answer," said Erin, "but I think you need to speak to that Detective—um, Caulfield, was it? The one who knew your sister? If you're that worried, and I agree that you should be, you need to get as much information as you can. Maybe Detective Caulfield can give it to you, or point you in the right direction."

"What if I'm just opening Pandora's box by going down that road?" asked Kate.

"It may be difficult, and it may turn your life upside down, but you need to remember that the thing left in Pandora's box was hope," said Erin. "And I think you need to hold on to that at the moment."

"Okay. I'll think about it," said Kate. "Now, distract me. What's new with you? How's work?"

"Work is going pretty well, actually," said Erin. "We have a presentation lined up this week to the new donors who gave us that research grant."

"That sounds positive."

"They're from a foundation that's interested in the progress we've made, so they want regular updates on how we're using their money to further our research."

"So much for no one ever investing in L.A.M. research," said Kate. "Your mom would be really proud of you. You know that, right?"

"I just wish I could have been able to do it while she was still alive, so I could have make a difference in her life."

"I know. But maybe because of this, someone else won't lose their mom."

Erin sighed as he sat back in his chair and looked from his computer screen to Akiko, who was watching him from across the table.

"I think we should personalize this," he said as he gestured at the presentation open on his computer. "We want them to keep investing in the research because they want to focus on rare diseases like L.A.M."

"The number of people who suffer from those diseases and are likely to receive any kind of tangible benefit from this research is limited at best," said Akiko. "From an economics perspective, who would invest millions and millions of dollars in researching a potential cure for something that currently affects about one thousand women across North America? We want to be making the argument that they should invest because the gene mutations involved in L.A.M. have also been linked to other conditions like bladder cancer, tuberous sclerosis complex, and focal cortical dysplasia of Taylor balloon cell type."

"Yes, this process may be able to be adapted to treat other conditions like cancer, which could represent a massive breakthrough in understanding it and those other conditions. But right now, it represents hope for thousands of women, children, and families affected by this disease. We shouldn't make light of that."

"I'm not trying to make light of it," said Akiko. "But I am trying to be realistic. We'll ensure continued funding if we can show that there's a business case for this research, that they can market this in some way—and to be honest, a potential cancer treatment fits that bill much better than a treatment for L.A.M."

Erin drummed his fingers for a moment before he asked, "Do you know why I started researching in this area?"

"No."

"My mother was diagnosed with L.A.M.," said Erin. "I watched her suffer through breathing problems that just got worse and worse. She had collapsed lung after collapsed lung. I watched her in so much pain day after day until she died. I spent every day so worried about not just her, but what would happen if I got something as simple as a cold, because I knew that could mean pneumonia for her. Every day was so exhausting. It was months and months of hell."

"I didn't know," said Akiko.

"Do you know the thing that sticks out for me the most, though?" asked Erin. "More than the pain and the suffering? A doctor saying basically what you said. Telling us that because L.A.M. affects so few women, there will never be any research or any treatment, let alone a cure. My mom was basically told to go home and die, because there was nothing they could do. I don't want anyone else to be told that. I don't want anyone to think their lives or their families' lives don't matter just because only a few people are impacted. Each human life matters."

CHAPTER TWO

"Hey," said Alex as she walked into the Upper East Side apartment. "What are you doing here?"

"Well, I live here," said Kate.

"I just wasn't expecting you to be home already."

"I think everything that has happened is just beginning to sink in right now."

"Kate, what's wrong?" said Alex as she caught sight of Kate's face for the first time.

Kate knew her eyes were red and that there were dried tears on her cheeks. She took a deep breath and bit down on her lip sharply in an effort to stave off more tears.

"Hey," said Alex as she crossed the room to sit beside Kate, "whatever it is, it'll be okay."

"No, it won't," said Kate. "It's not going to be okay."

"You need to tell me what's going on."

"We need to talk about something."

"That's your serious voice," said Alex. "Why are you using your serious voice?"

"A lot has happened over the last couple of days," said Kate, "and I really think we need to clear some things up. Some things about us."

"Okay," said Alex slowly. "Now you're scaring me."

"We can't." Kate shook her head. "I can't keep putting this off. I can't keep going along with you every time we talk about it."

"Talk about what?"

"About getting married and having a family."

"I'm not sure I understand," said Alex.

"I was offered a Rhodes Scholarship. So I have an opportunity to study my Master of International Relations at Oxford."

"That's incredible news, honey," said Alex, "but I don't understand what that has to do with us."

"It has everything to do with us. I'm talking about spending the next two years studying at Oxford. What does that mean for us and our relationship?"

"This isn't the time for this," said Alex. "Please don't do this."

"Don't do what? What's best for me?" asked Kate. "I have waited for you for three years. I have lived on your terms for three years. I have always set aside what I wanted and what I needed just to make you happy. I can't do that anymore. I won't do that anymore."

"So, what do you want me to do?"

"I want you to tell me the truth," said Kate. "I want you to tell me whether what you want is the same thing as what I want. You are the reason that I even want to have kids. I didn't want to bring someone else into the craziness that is my family, but then I met you. I saw how you were with kids and how much love you have to offer. It made me want more."

"It's not like I haven't thought about it," said Alex.

"Then why have you always been so definitively against us having more than this?"

"Because I'm terrified," said Alex. "I'm terrified of how much I would love our child and I'm terrified of losing that child. I'm terrified that I will lose you the way that I've lost others. I am terrified that if for some reason we can't have children, and what we have right now is not enough, then I will never be enough for you."

"Who isn't terrified of the future?" asked Kate. "Yes, see, *that* is the look I need right now. The 'I don't know what to do' look. That's the 'You're my partner, let's work it out together' look. Believe me when I say that it's a lot better than the 'I'm going to stubbornly make all the decisions for both of us until the end of time' look."

"You must hate that look," said Alex.

"I hate that look like you wouldn't believe," said Kate. "But if you really feel like marriage and kids can't ever be on the table for us, then you need to tell me."

"Will you still go to England?" asked Alex.

"If the answer is no, we should spend some time apart so that I can process," said Kate. "But if it's something that you're really open to discussing one day—and I mean truly open, not just trying to get me to stay—then tell me that too."

"Regardless of what my answer is, you need to go to Oxford."

"What?"

"You mean the world to me," said Alex. "And this is your dream, so I'm taking myself out of the equation. You need to do this for yourself and your career and what you want to achieve."

"Okay," said Kate slowly. "But we still need to talk about what this means for us. And it's okay if you don't have an answer right now. I'm fine to keep talking about this as long as you're open to it."

"I don't want to wait," said Alex. "I have an answer."

"You do?"

"I do, and I know what having a family, building a family, means to you," said Alex. "While I don't want to lose you, I can't ask you to sacrifice something this important. And with everything going on right now, I won't draw this out. I can't give you what you want if that's what you want. You need to decide if I'm enough for you. I need you to decide whether what we have right now is going to be enough."

"I said I would need time to process, but in the meantime, I think we need to take some time apart."

"If that's what you want."

"It isn't," said Kate. "But you just made it abundantly clear you aren't even willing to consider what I want."

Kate shook her head to clear away the cobwebs of the day she'd been offered a scholarship to study at Oxford. The day that she and Alex took one of the first breaks of what had become a very turbulent stage of their relationship. She didn't know why she'd been thinking about it. It had been years since she had, and she'd thought she had put it well and truly behind her. There must be something wrong with her. She needed to do something about it, which was why she was standing outside the police station, waiting.

"Detective Caulfield?" asked Kate as the woman she was waiting for stepped outside.

"Ms. Matthews," said Eddie as she walked toward Kate. "It's good to see you again."

"You can call me Kate."

"Eddie."

"Um, can I ask you something?" Kate looked at her feet and fiddled nervously with the buttons on her shirt.

"Sure," said Eddie.

Kate glanced furtively up at her. "Do you know if Rowan knew anything about our biological parents? Did she know who they were?"

"No," said Eddie. "She knew that it was a closed adoption, but she didn't want any further details. She didn't want to know them."

"Well, at least we have that in common."

Kate looked away as she felt a slight pang of loss at the realization. She had not thought she could miss this person she had never known, but going down this rabbit hole to find her birth parents would have been easier if there was someone going down it with her.

"Is there any way to find out who they are?"

"I don't think so. At least, not without a court order permitting you access to the adoption records," said Eddie. "Why?"

"I just want to look into their medical history, specifically whether there's any history of mental health problems."

"Is everything okay?"

"No." Kate's voice wavered and her eyes burned with unshed tears. "Everything is not okay. I'm not okay."

"What's going on?" asked Eddie.

"About three or four months ago, I started having these dreams," said Kate. "They were all about places in Seattle, like the Space Needle and the Ferris wheel at the Pier. They were all places I had been, so I thought nothing of it."

"And now?"

"When the realtor was showing me my apartment, it was like I blinked and suddenly the room was filled with all this furniture that wasn't mine. Then someone who looked like me walked in."

"That's why you asked about Rowan's furniture," said Eddie.

"Yes."

"Have you seen anything else?"

"It's just glimpses. When I'm at the coffee shop or the university or the market. It'll be a blink and someone who looks just like me but in very different clothes will be there," said Kate. "That's how it started, but now it's memories. Memories that are so vivid and so real it's like I'm back there living them again. I'm just worried that I'm having some delayed psychotic break, and I thought I should find out about my family history."

"Will more information help?" asked Eddie.

"Yes. I want to give my doctors as much as I can."

"Okay. I'll see what I can do, but I do have one last question. Why would you think it was a delayed psychotic break?"

"The, um, dreams started just after my wife died," said Kate. "She was from Seattle."

"You just thought it was memories of her?" asked Eddie.

Kate nodded. "And then I found out about Rowan, and I'm just scared that something is really wrong."

"Come here," said Eddie, pulling Kate in for a hug. She dropped a kiss on Kate's hair before she tucked the other woman's head under her chin. "How about I take you home? I'll need to leave you there and go see someone else, but I'll come right back."

Kate drummed her fingers against her leg as she looked around her apartment. After Eddie had left, she had settled on the couch, hoping she would finally be able to silence the torrent of memories flooding through her mind now that she was taking proactive steps to get help.

Despite how much she tried, though, she could not switch her brain off. She could not help but feel like she was drowning on dry land, like her thoughts was suffocating her and she was helpless to stop them. Her memories of Alex were a weight dragging her down.

Her gaze landed on an ornament sitting on a shelf across the room. It was a small white plastic lion with a blue-and-red mane with the face and mane of another lion emblazoned across its chest. It was one of a set of three from some Olympic Games merchandise she had purchased when she first arrived in the United Kingdom. She had given one, a red lion, to the roommate she had lived with at Oxford. The final lion, a blue one, she had given to a woman called Monty.

As if drawn by a magnet, Kate's gaze moved to a photograph on another table. It showed her, smiling, sitting beside a woman with long blonde hair, green eyes, and a warm smile. Monty's smile had once made Kate feel safe. She remembered the moment from the photograph when she and Monty had visited the Hotel Sacher in Vienna for a weekend away. It was still early in their relationship, when they were happy and didn't fight more often than they talked. Kate sighed. Monty felt like such a distant memory instead of someone she had thought she loved and was willing to stay in the United Kingdom for, until things went sideways.

Kate closed her eyes as her mind was suddenly flooded with a memory she had tried so hard to forget—a memory she had replayed time and time again for years, hoping for a different outcome whenever things got difficult with Alex. In an instant, she was back in the small apartment she had lived in at Oxford.

There was Monty, standing on the other side of the room, watching as Kate gathered up the last few things she needed before they went out for dinner. Before Kate could finish, her phone rang.

"Sorry, I'll just be a second." Kate smiled apologetically at Monty and answered the call. "Hello, this is Kate."

"Hi, Kate. It's Alex."

Kate closed her eyes and turned away from Monty.

"Alex," she said. "I assumed you'd forgotten my number."

"There's something I need to tell you," said Alex, her voice unusually small and quiet.

Kate frowned. "Are you okay?"

"Um, well, I've been better."

"What's going on?"

"It's my mom," said Alex. "She's pretty sick, and the doctors say she doesn't have too long. I know this is selfish, but I need you right now."

Kate sighed as she turned back to look at Monty standing there, waiting for her. She closed her eyes again and said, "I'll take a flight to Seattle as soon as I can."

"We need to tell Kate the truth," said Eddie as she paced in front of Nolan's desk in the mayor's office.

"I don't think that is an option," said Nolan.

"Why?"

"You've had how many opportunities to tell her now? What makes this time any different to all the others?"

"She's so scared that something is wrong, and telling her will help reassure her," said Eddie. "It won't matter that I could have told her earlier."

"You really don't know her, do you?" asked Nolan. "She is not her sister. It will matter to her. She is guarded and insecure, with a bucketload of trust issues. You tell her now and you just become one more person who's lied to her. One more person she cannot trust. Where would that leave her? Where would that leave you?"

"So I'm just supposed to sit on my hands and do nothing?"

"Yes," said Nolan. "That is in your, and Kate's, best interests. You tell her now, you aren't helping her; you're just absolving your own guilt."

"I'm not sure I feel comfortable with doing nothing," said Eddie.

"You do not have a choice."

"You don't have to do this if you don't feel up to it. It's fine if you just want to drop me off," said Erin as Kate parked her car behind Phillip Quinn's in the double garage of the Quinn family's townhouse. "I can explain everything if you want, and I'm sure Alex will understand. It will be enough that you came all the way here."

Kate turned off the car and turned to face Erin with a small, soft smile. "I appreciate it, Erin, but I want to be here for you and Alex. I want to help, and I just can't think of anything else to do."

"If you're sure, then."

"Yes, I am."

Kate opened the trunk of the car and watched Erin pull out the two bags of souvenirs she had bought for the Quinn family before she left the United Kingdom.

"Are you sure you're okay?" she asked as she closed the trunk.

"Yeah, I think so," said Erin. "I think I'm still processing all of this."

"Okay, but if you ever want to talk to me about this or anything else, you can."

"I know, but I hope you know that that goes both ways."

Kate smiled. "I know that, and I appreciate it."

As the pair walked into the living room, Phillip got up from the couch. "Kate, honey, thanks for coming."

"There's nowhere else I'd rather be," said Kate. She accepted the hug he offered as Erin put down their bags.

"Hey, you," said Alex from behind them.

Kate and Erin turned to Alex as she walked down the stairs. Kate frowned as soon as she saw her. "Is everything okay?"

Phillip looked toward his daughter, then turned back to Erin and said, "How about we go check on your mom before lunch?"

"Sounds good to me."

Kate watched them leave, then sat on the living room couch. Alex took a seat beside her.

Kate reached out to take her hand. "Talk to me, Alex."

Alex visibly deflated as she turned to Kate with tears in her eyes. Kate's heart ached. She had never seen her look so broken. Without thinking, she pulled Alex into her arms.

As soon as Kate's arms were around her, she burst into tears. Kate maneuvered her so that she was curled into her side with her face pressed against Kate's neck. They were so wrapped up in one another that neither noticed Erin had walked back in until he placed a glass of water on the coffee table.

He sat down next to his sister. "What's going on, Alex? Can you tell us? Do you want some water first?"

"Yes, please," said Alex softly.

Erin passed the glass to her. As she took a small sip, he grabbed a box of tissues off of the coffee table and placed it on top of her legs.

"It's just about Mom," said Alex. "It's all a bit too much right now. I don't want to lose her. I can't lose her."

"How is she?" asked Kate as she brushed a piece of Alex's hair behind her ear.

"It's not good." Alex shook her head. "The doctors have told her she has Lymphangioleiomyomatosis, or L.A.M."

"That's a mouthful," said Kate. "What does it mean?"

"It's a lung disease without a cure and not a lot of viable treatments. Her lung keeps collapsing and she's coughing up blood. They keep using needle decompression to treat each collapse, but it's probably just going to keep happening. It kind of feels like they're using a band-aid for a bullet hole."

"I'm so sorry, Alex." Kate reached out to take Erin's hand, too. He offered her a watery smile.

"You didn't have to come," said Alex as she turned back to Kate. "I shouldn't have called you. I shouldn't have interfered with your life like that."

"I'm glad you did," said Kate. "I want to be here to support all of you through this. I mean it. There is no place I'd rather be, so stop worrying about me. Are you going to be okay?"

"It's hard seeing her like that," said Alex. "She was asking yesterday how high her window was from the ground."

"Why?" asked Kate.

"She wanted to jump," said Erin. "She's given up. She thinks she's a burden, and she just wants it to be done."

"Have the doctors said how long she has?" asked Kate.

"They don't know, but treatment from here is largely palliative."

"Do you think she'd be up for a visit after lunch?"

"I think she'd like that," said Alex.

"When was the last time you slept?" Kate asked her.

"I don't know."

"How about you go lie down?"

"What about lunch?"

"I'll make sure you're awake for dinner," said Kate. She slowly shifted Alex from her lap and stood up. "Come on."

She pulled Alex to her feet and to her room. Alex lay down on the bed. Kate shut the door softly and sat on the bed beside her. She reached out to squeeze Alex's hand.

"Do you need anything?"

Alex entwined her fingers with Kate's. "Stay. Please."

Kate lay down beside her and pulled Alex into her arms. "Always."

"Detective. Eddie. Hi," said Kate as she opened her front door to reveal Eddie on the other side. "Come in."

"How are you? Are you feeling any better?" asked Eddie.

Kate beckoned her through the door. Inside, Eddie stopped short awkwardly. She placed her hands in the pockets of her jeans as she rocked back on her heels.

"Not really," said Kate with a shrug as she closed the door.

"Well," said Eddie, hesitating and looking down. "How about I see what I can do to try to get you those adoption records?"

Kate frowned as Eddie continued to look at her feet. There was something about the sudden change in her demeanor that unsettled Kate. It reminded her of how Alex had acted in the weeks before she proposed. While the proposal had pleasantly surprised Kate, she remembered being on edge during those weeks, waiting for the other shoe to drop. She'd called Erin almost daily in a near panic, telling him of the stories her mind was concocting about why Alex had been showing the same kinds of concealment and deception markers Eddie was showing now. Kate couldn't fathom any good news that Eddie could be keeping from her, particularly as this was not the first time she had felt that Eddie was hiding something.

"Is there something you aren't telling me?" asked Kate as she crossed her arms in front of her chest. "Do you know something about who my parents are?"

"No," said Eddie as she shook her head slightly. "I don't know anything."

Kate narrowed her eyes. "Why are you lying to me?"

"I'm not." Eddie tugged on her ear. "I promise. I'm not lying to you."

"For a police officer, you're a very poor liar." Kate reached out to grasp the handle of the front door.

"Please, just let me help you," said Eddie. She took a small step toward Kate and reached out.

"No," said Kate as she tightened her grip on the door handle. "I don't want your help."

"Kate—"

"You need to leave." Kate opened the door, averting her gaze.

"I'm sorry," said Eddie, shoulders slumping in defeat as she walked out.

Kate didn't wait for her to say anything further before she closed the door. She leaned back against it and sank to the ground, tears spilling from her eyes.

CHAPTER THREE

Kate turned her head as the bedroom door opened behind her. Erin walked in and quietly knelt beside the bed.

"Is she asleep?" he asked.

"Yes. Do you want me to wake her up?"

"Pizza is on its way, and she missed lunch, so she should probably eat something."

"Okay," said Kate. "We'll be out soon." She waited until Erin had closed the door behind him before she turned back toward Alex. "Alex, honey."

"I'm awake," said Alex as she opened her eyes.

"How are you feeling?" Kate tucked a strand of hair behind Alex's ear.

"I'm feeling a lot of conflicting emotions."

"Why?"

"I feel sad."

"I'm sure you do. I'd be concerned if you didn't. What else?" asked Kate. "You can tell me whatever you want to. I'm here for you."

"I feel guilty," said Alex.

"Why do you feel guilty?"

"I don't want to lose her, but I don't want her to suffer like this. What kind of person wants their mother to die?"

"Oh, honey," said Kate. "I don't think you want her to die. What you want is for a person you love to no longer be suffering. That doesn't make you a horrible person, but a very humane one."

"I'm sorry for dumping this on you."

"I don't ever want you to apologize for talking to me," said Kate. "We were together for three years. I will always love you, whether or not we are together. You will always be an incredibly large part of my life and I don't want that to change just because we aren't together. I want you in my life in whatever way you feel comfortable being. If you need a shoulder to cry on, I'm happy to give you mine."

"I will always love you too," said Alex.

Kate sighed and ducked her head as she sat up on the bed. Alex reached out and grasped her hand before Kate could move too far away.

"Why does that upset you?" she asked.

"It's not important," said Kate.

"You're a large part of my life too," said Alex, "and I also want you to feel comfortable sharing whatever is going on in your life."

"Being here with you in this house, where we spent Christmases and Thanksgivings and holidays, just makes me miss you and our home and our life so much."

"So why don't you move back to New York?" asked Alex. "Why don't you come back to me?"

"I can't do that."

"Why on Earth not?"

"I got into the political science doctoral program at Yale," said Kate. "I start my Master's and PhD in the fall. It means I'll be moving to New Haven."

"So? It's not like New Haven is that far from New York. We can make it work." Alex paused. "Unless it's about something else? Like getting married or having kids? Because since you said it, I haven't been able to stop thinking about a little girl with your hair and my eyes."

Kate sighed. "I can't have this conversation with you right now."

"Thanks for meeting with me," said Agatha as she settled into a chair across from Hunter at the Broadway Coffee House.

"It's okay." Hunter took a sip of his coffee. "You made it sound important."

"It's just about last night," said Agatha. "Isn't it unusual to see Encantados this far north?"

Hunter tilted his head slightly, his brow furrowed. Eventually, he said, "Usually, they wouldn't stray too far away from Encante unless there was a very specific reason for them to do so."

"It's not just Encantados, though, is it?" asked Agatha. "There has been the Alp and the Kitsune."

"Exactly," said Hunter. "Why does it seem like so many Lesser Fae have been traveling to Seattle?"

"Maybe ..." Agatha trailed off and drummed her fingers against the table.

"What are you thinking?" asked Hunter.

"I'm just thinking that Rowan would have used an awful lot of power to save your partner."

"And?"

"That kind of power acts like a beacon, drawing Lesser Fae beings and the like toward it."

"So, it probably wouldn't help that they're going to be looking for Rowan and find her identical twin in Kate?"

"No, it probably doesn't."

"Is there a way to ensure that this beacon dissipates faster?" asked Hunter. "I only ask because it sounds like the most logical play. If that's the thing drawing the Lesser Fae here and putting Kate in harm's way, we need to get rid of that beacon somehow."

"There isn't a way, or at least not a way that I know of." Agatha rubbed her chin. "But there could be a way to shield Kate. I'll look into it."

"Night, you two," said Erin as he headed off to bed, leaving Kate and Alex standing on the balcony.

Kate smiled softly in acknowledgment before she turned back to look out at the stars. Alex moved to stand behind her with her arms on either side of Kate's against the railing and her head resting on Kate's shoulder. Kate bit her lip to prevent another smile from breaking across her face at how safe Alex made her feel. It didn't matter how chaotic or overwhelming her life was; Alex's presence always seemed to put her at ease and make her feel like nothing could ever hurt her.

"Dinner was nice," said Kate softly. "Thank you for calling me."

"We all wanted you here," said Alex.

"I hope your mom had a good day."

"I'm sure she did."

After a few moments of silence, Kate sighed. "Did you mean what you said before?"

"About what?" asked Alex.

"About the little girl with my hair and your eyes? Have you really been thinking about it? I mean, it's been almost two years since we broke up and I went to Oxford."

"Of course I have," said Alex. "It's human nature to think about something like that after someone mentions it. You put the idea in my head."

Kate turned around to face her. "But your mind hasn't changed?"

"What does it matter?" asked Alex.

"I don't want you to just tell me things I want to hear," said Kate. "I don't even need you to be sure. I just need you to be my partner. I want whatever our future could be, whether that involves kids or marriage, to be something we work out together."

"I want you," said Alex. "You are all that I need. I love you."

"I love you too," said Kate. "But that just isn't enough for me anymore. I don't want us to keep doing what we've always done."

"What is that supposed to mean?"

"It means that you make all the decisions for both of us. I want to be your partner. I want us to work through these things together. But you don't. You only want me to do everything you say. You still treat me like I'm your nineteen-year-old student. Well, newsflash, I'm not."

"I know that you aren't—"

"Well, stop treating me like I am," snapped Kate. She sighed in frustration and pushed past Alex.

Before she could get more than a couple of steps away, Alex reached out to grab her wrist. She turned Kate back to face her.

One moment she was glaring at Alex, and the next the two women were pressed against one another. Kate pushed Alex back against the railing and pulled her mouth down to meet hers. Instinctively, both of her hands dropped from Alex's face to rest on her waist. Alex lifted one hand to caress Kate's cheek as her other pressed against Kate's lower back.

Kate pulled away. She breathed heavily for a few moments before she said, "This doesn't change anything."

"I know, baby," said Alex as she ran her thumb along Kate's cheekbone. She slipped her hand behind Kate's neck and drew her forward slowly to press their lips together once more.

After a few more moments, Kate pulled away again. "This is a bad idea."

"I know, baby," Alex repeated as she pressed her mouth back to Kate's. She moved forward, pushing Kate into the house and toward her bedroom.

Eddie leaned back against the wall. From where she was standing, she could see her partner at a table in the Broadway Coffee House. Unfortunately, she could not see much of the woman sitting across from him. Eddie had been standing there for almost an hour and had yet to see more than the woman's back. Any parts of her face that may have been visible were obscured by the wavy blonde hair that fell to just below her shoulders.

Eddie sighed in frustration. She hoped she wasn't wasting her time. But she also hoped that she was wrong about Hunter. She wanted to trust him, and she hoped that the thing holding her back was just her own fears. Her prejudices. Her preconceived notions. It would not be easy—*but,* said an inner voice that sounded oddly like her partner's, *you can work on those, if you need to, for the sake of our partnership.*

Movement through the window caught Eddie's attention. Focusing on Hunter's table, she caught her first glimpse of the woman as she stood up.

Eddie frowned. For some reason, the woman looked familiar. She ducked down and hurried across the road, then crouched in the gap between two cars just outside the door of the coffee house as Hunter and the woman stepped outside. She searched her memory, trying to place the woman and explain why she felt like she had met her before.

Eddie was still lost in thought when she overheard Hunter saying, "Let me know what you find out, Agatha."

"Will do."

That was it. The woman's name was Agatha. Eddie had met her at Rowan's funeral. Rowan's mother had introduced the two of them, saying that Agatha was a realtor who was going to help them find a tenant for Rowan's apartment.

There was something important about that. Something significant about Agatha being a realtor. What was it? She rapped her knuckles against her thigh in frustration. Why was it so important that Agatha was at the funeral? *Wait,* thought Eddie. *Why would a realtor Rowan's parents had just hired be invited to her funeral?*

Rowan's mother had said she was having Agatha assist them again, as she had assisted with their purchase of the property. She had even mentioned that they had known Agatha from when she had met Rowan in college.

But if Agatha was in league with Hunter and Cornelius, that meant they had known where Rowan was for years. How was that even possible? And why had it taken so long for them to kill her?

Kate awoke slowly to the feeling of warm sun on her back, cool air blowing against her skin from the overhead fan, and someone drawing small circles against the palm of her hand. She opened her eyes to watch Alex trace patterns on her skin.

"Hey," said Kate softly.

Alex smiled as she flicked her gaze up to meet Kate's. "Hey yourself." She moved to draw circles against Kate's hip. "How are you feeling?"

"That's a loaded question."

"It wasn't meant to be."

"I'm as okay as I can be, given everything currently going on. I think that's the best I can ask for in the circumstances," said Kate. "How about you? How are you feeling?"

"About the same, I guess," said Alex.

Kate sighed and rolled onto her back to watch the fan rotate above her. After several moments of silence, she said, "I should probably go."

"Are you sure you should be alone at the moment?" asked Alex.

"I'm not the one whose mother is sick. Plus, I can't stay here."

"You mean you can't stay here with me."

"Don't put words in my mouth," said Kate. She sat up and wrapped a sheet around herself.

"Are you sure you want to give up on this?" asked Alex. "Give up on something tangible and real for some notion you have about getting married and being a mom? Is it really that easy for you to give up on everything we have, after everything we've been through?"

"What do we have, exactly?" asked Kate. "I mean, I went from being the student you were having an affair with to being your roommate with benefits. I was only ever the other woman, the secret you would never admit to. I don't want that. I want someone who will love me openly, who wants to marry me and plan a future with me. You can't give me that."

Without waiting for a reply, she stood up and left the room.

Eddie slammed the door of her apartment shut behind her. She dropped her keys in a bowl on the table beside the door as she kicked off her shoes. She snagged a tennis ball off the kitchen table as she walked past, bouncing it as she paced her apartment and tried to figure out the significance of what she had seen at the Broadway Coffee House. Her instincts were screaming that the black-and-white version of events leading to her partner's death was suddenly far less simple.

She had been so sure, so certain, about who had killed Rowan and why. But now, things seemed less cut and dried. Maybe the simplest explanation was not the right one. *So,* thought Eddie, *what does that leave?*

She stopped suddenly as her gaze caught on a large corkboard hanging on the wall. Pinned to it were numerous photographs she had taken over the years, from school to college to the friends she had met while living in Seattle. Eddie stepped closer, her gaze settling on a photo of her and Rowan. She sighed as she pulled out the pushpin that affixed it to the corkboard.

"I'm going to find out who killed you." She blinked furiously, eyes burning as she looked at herself and Rowan standing arm in arm, smiling widely for the camera. "I promise."

Eddie set the photo down reverently on the kitchen table before she returned to the corkboard. She pulled it from the wall and carried it to the table, then flipped it over and reaffixed the photo of her and Rowan at the top.

She opened the file where she had placed her background check of Ainsley Cooper to find a photograph of Ainsley, then attached it to the corkboard along with pictures of the knives taken from the scene of Rowan's death and the attack on Kate at the park.

Eddie pulled out a piece of paper, which she tore into three. She wrote Cornelius' name on one and added it directly above Ainsley's photograph. She wrote Hunter's name on the next and Agatha's on the final piece, then affixed them on either side of Ainsley's photo.

Eddie bit down on her thumb as she looked at the gaping hole in the middle of the corkboard between the pictures of the knives and Ainsley. She did not understand why Cornelius would have killed Rowan when he did if he had known where she was since Agatha came into Rowan's life. It was not like anything had changed if that was the case. So there must be something she was missing.

Eddie sighed as she fished her phone out of the back pocket of her jeans. She scrolled through her contacts and dialed Rowan's mother.

"Mrs. Ashley. It's Eddie Caulfield. Would it be okay if I stopped by tomorrow?"

"What's this?" asked Alex. Her eyes were wide and her eyebrows raised as Kate placed a glass of wine on the table in front of her.

Kate had struggled to find her, despite it being Alex's birthday party. She knew Alex hadn't been deliberately avoiding her, as it wasn't unusual for her to take time out from festivities like this. Knowing Alex the way she did meant that she was eventually able to locate her tucked away in a quiet corner of the room.

"A long time ago, I promised you that on your birthday, we would have a glass of wine and talk about how to celebrate our upcoming milestone birthdays," said Kate as she settled down on the couch next to Alex. She sounded very matter-of-fact, even to her own ears.

"Ahh, yes," said Alex. "Thank you for reminding me that next year I'll be turning thirty."

"Don't they say that age is just a number?"

"Said by the woman closing in on twenty-five, not the big three-oh."

"You never know," said Kate. "I could be headed toward a quarter-life crisis."

"We don't have to do this if you don't want to," said Alex. "I don't want to make you feel uncomfortable."

"If I didn't want to do this or felt uncomfortable in any way, I wouldn't be here," said Kate, taking a sip of her wine. She placed it on the table next to Alex's untouched glass before she butted her shoulder against Alex's and leaned back.

"Did Erin call you?" asked Alex.

"Both Erin and your dad."

"Traitors."

"They were worried. They said that you've been distant and isolating yourself since your mom's death." Kate paused. "I didn't get to tell you how sorry I was about that, by the way."

"You just being at the funeral was enough," said Alex. "And I'm sure it would have meant a lot to my mom."

"Stupid question," said Kate, "but how have you been feeling since she died?"

Alex looked down at the two glasses. "I'm exhausted," she said quietly.

"Why?" asked Kate, dipping her head slightly as she tried to meet Alex's gaze.

"Because I miss you." Alex looked up. "I miss everything about you."

"Oh, baby," said Kate instantly, without a second thought.

Alex's eyes shone with unshed tears. Kate raised one hand to Alex's cheek as her other found Alex's hand. At that moment, she couldn't tell whether Alex had tugged her or she had propelled herself forward, but in an instant, she found herself straddling Alex's hips. A second later, their mouths crashed together like the tide coming home to the shore.

Alex tasted like everything she had been missing—a place to call home. They kissed for long minutes. They could not seem to stop, their lips starved for the taste of one another. It was bordering on deep and desperate until Kate deliberately slowed their pace. They gradually reached a point where they were kissing slowly and languidly, occasionally breaking apart for a gasp of oxygen before coming together again and again.

Kate was the one to draw back completely so that she could finally look at Alex again. She loved seeing Alex like this: with her cheeks tinged pink and her breath coming in tiny, warm puffs between them as she tried to compose herself. It was not a sight easily forgotten, but the reality was so much more potent than her memories.

Alex still had her eyes closed, so Kate took the opportunity to map her face carefully with the hand not intertwined with the other woman's, until Alex opened her eyes slowly.

"Wow," she said softly as she held Kate's gaze.

"Same here, darling."

Kate smiled as she slid backward off Alex's lap. She stood in front of her for several moments before using their still-entwined hands to pull Alex to her feet and draw her in for another kiss. This one was more urgent, with heavy breaths and wandering hands. A sense of purpose that neither of them wanted to ignore.

"Do you want to get out of here?" asked Kate in a whisper.

Alex licked her lips. In the darkened corner, her eyes looked almost black.

"Yes," she rasped, leaning in again.

CHAPTER FOUR

Kate sat up and looked around her apartment, startled by how dark her room suddenly appeared. She frowned as she reached across to pick up her phone. Her pulse skyrocketed when she realized she had spent at least six hours lost in memories of her wife. These moments of her life with Alex were replaying in her head so vividly that it was almost like she was back there relieving them.

Kate knew that was not normal. She was worried that something was very wrong with her. She knew that she needed help and that she should not be by herself. She unlocked her phone and opened her contacts, hesitating with her thumb over Detective Caulfield's name. She sighed as she scrolled past—she had already tried asking Eddie, but the detective had only lied to her.

Kate stopped when she reached Erin's number. She hesitated again. This was not something she wanted to burden him with. She scrolled back up to Ainsley's number and quickly started the call before she could talk herself out of it.

"Hi, Kate," said Ainsley.

"Hi, Ainsley. Sorry, am I interrupting you?"

"No, of course not. You okay?"

"Are you sure?" asked Kate.

"I'm sure," said Ainsley. "I was actually just on my way to see you."

"Okay." Kate blinked furiously as her eyes burned with tears.

"What's wrong?"

"Nothing. It's fine."

"You don't sound fine. What's going on?"

"I just ..." Kate raised a hand to her mouth and tried to muffle a sob. "I just think something is wrong."

"I'm coming over," said Ainsley quickly.

"No, you don't have to do that."

"Do you want me to come over?"

Kate paused before she admitted, "Yes."

"I'll be right there."

"Thank you."

Kate dropped her phone on her bed as she curled onto her side, sobbing. She shook her head in an attempt to chase away another memory. She closed her eyes, but suddenly she was closing the front door to her apartment in New York.

Kate was placing her keys on the sideboard when her phone started ringing. Seeing Erin's name on the screen, she answered as she walked into her living room.

"Hi, Kate. How did the interview at Princeton go?"

"Hi, Erin." She waved to Alex, who was sitting at the kitchen table, working on her laptop. Kate took a seat on the couch. "It went as well as it could have in the circumstances."

"That sounds a little ominous."

"Well, you know I'm a pessimist with unrealistically high expectations of myself."

"That I do," said Erin. "So, how would you say it went if you were me and not you?"

"I would say that the chances of me getting a postdoctoral research position are unlikely."

"That is nothing like what I would say, and that isn't an answer to my question."

"I know," said Kate, "but that's the best you're going to get."

"Okay. But you need to stop being so hard on yourself."

"Maybe one day."

"Consider it my life goal to get you there."

"That's why you're the optimist and I'm the pessimist."

"Yes, it is," said Erin. "Promise me you'll tell me how it goes, whatever the outcome."

"I promise," said Kate.

"That's my girl. Okay, that's enough from this proud pseudo-parent-cross-lifetime-cheerleader. I'll call you later."

"Thanks, Erin," said Kate. "I hope you know I appreciate it."

"I know," said Erin before he ended the call.

As Kate turned around, she noticed Alex watching her from the kitchen. "What?" she asked with a frown. "Is everything okay?"

"Well, I was just thinking." Alex stood and walked toward where Kate was sitting. "The Department of State has been looking for economists."

"Um, okay," said Kate. "I don't understand why you're telling me this."

"Well ..." Alex started pacing. "It could be an opportunity for me to put my name forward."

"You want to work for the State Department? In Washington?" asked Kate. "Since when?"

"It's something I've been thinking about for years."

"You have never once mentioned to me that that was something you wanted to do," said Kate. "And you have never once mentioned wanting to leave New York. In fact, your plan has only ever been New York, New York."

"Well, believe it or not, Kate, but I don't share everything with you," said Alex sharply.

Kate's mouth quivered as it formed a slight pout.

Alex closed her eyes and took a deep breath. "Sorry. I didn't mean for it to sound that way, but I never wanted to say anything because I didn't think I would ever actually be in a position where I could."

"Do you want to marry me?" asked Kate suddenly.

Alex stopped pacing abruptly. She turned to look at Kate. "What?"

"Just answer the question."

"Why are we back to this?" asked Alex. "I thought you had moved on from this when we agreed to get back together."

"So, what? I was just supposed to get over the idea of us being more than this? When did we discuss that? Oh, wait. We didn't. You just decided for the both of us again," snapped Kate. Alex still didn't answer her question. "Do you want to have kids with me?"

"I don't know," said Alex slowly as she sat down heavily beside Kate. "I've never really thought about it seriously."

"We've been together for the better part of the last six years and you've never thought about where we're going? How many times have I asked you? Or have I just been talking to myself the whole time?" asked Kate, incredulous. "I can't be the only one thinking about it, especially when I don't know where we're going."

"Well, I can't help you with that," retorted Alex, her tone frustrated.

Kate's face fell as Alex's words sank in. She rubbed a hand against her face as she got to her feet.

Alex reached out quickly to grab her wrist. "I didn't mean that."

"I think you did," said Kate softly as she turned to look at Alex. "I don't believe you meant to say it, but I think you meant it." She sighed. "I'm not angry, but I think there are some things we need to think about. I also think we both need some time apart right now, so I'm going to give Robbie a call—"

"When you say time apart, will you come back here? Tonight?" asked Alex. She sounded slightly panicked as she gripped Kate's wrist a bit tighter. "Because the last time you said that, you moved to another country."

"I'll be home tonight," said Kate as she placed her hand over Alex's.

"Okay," said Alex softly, tears welling in her eyes.

"Okay," whispered Kate. She placed a kiss on Alex's forehead before she moved away from the couch. She could feel Alex watching her as she gathered her things. She turned back one last time to look at Alex's stiff posture before she sighed and opened the front door.

Kate opened her front door to reveal Ainsley standing on her porch.

"Hey, you," said Ainsley.

"Hey," said Kate quietly as she leaned heavily against the door frame.

Ainsley pulled Kate into her arms for a warm hug. The burden of her fears lessened as she sank into Ainsley's embrace.

"It's good to see you," said Kate. She reluctantly pulled away and ushered Ainsley into her apartment.

"It's good to see you too," said Ainsley as she followed Kate inside.

As they settled on the couch, Kate watched as Ainsley's gaze drifted to the coffee table. She had left a bottle of wine there beside two wine glasses before Ainsley had arrived.

"Are you okay?" asked Ainsley. "Because you look like you could use some of that wine."

"Funny," said Kate dryly. "But, yes, I could use a drink, hence the wine."

"Huh," said Ainsley. "Here I thought it was just some kind of new decor you were going with."

"I also ordered Thai food," said Kate. "It shouldn't be too far away. But I can order pizza or dumplings or something else if you'd prefer."

"Thai sounds great." Ainsley reached out to pour wine into the two glasses and passed one to Kate.

"Thanks," Kate murmured as she settled back onto the couch.

"Is there something in mind that you want to talk about tonight?" asked Ainsley as she leaned back, pulling her legs up underneath her so that she was facing Kate.

"I don't know." Kate's eyes watered. "I'm just in such a weird headspace at the moment."

"Is there anything I can do to help with that? I'm here for you if you need it. In whatever way you want me to help, I'm here, okay?"

"Okay."

"Okay," Ainsley repeated. "Now, are you okay?"

"I'm sure it's nothing and I'm just being silly," said Kate. "I don't even know why I'm getting so upset about it."

"You're allowed to be upset and scared and anxious and anything else you're feeling," said Ainsley. "I just want you to talk to me so I can help."

"I'm having these memories or flashbacks of my life with Alex," said Kate as tears fell from her eyes. "They're so vivid and real. It's like I'm back there reliving it all over again. At first it was just momentary flashes, but now I'm losing hours and I can't stop it."

"Oh, sweetheart." Ainsley reached out to take Kate's glass from her hand, placing both glasses on the coffee table before she reached out to gather Kate into her arms.

Kate melted into her embrace, raising her arms to grip the back of Ainsley's shirt and secure herself to her.

"When was the last time you actually slept?" asked Ainsley as she ran a hand through Kate's hair.

"I don't know."

Ainsley gently wiped the tears from Kate's face. "Do you want to at least try to get some sleep before the food gets here?"

Kate nodded. "Will you stay?"

"Of course," said Ainsley. She slowly pulled them both into a standing position.

Kate looked up at her for a moment before she settled her head against Ainsley's shoulder. "Thank you," she said quietly.

"Any time." Ainsley pressed a brief kiss to the top of Kate's head and pulled her closer. "Okay, let's get you to bed. Then you and I need to talk about something."

"About what?" asked Kate, pulling away slightly to look up at her again.

"It's about you, and it's about your parents."

Kate stepped backward. "You know who they are?"

"Yes," said Ainsley. "I'm sorry I didn't tell you when we first met, but you had gone through so much and I didn't want to overwhelm you."

"So, you thought that you were—"

Kate stopped mid-sentence as a skull-splitting pain suddenly gripped her. She gasped, holding a hand up to her head.

"Kate?" asked Ainsley, her forehead creased in concern. "Everything okay?"

"It's just my head." Kate squinted, raising her hand to shield her eyes from the light. The room suddenly seemed too bright, sending shooting pain through her head. "I just got a sudden headache."

"Do you need me to get you anything?" Ainsley stepped closer, positioning herself between Kate and the light and placing a hand on each of Kate's elbows to steady her.

"I think I just need to—"

Kate cut herself off with a sharp wince. Her knees buckled and her vision grayed.

"Kate?" Ainsley tightened her grip and slid them both to the ground just as Kate's world turned black.

"You look absolutely stunning," said Erin as he looked down at the photo of Kate in the ivory wedding dress she would be wearing in a few days. It had a delicate lace bodice, a plunging neckline and V-back, and a soft, A-line chiffon skirt.

"Thank you." Kate blushed and looked down at her drink. She was glad that Erin had talked her into having an impromptu second bachelorette party, even if she knew both of them would regret it in the morning.

Erin grimaced as he swallowed another shot of tequila. "Are you sure you still want to do this?"

Kate's head snapped up to look at him. "Seriously?"

Erin shrugged. "I thought it was a valid question. You don't have too much longer to change your mind, so I thought I should ask the question."

"Do you want me to change my mind?" asked Kate. "Or are you simply a mean drunk?"

"I want you to be sure."

"That isn't an answer. And why do you think I wouldn't be sure about marrying your sister?"

"I didn't say that I don't think you're sure," said Erin. "I just want you to be sure that this is what you want."

"Why wouldn't I be?"

"Do you want my honest opinion?"

"At this moment, yes, that would be appreciated."

"Okay, honesty, sure," said Erin. "Now, I don't mean anything I'm about to say as an insult, and you know that I love you both dearly—but at the end of the day, you and Alex have never been equals. I've never really seen you as partners."

"Ouch," said Kate.

"What did I just say about not taking it as an insult?" asked Erin. "Because I didn't mean it to be."

"How did you mean it, then?"

"I meant that you are so giving as a person. You are so good at noticing what the people around you need and doing whatever you can to meet those needs. But you aren't very adept at recognizing your own needs."

"And that's a problem?"

"No, it's incredibly selfless, but you need someone who is going to take care of you and protect you when you aren't able to do that yourself. My sister, as much as I love and adore her, is not that kind of person. She will take and take and take until you have nothing left to give."

"I love her," said Kate.

"I know," said Erin. "But loving someone doesn't always mean you're meant to be with them."

"So, what I am supposed to do?"

"You can't let her walk all over you and make all the decisions," said Erin. "You need to ask for what you want whenever you want."

"You know I'm not very good at that."

"I know that, which is why you need to find someone who will support you and help you figure out what it is that you want. It's why you need someone who will make you feel safe enough to grow into the incredible person I know you can be. And whether that person is my sister or not, I will always love you."

"You rang," said Akiko as she settled herself into a chair in front of Nolan's desk.

"Yes," said Nolan without looking up from the document he was reading. "Why isn't Katherine Matthews dead yet? I paid you to kill her just like you killed her sister, but it seems like the most recent attempts on her life have been made by Lesser Fae with no connection to you."

"There have been some unexpected complications," said Akiko. "But those Lesser Fae left Kate uniquely vulnerable. That Alp left her with so much guilt, and the Encantados just drove the point home so exquisitely. It was so easy to get in her head. To use that guilt about her wife to slowly torture her and drive her insane. Breaking someone like that takes time."

"If you can't get it done, I will find someone who can," said Nolan.

"Don't worry," said Akiko. "She has already collapsed under the strain. She won't regain consciousness again, and from there, it's only a matter of time."

EPISODE SIX: APPLE

At the end of knowledge, wisdom begins, and at the end of wisdom, there is not grief ... but hope.
—Lloyd Alexander

CHAPTER ONE

Ainsley looked down into Kate's face to find her eyes closed. "Kate? Come on. Wake up, baby."

She leaned back slightly to keep Kate's limp body propped up against her own, gently guiding Kate's head to rest against her shoulder and smoothing her hair. When she was confident that Kate's body would not slip and sustain any further injuries, she wrapped her hand around one of Kate's wrists and tried to find her pulse.

After several moments of struggling to feel even the slightest movement, Ainsley breathed a small sigh of relief when she eventually found it. But her relief was short-lived when she realized how weak Kate's heartbeat felt underneath her fingers. Kate's breathing was also far too shallow.

"Kate," said Ainsley, shaking her slightly. "Come on, Kate. Just stay with me. I'll sort this out and you will be fine. Just don't ask me right now how I plan to sort it out—not that you're really in a talking mood, but you know what I mean. You might know what I mean if you can hear me and comprehend what I'm saying. I hope you can, because I really need you to be okay. And I'm clearly panicking, because not only am I rambling, I'm talking to myself, which is just great. Okay, just breathe for a second, Ainsley. What do I do? What do I do? I phone a friend. But to do that I need my phone, so ..."

Ainsley trailed off and looked around Kate's apartment. Her gaze landed on the couch, and she scooped up Kate and carried her to it, then pulled out her phone and called Agatha.

"Hey, is everything okay?" Agatha answered.

"She's barely breathing, Agatha. I need your help."

"Who is barely breathing? What's going on, Ainsley?"

"I'm at Kate's apartment. She's collapsed and I can't wake her. I need you here now."

"I'm on my way."

Kate entered the living room of Erin and Ainsley's father, Phillip. She had never needed much incentive to visit Ainsley's family. She had always found both Erin and Phillip so welcoming. It was a pleasant change.

She placed the pizza box she was carrying down in front of Erin and her brother, Robbie, before she sat down.

"So, Kate, what do you think of the new president?" asked Erin as he got himself a couple of slices of pizza.

"And what do you think about the United Kingdom leaving the European Union?" asked Robbie, reaching into the pizza box.

Robbie was as tall as Erin but lankier. His light brown hair was short on the back and sides of his head, with longer hair on top that was swept upward in a quiff. His green eyes were surprisingly similar to his sister's. It was one of the similarities that led people to assume they shared a biological connection. He also had a strong jaw where he was developing some stubble.

"Boys, no politics at the table while we're eating," said Alex as she sat down next to Kate.

"But, Alex," said Erin, "who's better suited to answer these questions than Kate, with her bazillion degrees in politics and international relations? You're basically saying that we can't talk about her study and work whenever we're eating."

"He does have a point there," said Kate, placing slices of pizza on her and Alex's plates.

"You aren't helping," Alex whispered before she turned back to the boys. "It doesn't matter. This is a family dinner, so we will not be discussing world politics."

"Okay, then," said Erin, smiling briefly. "Who else doesn't think that Lee Harvey Oswald was solely responsible for J.F.K.'s death?"

"Seriously?" asked Alex incredulously.

"This appears to be going well," said Phillip, exchanging a wide grin with Kate.

"Okay, new rule," said Alex, sounding exasperated. "No talk about politics, political figures, or the deaths of political figures."

"So, what are we supposed to talk about, then?" asked Erin, taking a bite of pizza.

"I think anything else would be great," said Alex.

"Okay," said Robbie. "I have something I want to talk about."

"Sure," said Alex.

"I want to ask when I will be getting a baby niece or nephew," said Robbie.

Kate's eyes widened in surprise as Alex raised her eyebrows and Phillip started coughing to hide his laughter.

"You what?" asked Alex at the same time as Kate said, "I'm sorry, what?"

"I think the two of you should have kids soon," said Robbie. "Kate is only going to be at Princeton for the rest of the year, and after that, you'll both be in the same place, wherever that may be. So, I think it would be a good time for you to think about filling your nest. But don't fill it too much. I don't want more than one or two."

"Erin, why do you think that Oswald didn't act alone?" asked Kate, deliberately avoiding any response to Robbie's comments.

"You still aren't helping," said Alex.

Kate raised an eyebrow. "I just assumed you didn't want to answer the other question."

"Okay." Alex took a deep breath. "No discussing politics, political figures, the assassinations of political figures, or the future of my relationship with Kate."

"What does that leave us with?" asked Robbie.

"Kate," said Erin, "you went on exchange during your studies, didn't you?"

"I went on a short-term exchange before I completed my Master of International Relations overseas," said Kate, reaching out and taking Alex's hand under the table.

"Where did you go again?" asked Phillip.

"The U.K."

"And by that she means Oxford," said Erin. "Seriously, Kate, you need to get better at accepting that you're a smart cookie, even if you don't seem to think so. Because honestly, not a lot of people get Rhodes Scholarships and the chance to study at Oxford."

Kate blushed and looked down at the table. "Can we please move on?"

"Okay, we can move on," said Erin. "But I want you to believe that you have achieved some pretty incredible things."

"Maybe one day."

"Why the U.K.?" asked Phillip.

"Do you want the P.G. version or the truth?" asked Erin.

"Hush, you," said Kate.

"You mean there's more than one version?" asked Alex with a slight frown.

"You didn't know there were two reasons?" asked Erin. "I thought that was why the two of you took some time apart when Kate went overseas."

"No, we broke up before we got much of a chance to talk about me going to Oxford," said Kate.

"What does Erin know that I don't?" asked Alex. "All I ever remember you saying was that the reason you applied for the Rhodes Scholarship was because you had been to Oxford on a short-term exchange and wanted to go back."

Kate squeezed Alex's hand. "That is true."

"Technically," said Erin.

"You really aren't helping, Erin." Kate glanced at him briefly before looking back at Alex.

"What else is there to the story?" asked Alex.

"See what you did?" Kate asked Erin.

"Like it isn't the first secret between the two of you," said Robbie.

Kate turned her gaze to her brother. "What is that supposed to mean?"

"Alex knows exactly what it's supposed to mean."

"No, I don't," said Alex.

"I'm not going to let you pretend that my sister is the only one who needs to explain things," said Robbie. "Particularly when you were still together when you did what you did, whereas you broke up with her before she even got the chance to tell you about Monty."

"Monty," repeated Alex. "Who is Monty?"

"Sorry, Kate," said Robbie.

"It's okay." Kate let out a deep sigh. "I was interested in going to Oxford a second time because it would be a great opportunity and because I had been there before." She paused. "But there was also someone there that I had dated briefly, and I wanted to see her again."

"Your first time was just before we met," said Alex slowly.

"I know. And it ended when you and I started seeing one another, but when you broke up with me, I decided that I wanted to go back and spend more time with her."

"Was she your lecturer?" asked Alex.

"Not when things started."

"But she was at some point?" Alex pressed.

"She was before anything happened, and during the time that I was completing my Masters."

"I see you have a type, then," said Alex coldly.

"That relationship was completely different," said Kate.

"How so?"

"She was manipulative, and she took advantage of my feelings for her. She treated me badly and knew that I would forgive her because of how I felt about her. In saying that, though, I want to be clear that I never intended to deliberately mislead you about that. The way things ended between us was difficult and humiliating. The things she said to me were so hurtful. When I got back, I didn't want to dwell on what she did to me. I don't hold on to that. I choose to remember my times overseas for all the good things that happened and not the one bad thing."

Clearly sensing that both women would prefer to continue discussing the topic privately, Phillip asked, "Is there something else we can talk about?"

"Who do we think will play in the Super Bowl this season?" asked Erin.

Ainsley ran her fingers through her hair in frustration as she walked from one side of Kate's living room to the other. Every few moments, her gaze was drawn in the direction of the couch, where Kate was lying limp and unmoving. Every time, Ainsley's blood ran cold—a sight that had once filled her with such warmth was now only tinged with fear and sadness. She didn't know what she would do without Kate in her life, and she promised herself that she would do anything she could to ensure Kate had a chance to go on living. The problem was that she had no idea what she could do. She had no idea what was happening. That uncertainty filled her with an intense and paralyzing sense of desperation.

A knock on the door shattered Ainsley's building panic. Agatha opened the door and walked into the living room without Ainsley inviting her in.

"What's going on here?" she asked, looking between Ainsley and Kate's prone form.

"I don't know," said Ainsley. She looked back toward Kate. Her voice wavered as she continued, "We were just talking, and then she was complaining of a headache and saying she was sensitive to light. Next second she collapsed, and now she's barely breathing. I need you to save her, Agatha."

Agatha hesitated for a second, then walked quickly toward the couch. She knelt on the floor beside Kate and reached out to take her wrist.

"Okay. You were right. Her vitals are incredibly weak," said Agatha. "But there's something else as well."

"What?" Ainsley quickly joined her.

"Something has a hold on her mind. Whatever it is, it's like a whirlpool sucking her down. If we aren't able to snap its hold on her, we'll lose her within a day."

Ainsley's eyes burned with tears and she started to breathe faster. "We can't let that happen. We need to get her out of this. We need to save her."

In an instant, Agatha had dropped Kate's wrist and brought her hands up to grab Ainsley by both shoulders. She shook her slightly until Ainsley's gaze met hers.

"Listen to me, Ainsley. I know this is hard and scary. If this was someone I cared about the way you care about Kate, I'd be breaking down too. But right now, I need you to focus on being strong for her. Okay? Because I can't help her if I need to worry about you hyperventilating. So, can you please do that for me? For her?"

"Yes, I think so," said Ainsley as she wiped the tears from her face.

"Okay, good," said Agatha. "Now, I'm going to try to get inside Kate's mind. If I can, I might be able to get her to wake up."

"What do you need me to do?"

"It's risky enough going inside someone's mind when they're stable," said Agatha. "Kate's mind isn't. It's like a vortex in there, which may suck me down before I'm able to do anything. So, if you see any changes or it seems to take too long, wake me up."

"Okay," said Ainsley.

"Okay." Agatha took a deep, steadying breath and closed her eyes. "Here we go."

Agatha opened her eyes and looked around. She was standing in the middle of a carefully manicured lawn under a bright blue sky, surrounded by neat rows of tombstones standing erect in silence. Most of the newer additions were smooth with their polished marble and black writing in the sun. But there were just as many weather and crumbling from age spread across the lawn. She could see the leaves from several large trees move silently, the wind moving through them failing to break the oppressive silence.

Agatha raised a hand to cover her mouth in shock as she looked down at the tombstone in front of her, which was new, with bouquets of flowers in front of it. The epitaph read: *In loving memory of Alexandra Emma Quinn (1987–2018)—Never say goodbye. Always say so long ... until we meet again.*

Agatha took a deep breath. "Kate. Where are you?"

"You won't find her," said a voice beside her.

Agatha turned, frowning as she saw a slimly built woman with alabaster skin, long, dark brown hair, and captivating emerald eyes. The woman she was looking for.

"Come on, Kate," said Agatha. "We need to get out of here."

The figure laughed darkly. "I am that forgettable, then? It's only taken a few months for my sister to replace me completely in your eyes?"

"Rowan?" asked Agatha. "How are you here?"

"If it weren't for you and your friends, she would be lying here," said Rowan. "She would have died. She should have died so Alex and I didn't have to."

"That isn't true," said Agatha.

"She was never good enough and she never will be," said Rowan. "She will never be deserving of your protection. If she was, she would have saved her wife; she would have protected Alex. She would have walked away or let Alex walk away when she wanted to. If Kate had never met Alex, or if she'd let her go when she was supposed to, Alex never would have died. But she was selfish and needy and now Alex is dead. Her death is Kate's fault, and yet you protect her. You're prepared to lay down your life for her."

"This isn't you, Rowan," said Agatha. "You were never cruel like this. This can't be you."

"Maybe I'm exactly who I should be after I've been betrayed by my friends," said Rowan. "You chose her over me. You threw me aside like I meant nothing.

You let me die at my own front door. And then, before my body was even cold, you were organizing for my replacement to move in and take over my life."

Ainsley had lost track of how long she had been sitting on the floor of Kate's living room, watching her best friend. She hoped that whatever Agatha was doing would help Kate wake up. She hadn't realized until this moment how much she cared about Kate and how desperately she wanted her to live. But she could not bear it if it came at the cost of Agatha's life. Agatha may not realize how much Ainsley needed her from how she acted. But Ainsley promised herself that if they made their way through this, she would make more of an effort to show Agatha how much she had needed her throughout their lives.

"Rowan," mumbled Agatha, suddenly tensing before Ainsley's eyes.

That can't be good, thought Ainsley. She reached out to jostle Agatha, hoping that would be enough to break her connection to Kate. Ainsley braced her friend quickly before Agatha could drop heavily to the floor. Agatha slowly blinked open her eyes.

"Are you okay?" asked Ainsley, helping her sit up.

"I am now. Thanks for getting me out of there."

"What happened?"

"Kate appears to be trapped inside this illusion," said Agatha. "Someone must have planted it in her mind."

"Can you break it?"

"Honestly, I don't think so," said Agatha. "I've never seen anything that elaborate before. I think even trying to break it would be more likely to kill Kate and me than save her."

"There must be something else that we can do," said Ainsley.

"There might be something," said Agatha slowly. "It's a Hail Mary, and it might not go our way, but I can't think of anything else."

"What is it?"

"On the Island of the Hesperides, there's a garden. One of the trees there grows golden apples, which have been known to cure the effects of all magical ailments."

"Okay, great," said Ainsley. "How do we get there?"

"We're going to need your boat," said Agatha.

Kate was lying on her side in bed with her back to the door when she felt a slight dip in the mattress as someone sat behind her. The person reached over and squeezed her hand.

"You keep far too many secrets," said Alex.

Kate sighed softly and turned so she was lying on her back. She looked up at Alex. "I know."

Alex rubbed comforting circles across the back of Kate's hand. "Are you ever going to change?"

"I read this article once." Kate shifted over and pulled Alex down beside her. Alex quickly gathered Kate in her arms before silently encouraging her to continue. "It talked about the trust issues that can develop when kids grow up in similar circumstances to what I did. I think, as a result, I create these boxes to hide parts of myself in. I can't put everything in one box, but each one has a memory or a moment or a person. That way, when I first meet someone, they don't see everything, just one or two small parts. Over time, they may see more and more boxes. But they never see everything. But I can promise you that no one on Earth has seen them all or knows what is in every box. I even think that if you gathered every friend and family member and colleague of mine together, you wouldn't have the whole picture—you wouldn't know everything that was in them. I don't say this as an excuse, but you have seen the most of those boxes. I can't promise you that I don't have any more secrets or parts of my life that you don't know about, because I do. But I can, and will, promise you that I will spend the rest of our lives together opening as many of those boxes for you as I can. Hopefully, one day we'll reach the point where there are no more secrets hidden away."

"I'd like that," said Alex, pressing a kiss to the crown of Kate's head.

Kate smiled and rested her head against Alex's shoulder. "Robbie was right about one thing, though."

"What's that?"

"Well, we do have our house all to ourselves," said Kate. "Any ideas about how we'll fill the time?"

"I have some." Alex sat up and moved to straddle Kate, placing her hands on either side of her head.

"Care to share?" asked Kate, biting her lip.

Alex leaned down. "I'd rather show you."

CHAPTER TWO

E ddie took a deep breath as she reached for the door to Kate's apartment. She had spent most of the night stewing about the way that she had left things with Kate. She desperately wanted to speak to her to repair some of the damage done by their last conversation. She had time before she stopped by to visit Rowan's parents, which was why she was standing on Kate's doorstep. Eddie took one more steadying breath before she knocked.

She fidgeted awkwardly for several moments as she waited for the door to open. Eddie looked down at her watch and frowned. She thought she was here early enough that Kate would still be home.

"Kate," she called as she knocked on the door again. "Are you home?"

After several moments of silence, Eddie pulled out her phone and dialed Kate. The call went to voicemail.

"Hi, Kate, it's Eddie," she said as she started back in the direction of her car. "I was just calling to check how you're feeling, so give me a call when you can."

"Here you go," said Alex as she placed a glass of wine on the table in front of Kate.

"Thanks." Kate looked down at the table as she ran her fingers up and down the stem of the glass. After several moments of silence, she noticed that Alex was not paying attention to her discomfort and was instead looking around. She watched through her eyelashes as Alex noticed someone on the other side of the room.

"Are you fine here for a second?" asked Alex suddenly. "There's just someone I want to speak to."

"Sure, okay." Kate watched Alex walk away from the table, then looked around the mixer filled with students, faculty, and alumni from Columbia University. The groups of people closest to her were chatting enthusiastically. She turned back to her drink.

"Hi," said a woman as she appeared at the table across from Kate. "I'm Anika."

"I'm Kate." She smiled tightly at the woman, who had green eyes and straight auburn hair that fell to below her shoulders.

"I know. Sorry, that was creepy. I meant that I've seen you in pictures with your family." Anika paused and scrunched up her face. "That wasn't any better, was it?"

"No, not really."

"Okay, then. Well, moving on—I saw that you were with Alex Quinn."

"Um, yes, you did," said Kate. "How do the two of you know each other?"

"Well, Alex was my T.A. when I was studying at Columbia," said Anika.

"Oh, really? That's how I met her as well."

"Oh, you were another one of her conquests, then?"

"Conquests?" asked Kate.

"I just meant that for as long as she's been at Columbia, Alex has had a reputation for bedding her pretty female students," said Anika. "I knew she wouldn't be interested in me for longer than a semester but, hey, why not, right?"

"Sure," said Kate slowly.

"So, is that how you two know each other?"

"We're actually married."

"Oh, wow," said Anika. "I wouldn't have picked Alex as the marrying kind, but maybe she's changed her ways."

"Who's changed their ways?" asked another woman who had been eavesdropping as she drifted past their table.

"Alex Quinn, when it comes to marriage," said Anika.

"That leopard is never going to change its spots," said the woman. "I think the only reason she got married was that she saw a chance to land Neil Matthews' granddaughter. But then again, when you're someone with Alex's political aspirations, who wouldn't take that opportunity? It's up there with bagging a Kennedy or a Clinton. It wouldn't surprise me either if she was sleeping around. She was a big fan of the overlap."

"The what?" asked Kate with a frown.

"The overlap," the woman repeated. "When you know that a relationship is reaching its end, you start dating someone else so that you have someone ready to go and never have a cold bed to sleep in."

"I don't think this is an entirely appropriate topic of conversation," said Anika.

The woman frowned. "Why would you say that? I'm pretty sure you were the one who started it, Anika."

"I know, but ..." Anika gestured in Kate's direction.

"What?" asked the woman.

"I'm Kate Matthews," said Kate.

"Oh." Her eyes widened. "I'm sorry. I'm sure she isn't cheating on you or using you or anything."

"I think you should go, Tamara," said Alex from behind them. "You too, Anika."

Kate waited for both women to leave her alone with Alex before she asked, "Is that what Robbie was talking about?"

"Come with me." Alex grasped Kate's elbow and pulled her into a more secluded corner of the room.

"You heard me," said Kate. "Is that what Robbie meant?"

"What are you talking about?"

"When we had dinner with him, Erin, and your dad last month, Robbie insinuated that you were keeping a secret from me. Is this what he was talking about?"

"No, it wasn't," said Alex.

"So, there is something else as well?"

"Yes."

"What is it?"

"I applied for the job at the State Department."

"So, are you just going to move to Washington, then?" asked Kate. "Without even telling me?"

"No, I'm not, because I didn't get it," said Alex. "Not everything comes as easily to me as it does to you, Kate."

"What is that supposed to mean?"

"It means everything you have achieved has just been handed to you on a silver platter," said Alex. "You haven't had to work for anything. You are so privileged and entitled and you don't even realize it. Everything in your life has just been so easy."

"Easy? You think my life has been easy? Yes, my parents' money and connections have made it easier to go to certain schools, but I've still had to work incredibly hard to get to where I am. I've had to spend every day of my life proving to my parents over and over again that I was good enough for them, that they didn't make a mistake when they picked me. That I was worthy of not just their time, but their love. Because at the end of the day, they didn't love me, not really, not after they had Robbie. He was what they wanted and he was theirs. I was just the spare adopted kid that they picked up at an orphanage, and they never let me feel like anything else. They made me feel like I wasn't, and still aren't, deserving of their name or their connections or their money. So, yes, I was given opportunities that others weren't. I was sent to schools that most people would never have been able to afford, but that was only because they didn't want me in their home. They wanted me out of sight and out of mind so that they could have the family they really wanted while convincing all their fancy friends that they'd done the charitable thing by adopting some poor kid."

Kate stopped and looked up at her wife.

"And if you're going to be just like them, using me for your own ends without loving me for who I am, tell me, so we can end this now."

"Are we getting close?" asked Ainsley as she stepped into the aft cabin of her yacht. She looked at Agatha, who was seated next to Kate's still-prone body on the bed.

Agatha raised an eyebrow. "As the captain of the ship and the one to whom I gave the coordinates, that would be a question answered better by you." She looked at Ainsley closely. "Not even a smile. You must be stressed."

"I just want to get there," said Ainsley. She moved closer to the bed and smoothed down Kate's hair. "I don't want it to end this way."

Agatha frowned. "You need to realize that this is the Hail Mary. If this doesn't work, there are no other options. This is it. This is the end."

"This will work," said Ainsley without taking her gaze away from Kate. She smiled softly as Kate turned her cheek into Ainsley's hand.

"Ainsley—"

"We will get there." Ainsley fixed her gaze on her friend. "And this will work."

Agatha nodded. "Okay."

Ainsley stroked Kate's cheekbone. "How is she?"

"She's getting worse. She's having bouts of delirium, and she appears to be more restless and agitated for longer periods."

"You never mentioned what you saw when you were examining her earlier," said Ainsley.

"No, I didn't."

"Would you tell me if I asked?"

Agatha looked down at her hands before she sighed and looked back up at Ainsley. "You need to promise me that if she makes it through this, you will tell her the truth about Alex."

"I'm not sure that's a good idea," said Ainsley.

"She is torturing herself," said Agatha. "She may be getting some unwanted assistance, but she is literally torturing herself about what happened to her wife. It's irrelevant whether or not it's a good idea—she needs to know."

Ainsley looked out of the yacht's porthole as she contemplated her response. A small island suddenly materialized. It had a white sandy beach surrounding a cove filled with blue water that sparkled in the early morning light. The island also had what looked like a tiny fishing village with a smattering of syrmata-style houses, made of white stone with blue doors and accents.

"I think we're here," said Ainsley.

"Yes, we are." Agatha looked out of the porthole before rising from the bed. "Welcome to the Island of the Hesperides."

"How have you been, dear?" asked Natalea Ashley, placing two mugs of coffee on the table where Eddie was seated in the kitchen of the Ashley family home.

"I'm okay," said Eddie. She wrapped her hands around the mug. "It's hard, but I'm just taking it one day at a time. But I'm sure what I'm feeling is nothing compared to what you're going through."

"As difficult as it is to admit, there was a part of me that knew this would happen," said Natalea. "It's one of the difficult things about being the mother of a police officer. You spend every day incredibly proud of their service to their city, but also terrified that it will be the day they don't come home."

"I guess I've never thought about it like that," said Eddie.

"I hope you don't take offence to this, but why would you?" asked Natalea. "It's far easier to risk your life than it is to be the one waiting at home."

Eddie looked down at the table. "Sorry."

"Nothing to be sorry about," said Natalea as she reached out to pat Eddie's hand. "As I said, it's something that I came to terms with a long time ago. I would have been a basket case long before now if I hadn't." She paused. "But enough of that. You said you wanted to talk to me about something?"

"Yes," said Eddie. "The realtor who helped you with leasing Rowan's apartment—I recall meeting her at the funeral, but do you remember her name?"

"Agatha," said Natalea. "Agatha Truman. She helped us purchase the apartment in the first place, so it made sense to ask for her help when we were leasing it out."

"Sure," said Eddie, "but—and no offence here—why did you invite her to the funeral?"

"We've known Agatha for years," said Natalea. "So had Rowan. It only made sense to have her there."

"Oh, really? How did you meet her? More property purchases I don't know about?"

"We aren't that wealthy, so don't go thinking of us as some property tycoons," said Natalea. "No, she was Rowan's roommate in her first—no, must have been her second—year in college. Then when we were looking to buy, well, it just made sense to get some help from someone we knew, someone who would tell us the truth and not just what we wanted to hear."

"It makes sense, the two of you wanting to be comfortable with your realtor."

"Do you mind if I ask why all the interest in Agatha?"

"I just thought I saw her the other day, and I guess it left me a little curious and wanting to put together the pieces of Rowan's life. I wasn't really up to asking those kinds of questions at the funeral. I just …" Eddie paused. "There's so much I don't know about someone I thought I was so close to."

"Oh, honey. You knew her. You knew the important things, the things that mattered." Natalea placed her hand over Eddie's. "I have an old box of photos of Rowan—mainly from her last years in high school, college, and her first couple of years on the force. Would you like to borrow it? Go through it?"

"I'd like that," said Eddie.

Natalea smiled and got to her feet. "Let me just go get it."

Eddie waited until Natalea was out of the room before she pulled out her phone and dialed Kate's number. "Kate, it's Eddie," she said when the call was eventually forwarded to voicemail. "Please call me back."

"Michelle mentioned that you were thinking about extending your postdoctoral research," said Greg Spinda as he and Kate stopped outside the faculty building at the end of a long Friday afternoon.

"I wouldn't go that far yet," said Kate. "I'm just making sure I have all the information to consider my options for next year."

"Well, I think that is a very wise decision," said Greg. "Admittedly, I feel I'm slightly biased in saying that I would like you to stay at Princeton."

"Thank you for saying that."

"I say it because I mean it." Greg's gaze drifted over Kate's shoulder. "But I should let your lovely wife take you off my hands. Have a good weekend, ladies."

"Thanks, Greg," said Kate.

"What was he talking about?" asked Alex.

"It was nothing."

"It wasn't nothing. What aren't you telling me?"

"I've just been talking to the Head of the Department about potentially extending my postdoctoral research here."

"No," said Alex, "that's not what we agreed."

"Agreed?" repeated Kate. "We haven't agreed to anything."

"It was implied."

"What was?"

"That next year you would be taking a job at Columbia or NYU or something," said Alex. "We need to be in the same place."

"We are in the same place, and we spend plenty of time together."

"You spend more time on the I-95 each day than you do with me."

"That's not fair," said Kate. "You know how great an opportunity this is for me."

"I know it is, which is why I agreed to it in the first place," said Alex. "But this is when you commit to us. You need to agree to only look for a job in New York next year."

"And what if I don't?"

"Then we need to talk about our future."

"Seriously? That isn't fair," said Kate. "You can't guarantee that a position will even be available in New York next year. Do you want me to turn down an actual paid position just so you can see me for an extra two or three hours a day?"

"I want you back in New York full time," said Alex.

"Well, babe," said Kate, "you don't always get what you want."

"No," said Alex, "but you get what you need, and I need my wife in New York."

"Okay, so we're here," said Ainsley as she tied her yacht up to the side of the dock. "What next?"

"It's been a while since I've been here," said Agatha. She stepped down onto the dock. "I'm not sure what to expect, but I think we should just leave Kate where she is right now until we sort it out."

"Why have you come to our home?" asked a voice.

Ainsley's head whipped up. They were suddenly surrounded by seven women standing in a loose semi-circle around them. They were almost ethereally beautiful with soft, youthful features and long wavy hair. Each wore a heavy full-length woolen tunic with leather sandals.

Ainsley and Agatha exchanged a glance before Agatha said, "We're here about our friend. She's in the cabin below. She has been stricken by a magical ailment and needs one of your apples."

"It is not our role to interfere in the lives of the Faeries," said one of the women. "We are the Nymphs chosen to protect the Garden of the Hesperides from the interference of others. Too often have the children of the Fae come to our shores, seeking the golden apples for their own selfish ends and betraying their comrades once their hand is on one of the apples."

"Please," said Ainsley. She sensed that the Nymphs were about to refuse her request. "We need—*I* need your help. I need you to help her. She doesn't deserve whatever is happening to her. She is good and kind and one of the best of us. Please, don't refuse her because of what others have done. She is pure, innocent, and far more deserving."

The two Nymphs who had spoken looked back at the one in the middle of the semi-circle. This Nymph looked slightly older than the others, with a silvery hue to her hair and slight crow's feet at the corners of her eyes. She took a slight step forward before she asked, "Why is it so important that we save this Faerie friend of yours?"

"Kate. Her name is Kate," said Ainsley, "and she is the great-niece of Prince Cornelius and the heir to our people's throne."

"We know her identity," said the Nymph. "What we would like to know is why it is so important to you that this woman survives that which ails her."

"I can't let her die thinking it's her fault that her wife and sister are dead," said Ainsley. "I can't let her die before she's had a chance to live and see all the good and beauty that this world has to offer. She deserves that. A chance to see that the world isn't just what it has put her through so far. A chance to know about who she is and where she came from."

"And did her sister not deserve all of the same things?" asked the Nymph. "Why would you go to such lengths to save one twin but not the other?"

"Because Kate is special," said Ainsley. "She is the epitome of what it means to be human or Fae. She is flawed and has seen the worst of this world, but she still believes that there is so much good in it that's worth fighting for. She is compassionate and merciful despite everything, and yet she doesn't even know how inherently good she is."

"That is a fair and convincing assessment of her," said the Nymph. "But words will not be enough to save her. You will need to prove yourselves worthy."

"I thought we had just done that," said Agatha.

"No," said the Nymph. "You proved why Katherine was worthy of saving. Now, you need to prove yourselves worthy enough of saving her."

Chapter Three

Eddie placed the box of photos Natalea had given her onto the kitchen table. Fishing her phone out of her pocket, she sighed when she saw that she had not missed any calls from Kate. She bit her lip for a second before she dialed Kate's number and raised the phone to her ear.

She sighed again as the call went to voicemail once more. "Hi, Kate, it's Eddie. Detective Caulfield. Look, I know I'm approaching creepy stalker territory, but I'm just worried about you. I know we didn't leave things in a good place, but I just want to know you're okay, so please, just call me back."

Eddie ended the call and sat down, running a hand through her hair. Opening the box, she flipped through photos filled with happy, smiling faces. One bundle was filled with photos of Rowan wearing her varsity soccer jersey—some showing her posing casually with teammates, others holding various trophies, and even a couple of her playing. The next bundle included photos taken on Rowan's graduation day—Rowan standing proudly in her cap and gown beside her parents, who looked just as proud.

Eddie struggled to connect the next photos together for several moments until she realized that they showed the steps along Rowan's path to being accepted to the University of Oregon, including the day she'd received her acceptance letter through to her packing up her room and her first day on campus.

Eddie's fist clenched as she flipped to the next photo and saw Agatha with her arm around Rowan. The next several photos were dominated by Rowan and Agatha, but it was one of the last that made Eddie sit up suddenly. It appeared to have been taken at a party to celebrate Rowan's twenty-fourth birthday and showed her sitting between Agatha and Ainsley Cooper.

So now there was evidence that Agatha and Ainsley had known exactly where Rowan was for at least four years before she died, and long before Nolan had ever mentioned her. So, if Cornelius wanted her dead, why had it taken so long for him to do it?

"My name is Arethusa," said the older Nymph as she led Ainsley and Agatha away from the dock.

Ainsley looked back at her yacht. "Shouldn't we be getting Kate?"

"Aigle, Erytheis, and Hestia will bring Katherine to our house of healing," said Arethusa. "She will be safe in their care, but if you would like Agatha to assist, she may."

Agatha and Ainsley shared a look, then Agatha said, "I'll be right back."

Arethusa waited for Agatha to leave her alone with Ainsley before she said, "In making your justifications, I am surprised you omitted the most important reason of all."

"I didn't omit anything," said Ainsley. "I told you why Kate deserved a chance to live."

"Yes," said Arethusa, "you told us about who your Katherine is. You told us all the reasons why you love her without telling us you want to save her because you love her."

"I don't," said Ainsley quickly. "Or at least, not in the way you're implying."

"That is interesting," said Arethusa. "It is not that you are incapable of admitting the depth of your feelings, but that you fear how much of those are the transference of your feelings for her mother."

Despite the decades that had passed, it still felt like a knife in her chest when Arethusa mentioned Titania. Ainsley had known Kate's mother for most of Titania's life. She remembered meeting Titania when she was young, precocious, and vociferous. The young princess had been a force of nature, which had quickly endeared her to Ainsley. Over the years, that juvenile affection had evolved into something deeper as Titania matured into a charming and effervescent woman. Ainsley had easily become infatuated with Titania by that point. And for a time, she had harbored hopes that the infatuation, combined with their deep friendship, could become something more. But she had never been more wrong. And Titania had shown no reservations about throwing Ainsley's misconceptions right back in her face.

"Titania made it clear she could never love someone of my status," said Ainsley. "She never really loved me."

"No," said Arethusa, "she probably did not, or at least not in the way you wanted her to love you. But that does not mean that her daughter cannot love you how you want."

"Kate is still in love with her wife," said Ainsley. "There is no replacing that. And I am not a consolation prize."

"I strongly doubt that the feelings she has for you are a consolation," said Arethusa. "As the feelings between you grow, you will come to realize that the two of you are more closely bonded than you know."

Ainsley stared at Arethusa for several moments, searching for signs of deception to extinguish the glimmer of hope that had suddenly flared in her chest. There had been moments when she had held Kate where she had hoped for something more, but she had always tried to lock that feeling down. She had convinced herself that she would just be happy to have Kate in her life in whatever way Kate wanted, even if it was just for some sexual sorbet.

Ainsley blinked and looked away from Arethusa, noticing that Agatha was approaching them.

"Okay, so Kate is safely tucked away with the Nymphs in the healing house," said Agatha.

Uninterested in sharing their conversation with Agatha, Ainsley asked the Nymph, "So what do we need to do to prove ourselves worthy?"

"To prove yourselves and help Katherine survive, you will need to survive two challenges," said Arethusa. "The first involves picking a golden apple from our orchard."

"So," said Ainsley, "the only thing we need to do is pick an apple from a tree? That sounds pretty easy."

"Things are not as easy as they sound," said Arethusa.

"What is that supposed to mean?" asked Ainsley.

"I think it's supposed to mean there's a dragon between us and that golden apple," said Agatha as they reached the opening to the orchard. Ainsley turned and saw a large dragon coiled around the orchard's sole tree.

Nolan answered his phone. "Nolan Fitzroy speaking."

"It's Akiko. I wanted to let you know that Kate is deteriorating far more rapidly than I thought."

"Why would that be the case?"

"Sometimes it happens when the individual in question does not want to go on living. They are more inclined to just give up and seek the oblivion that the illusions provide. When it happens, it can be a rapid decline, similar to someone taking a step off a cliff."

"At least something is going in our favor," said Nolan.

"I do not imagine her living past sunset," said Akiko.

"Come see me later today and we will discuss this further," said Nolan before unceremoniously hanging up the phone.

He sat back in his chair and looked out the window of his office. He didn't even try to hide the smug smile that spread across his face. It may have taken the better part of three decades, but soon there would only be one person left between him and the throne that was his birthright, and no one was any the wiser. He was prepared to do anything to get what was his—particularly as the death of another great-niece would largely be inconsequential when he already had the blood of her sister, mother, father, and grandfather on his hands.

"Okay, good dragon," said Ainsley as she edged closer to it with her hand outstretched, like the dragon was just an overgrown dog capable of being calmed by a soft touch. "Will the good dragon let us take an apple?"

The dragon rose up. Not one, but several heads snapped viciously in their direction.

"I'm going to take that as a no," said Agatha.

"Ladon, with his hundred heads, never sleeps as he guards the golden apples, which are the treasure of the Garden of Hesperides," said Arethusa.

"Great," said Ainsley.

"What do we do?" asked Agatha.

"Um, well, we ..." Ainsley looked from the dragon to the apple tree and back again. "Ah, sleep. That's it."

"How is sleep 'it' when she just said the thing doesn't sleep?"

"We make him sleep." said Ainsley.

"Oh," said Agatha. "Oh, right."

"Okay, on three." Ainsley reached out to take Agatha's hand. "One, two, three."

Ainsley and Agatha stretched out their free hands in Ladon's direction. The dragon continued to snap viciously, but eventually, his many eyes blinked heavily. Ainsley took a step closer to Ladon's heaving bulk. Several of his heads snapped the air near her, but each one was now blinking rapidly. Ainsley took one more step. Ladon started to wobble, then slumped to the ground.

Ainsley froze, waiting for several moments to ensure that the dragon was slumbering safely. Then she dropped Agatha's hand and sprinted in the direction of the tree. She barely wasted a moment before jumping up to grab one of its golden apples. The fruit felt heavy and cool to the touch. When it was safely in her grasp, she returned quickly to where Agatha and Arethusa were waiting.

"Are we worthy now?" asked Ainsley as she held out the apple. "Will you do what you need to do to save Kate?"

"It is the apple that will save her, not I," said Arethusa. "But even this will not be enough."

"What?" asked Agatha.

"You lied to us," said Ainsley as she stepped toward Arethusa, her fist glowing.

"I have done no such thing," said Arethusa. "The golden apple is only able to repair the damage that the illusion has caused to Katherine. It will still be up to you to draw her out of it in one piece—and to keep yourselves in one piece as well."

"I thought you said you were heading off about an hour ago," said Greg as he walked past Kate, who was seated just inside the door to the faculty building.

Kate looked up from the book she was reading. "Alex is supposed to be picking me up so that we can go away for the weekend. Apparently, she's running late."

"Is everything okay with you two?" asked Greg as he sat down beside her.

"I don't even know at the moment," said Kate. "Things have just been really tense since that mixer late last year."

"Do you think it has anything to do with the job offer Michelle gave you? Which you haven't responded to yet, by the way."

"I wish it were that simple. But Alex doesn't know about that yet."

"I don't know about what?"

Kate looked up. Alex was standing in front of her, wearing a white button-down and denim jeans under a tan coat, and a frown on her face.

"Sorry," said Greg, slowly edging away.

"What don't I know about?" repeated Alex as she glared at Kate.

"Can we talk about this in the car?"

"Fine." Alex stormed outside.

Kate stood up and reluctantly followed her. She remained silent even after taking her seat in the car.

"Are you going to say anything?" asked Alex as she pulled out of the parking lot.

"What do you want me to say?" asked Kate.

"I want you to tell me what Greg seems to know. Because clearly you've been keeping something from me, you hypocrite."

Kate sighed. "Michelle offered me a position at Princeton after I finish my postdoctoral research in a couple of months."

"We had an agreement," said Alex. "When you finished your postdoctoral appointment at Princeton, you would take a position at either Columbia or NYU."

"Now is not the time to be having this conversation again," said Kate as she looked out the window at the snow that had started to fall, more heavily than it had been for most of the day. "And you need to slow down and be careful. There's ice everywhere."

"Princeton is not in New York," said Alex. "How can we have a relationship if we're not even in the same place? Would you work at the University of Washington, if they offered it?"

Kate watched Alex press harder on the accelerator. "Please, just slow down—"

"Washington is on the other side of the country," said Alex, just as the car hit an icy patch of the road and fishtailed out of control.

"Alex!" screamed Kate.

The loud screeching of tires filled the air and a blinding white light filled her vision.

"It will be best if the two of you lie down on either side of Katherine," said Arethusa as Ainsley and Agatha followed the Nymph into the healing house. Kate was lying on a bed in the center of the room. "You should each take one of her hands in yours."

"Just a second." Agatha reached out and grabbed Ainsley's wrist to prevent her from crossing the room.

Ainsley looked back at her. "We don't have time to take a break."

"We do for this," said Agatha. "Who do you see when you look at her?"

"What?"

"When you look at Kate, do you see her or do you see Titania?"

"I see her," said Ainsley. "I don't see Titania or Rowan or anyone else. I see her. I see a woman who is compassionate and kind and loyal. I see the woman who has gone through hell and deserves a chance to see that there is good in this world. This isn't about Titania, or getting someone connected to her to owe me or anything. This is about Kate. The woman that I have spent the better part of twenty-eight years watching grow into this incredible person. The woman I think can bring so much good to this world if she is given the chance." She paused. "Will you just trust me?"

"I trust you. I have always trusted you," said Agatha. She looked over at Arethusa. "Okay, then. We're ready to go."

Ainsley opened her eyes and looked around at the room that she and Agatha suddenly found themselves standing in. It looked like an emergency room at a hospital, filled with frantic energy as people moved purposefully across the space.

"Ms. Matthews," said a voice behind a curtain to Ainsley's left. Ainsley stepped forward and opened it as the voice continued, "I need you to say something. Ms. Matthews?"

"I think you need to give her some space," said another doctor standing beside the bed that Kate was on. She was petite with greenish-blue eyes and long red hair pulled back from her face.

Ainsley frowned. Something about the doctor seemed incredibly familiar.

The first doctor said, "I hope you know what you're doing, Dr. Campbell."

When Dr. Campbell fixed her colleague with a resolute gaze, he huffed and walked away, leaving Kate and Dr. Campbell with Ainsley and Agatha.

Dr. Campbell took a seat on a stool beside Kate. "It's Kate, right? My name is Cailin. I am a doctor here and I need to check you out to make sure you're okay." She paused for a moment. "Kate, can you hear me?"

"Kate? We need to leave. Kate? Can you hear me?" Ainsley reached out to touch Kate's shoulder, but her hand went right through Kate's arm. "What's going on?"

"I don't know," said Agatha. "Maybe this isn't Kate, and we're in her memories."

"So where is Kate?" asked Ainsley. "There must be a reason why we're here."

"Where's Alex?" came Kate's voice from the bed.

"The other doctors are over there doing everything they can," said Dr. Campbell as she gestured behind her. "But right now, Kate, we need to focus on you and make sure you're all right."

"Oh. That must mean ..." Agatha trailed off.

"This is the day that Alex died," finished Ainsley.

"Okay," said Kate softly in response to Dr. Campbell.

"Okay. Do you have any pain that I need to know about? Head, neck, back, or chest?"

"No, I'm okay."

"You were in a car accident—you shouldn't be fine. Although ..." Dr. Campbell frowned. "You do remind me of someone I haven't seen in a long time." She paused again before she leaned closer to Kate and asked, "Is there a reason for that? Is there something that you want to mention to me about who you are?"

"Wait," said Agatha, "what did that doctor say her name was?"

"Kate," said Ainsley, ignoring Agatha's question as she noticed a second Kate standing at the opposite end of the room. Ainsley took a step toward her just as the hospital room flickered away, leaving Ainsley and Agatha standing on a rooftop. Ainsley looked around. "Kate?"

The rooftop was lit only by the moon, partially obscured by clouds. There was a table in the middle with several plates of half-eaten food alongside candles and flowers. As Ainsley stepped closer, she noticed that everything was covered in water, like it had been raining heavily earlier. The rain must have interrupted what was intended to be an intimate and romantic evening.

"I think you need to do this by yourself," said Agatha.

Ainsley turned to look at her. "What do you mean?"

"We need to get through to her and be honest with her," said Agatha. "You're the one she trusts and the one she has a connection with. I'm just going to get in the way."

"Are you sure?"

"Positive," said Agatha. "You can do this, Ainsley. Bring her home."

Ainsley nodded. Agatha smiled for a second before she suddenly disappeared. Ainsley stood in silence for only a moment until the fairy lights around the rooftop abruptly flicked on.

The skies opened and rain poured down. Two figures, one standing and the other kneeling, appeared on the rooftop.

"Kate?" asked Ainsley as she took a step closer. Kate was the one standing in front of a woman she recognized as Alex. Alex was down on one knee.

"It was one perfect moment," said a voice to Ainsley's left. She turned to see another Kate next to her. "It didn't matter that it was raining or that the food was cold and wet, or that after about five more minutes the lights stopped working. None of that mattered because right then, right here, we were together and in love."

"Kate," said Ainsley. "I need you to wake up."

"It was also the moment that I realized we would never be as happy as we were right then," said Kate.

Ainsley's curiosity got the better of her. "What do you mean?"

"She didn't want to marry me," said Kate. "She only proposed because she thought I would leave her if she didn't. If I hadn't forced the issue, or even if I had said no, then she wouldn't have died."

Ainsley turned to face her. "Kate, what happened to Alex is not your fault."

"Of course it is," said Kate. "And this is my punishment—watching the moments of our lives over and over again."

"No, Kate. This is an illusion." Ainsley reached out to take Kate's hand, relieved to find it solid and warm to the touch. "Someone is doing this to you."

"No one cares enough to do something like that," said Kate. "And so what if they did? What exactly is going to happen to me in here?"

"Kate," pleaded Ainsley, "if you stay here, you will die."

"Would it matter if I did?" asked Kate, looking at Ainsley for the first time since she had appeared on the rooftop. "I mean, as bittersweet as this moment is, I was happy. Why should I walk away from that?"

"Because we need you to live."

"We?"

"Yes," said Ainsley. "Your people need you to live, because you are so much more than what you think you are. It's not even enough to say that you're a Faerie, because you're a Faerie princess. You are my Faerie princess, and I swore when you were born that I would do anything in my power to protect you."

"What would you need to protect me from?"

"You were born in the middle of a civil war between your parents and your great-uncle, Cornelius," said Ainsley. "After your parents died, there were so many people who wanted to hurt you, but I have always tried to protect you and I need you to let me do that again. I need you to wake up and let me protect you from this."

"You mean they didn't give me up?" asked Kate. "My parents?"

"They only wanted you safe," said Ainsley. "They wanted you protected and they wanted to give you the best possible chance. Now, please, Kate. Come with me."

"I don't know if I can," said Kate. "I don't know if I can leave her. It just hurts so much."

"I know it does, baby. But you will be able to get through this."

"I don't want to forget her."

"You won't. I promise you. She will always be a part of you, and I will be there every step of the way if you need me." Ainsley held Kate's gaze for several moments. "Now, please, can we go?"

"Okay," said Kate slowly.

"Okay," said Ainsley, pressing a kiss to Kate's forehead and closing her eyes.

"We did it," said Ainsley as she opened her eyes and sat up. Arethusa and Agatha turned to look at her. "She's waking up. It's all going to be fine."

The gazes of the two women slid from her face to her side, where Kate was lying. Their expressions shifted from disbelief to relief, and then, after several moments, to concern.

Ainsley looked down. Kate's body remained still, without any indication that she was stirring.

"Kate," she said, shifting back to get a better look at her. "Wake up. Please, just wake up."

CHAPTER FOUR

"I thought you said she was waking up," said Agatha. She sat down on the other side of Kate.

"That's what I thought." Ainsley brushed Kate's hair behind her ear. "Why isn't she waking up?"

"I don't know," said Agatha, exchanging a glance with Arethusa over Ainsley's head. The Nymph raised her eyebrows at Agatha before quickly leaving the two women alone with Kate.

"Kate. Come on, baby. Wake up." Ainsley turned to Agatha. "There has to be something else."

"There isn't," said Agatha.

"There must be something else we can do. Something else we can try."

"This was the Hail Mary, Ainsley. There is nothing else. If she doesn't wake up, then we're out of options."

"We can't just let her die."

"We gave her every chance to live."

"I refuse to give up on her."

"Look, I know you care about her," said Agatha, "and hey, so do I, but wouldn't it be simpler this way?"

"What are you talking about?" asked Ainsley.

"Surely you've thought about it."

"What?"

Agatha took a deep breath as she steeled herself. She hated herself for what she knew she had to say to her friend. Ainsley would hate her for saying it, but a surprising sense of relief had filled her when she'd seen that Kate wasn't waking up. While she didn't have the connection to Kate that Ainsley did, she had never wanted any harm to come to either of Titania's daughters. But at the same time, the civil war would finally be over if there was no one else vying for the throne. It would be time for the divisions to end and the wounds left behind to finally heal.

"Well," said Agatha, "if Kate dies, with Rowan already dead, then there are no other heirs out there. No more royals for the rebels to rally around. No more civil wars."

"Why would you say that?" asked Ainsley.

"Come on, surely that thought has entered your head." At Ainsley's blank look, Agatha continued, "Haven't you thought that Kate's death would solve a lot of problems?"

Ainsley's eyebrows furrowed. "What do you mean?"

"Oh, come on, Ainsley. Rowan's death, the Kitsune, this happening to Kate—someone is targeting them for a reason. Someone wanted both of them out of the way for a reason, and it has to be to reignite the civil war. Wouldn't it be better for everyone if that doesn't happen? If it all just ends?"

"We've already talked about this," said Ainsley.

"Well?" asked Agatha.

"Well, what?"

"Wouldn't it be better just to let whoever is behind this succeed? Just to end the pain and bloodshed?"

"How can you say that?" asked Ainsley.

"Easily," said Agatha. "I thought about the greater good, then opened my mouth and let the words come out."

"Now isn't the time for this."

"Ainsley, you need to prepare yourself for the very real possibility that she won't wake up."

"She needs to wake up. We need her to wake up. I need her to wake up," said Ainsley. "Please wake up, Kate."

Kate looked around as the darkness of the rooftop fell away. She was standing in a large room with white walls and plush white rugs covering a hardwood floor. The large windows bathed the room in bright golden light. It enveloped Kate with a feeling of warmth and safety—a feeling she thought had died with the person who had filled this bedroom with laughter, hope, and warmth since they had moved to New York.

"You shouldn't be here," said Alex from the window seat.

"Alex," said Kate. "What are you doing here?"

"I will always be here," said Alex as she beckoned Kate closer. "I'm a part of you, so I will always be right here when you need me. But it's not your time."

"I can't leave you," said Kate. She sat down beside Alex. "I've lost you once and that was hard enough. I can't walk away from you again."

"I know, honey, but you were meant for so much more than this, and you need to move on," said Alex. "I want you to move on. To live your life. To be exactly who you were born to be and be happy."

"Alex—"

"I'm serious, honey. I don't want you to put your life on hold for me anymore. We had our time, and it wasn't as long as either of us wanted, but we were happy. We had our chance to be happy, and that is more than I could've ever asked for. You made me feel loved, but you need to let other people love you now. You have so much love to give. I want you to have that again."

"But—"

Alex placed a finger on Kate's lips, silencing her. "No buts, sweetheart. You deserve to find happiness and I don't want you to feel bad for moving on. That's what I want for you. I want you to find someone who will make you happy and love you in a way I never could."

"You and I are going to have to talk about this," said Agatha as she looked across the room to where Ainsley was seated beside Kate.

Ainsley turned to her. "Talk about what?"

Agatha gestured at Kate's prone body. "You are in love with her."

"No, I'm not."

"Ainsley."

"Agatha."

"I have known you for the last century of our lives," said Agatha. "I have seen you in countless romantic relationships over that time."

"Your point?" asked Ainsley.

"No matter how much you may have thought you loved some of them, including Titania, you've never looked at her or any of them the way you look at Kate."

"She's special."

"I know she is," said Agatha. "I really do know that, and I know it's not just because of her being Cornelius' niece, so I'm sorry for saying what I said."

"Thank you," said Ainsley. "But you were right, though. Someone targeted Rowan and is targeting Kate. But a rebel wouldn't do that—they would have rallied around the twins."

"Anyone loyal to Cornelius wouldn't have done it either. They would have known how he felt about them."

"Right," said Ainsley slowly. "So, if you take the rebels and the loyalists out of the equation, who does that leave behind?"

"Someone else who wants to see the House of Connachta fall?" asked Agatha.

"I don't know." Ainsley stood and walked over to her. "But we will figure that out together."

"I like the sound of that."

"Ains," mumbled a voice from the direction of the bed.

The pair turned to find Kate blinking blearily at them.

Ainsley smiled warmly. "Kate."

"How much longer do you think it will take?" asked Nolan, drumming his fingers against his desk.

"Not long now. The damage has been done. She is close to giving—" Akiko stopped abruptly. "No, that's not possible."

"What?" asked Nolan.

"She's awake," said Akiko. "She has found a way to break free of the illusions clouding her mind."

Nolan stood up and slammed his hands down on the desk. "You said that wasn't possible."

Akiko shrugged. "It shouldn't have been."

Nolan clenched his hands into fists as a muscle in his jaw pulsed. He picked up one of the crystal tumblers on his desk and threw it at the wall.

"Don't you think you're overreacting?"

"I told you that I wanted this done," snarled Nolan.

"It will be. Just stop and think about this for a second," said Akiko. "The only way they could have saved her would have been through something very old—ancient, even."

"That would be a risky and desperate play," said Nolan. "Anything that old, that powerful, comes with consequences. To bring someone back that way would have cost something significant. I wonder what the fools who saved her have sacrificed to do so."

"What should we do, then? Just wait?" asked Akiko.

"No," said Nolan. "I think it's time that we got creative."

Kate stepped out of the guest house, leaving Agatha with Aigle and Erytheis. It was the first opportunity she'd had to look closer at the picturesque port and beach of the fishing village on the Island of Hesperides.

She pulled out her phone and dialed Erin.

"Hi, you," he answered.

"Hey, E. Sorry I missed your calls."

"Where are you? You just disappeared."

"Just had to sort out something. I should be back tomorrow. We can grab a bottle of wine and I can fill you in on all the details. Anything new with you?"

"Actually, yes. We've made a breakthrough in the research. I think we might finally be getting somewhere."

"That sounds great. Really promising."

"It is."

"So why don't you sound over the moon? You've been working toward this for years."

"I just have this feeling that it's too good to be true, but we can chat about it when you're back."

"Are you sure?"

"Absolutely. I'll see you when you get back. Bye, Kate."

"Bye, chicken."

Kate placed her phone back into her pocket as she walked in the direction of the white, sandy beach. She filled her lungs with deep breaths of the salty sea air. As she got closer, she noticed Ainsley seated on the sand, looking out at the sparkling blue water that filled the bay. Kate smiled as she stopped just behind her.

"Are you going to say something, or are you just enjoying the view?" asked Ainsley without turning around.

At that moment, Kate felt oddly bold. "I can assure you that I like the view very much."

She smiled as Ainsley whipped around to face her. Kate was quietly delighted by the faint blush that stained her cheeks. She raised an eyebrow at Ainsley in response.

"I think it goes without saying that you weren't who I expected to be standing there," said Ainsley.

Kate crossed her arms and took a half-step away. "Sorry to disappoint."

"There is absolutely nothing about you that is a disappointment," said Ainsley. "It was just a surprise. A very attractive and intelligent surprise, but a surprise all the same."

"That's good to know," said Kate. She took a small, hesitant step closer. "I mean, I can't help but think that you've been a wonderful surprise as well."

"I wasn't fishing for compliments, but thank you for saying that." Ainsley reached out and grasped Kate's hand. Kate allowed Ainsley to pull her down onto the sand so that they were seated side by side. "Did Agatha give you a clean bill of health?"

"Yes, she did."

"Well, that's good. How are you feeling about all of this?"

"I will say that I've been better," said Kate. "I mean, I feel like everything I thought I knew was and is so completely wrong."

"I'm sorry."

"It isn't your fault. From what I can tell, none of this is your fault."

"I'm sorry that I didn't tell you sooner, though," said Ainsley. "If I had, maybe you wouldn't have gone through everything you've had to go through since you came to Seattle."

"At least you told me," said Kate. She looked out at the bay and sighed. "Did Cornelius kill my parents? I mean, my biological parents."

"You and the non-sequiturs," said Ainsley. "Your father died at Cornelius' hand, but it was a battle, and I strongly believe that he never wanted to end your father's life."

"And my mother?"

"Honestly, I'm not sure who exactly was responsible," said Ainsley. "Those outside of Cornelius' inner circle have always said it was him, but I don't see how that was possible—logistically speaking, that is. But I also know that he always hoped the civil war had not ended with either of their deaths."

"Why should I believe you?" asked Kate. "Why should I trust you?"

"He loves you, Kate, and he always has," said Ainsley. "He has doted on you, both you and Rowan, your entire lives. He has always been so proud of every one of your achievements. I refuse to believe that someone who loves you as much as he does would ever have done anything to harm you. Every child should have their parents in their life to protect them and make them feel loved. He never wanted to take that from you, to take them from you. He has always done everything that he could to protect you."

"What do you mean?" asked Kate. "How has he protected me?"

"We have always known where you were. He made sure that he saw every award, every graduation, even your wedding, and he could not be prouder of everything you've accomplished. He only wishes—" Ainsley paused. "I only wish I could have done more."

"That doesn't answer my question. How has he protected me?" asked Kate. "And what else could you have done?"

"It wasn't some fluke that you survived the car accident," said Ainsley.

"Alex?"

"I wish I could have saved her too, but there just wasn't a way. I wasn't strong enough, and I'm so sorry."

"For months after the accident, I tried to—" Kate stopped. "Well, I tried to understand why I lived and she died. I tried to find an explanation for what happened, and I couldn't. No one could explain it. For the longest time, I thought the guilt and the grief were driving me crazy."

"That was never my intention. I would have said something if I knew."

"I didn't mean to make it seem like I blame you for that."

"You don't?" asked Ainsley.

"No," said Kate. "Not in the slightest."

"Do you mind if I ask why? Not that I'm not grateful, I just ..." Ainsley paused. "I just don't understand."

"I will admit that the grief of losing Alex was, and is, overpowering at times," said Kate. "There are so many moments each day when it consumes me. Some days, particularly right after it happened, I was just numb. It was like I was on autopilot. I had a funeral to plan and lawyers to see. But there came a point when I ran out of things to do. That was when the despair set in. I would spend days crying and hours on the phone to Erin, questioning the point of life. Then I got a job offer from Columbia. That was the day the rage set in. That was the day I looked at the life that Alex and I had built and realized it didn't make sense without her in it."

"So, what did you do?" asked Ainsley.

"I decided to change my life," said Kate. "I knew it couldn't be the one I planned to live with Alex. So I took the chance to live the life that I wanted. Despite everything that has happened since I moved to Seattle—and it has been a rollercoaster—I'm finding a way to embrace the life that I have. Every day I choose to embrace the simple fact that I still have a life to live. I have the ability to make that choice because of you. Because you saved me."

"You wouldn't change a thing?"

"Unless I have some Faerie power that enables me to travel back in time ...?"

"You don't."

"Then there's no point thinking about changing something that can't be changed," said Kate. "For better or worse, I wouldn't be who I am or where I am today if everything that has happened hadn't happened."

"Well, um, if there's ever anything I can do, don't hesitate to ask, okay?" said Ainsley. She watched Kate carefully for a moment before she nodded to herself and stood.

Before Ainsley could get too far away, Kate scrambled to her feet. She wrapped a hand around Ainsley's elbow and pulled her closer. "There is one thing you can do."

"What is that?"

Kate took a deep breath as her gaze flicked from Ainsley's eyes to her mouth and back again. She slowly bit down on her lip as a blush spread across her cheeks. Kate took another breath before she said, "Kiss me. Please."

"Are you sure?" asked Ainsley softly, reaching out to cup Kate's face.

"I know how you feel about me. I've known since the other night, and trust me, the feeling is mutual. So, what's stopping us?"

"What about Alex?" Ainsley stroked her thumb along Kate's cheek. "I don't want to rush you into something you aren't ready for."

"I love Alex," said Kate. "I will always love her and she will always mean a lot to me."

"I know," said Ainsley. She closed the remaining distance between them.

"But you mean something to me too," said Kate as she reached out to take Ainsley's spare hand in hers. "I know we're still figuring out exactly what we are, but I don't want to go back to pretending that the only thing between us is friendship. I don't want to pretend like nothing is happening here."

Ainsley interlinked her fingers with Kate's. "I don't want to pretend that either, but how do I know that you won't compare me to her?"

"I don't want you to be her, or ever think that I want you to compare yourself to her. I'm attracted to you for who you are, and I don't want you to change that. Right now, I'm fine with you setting the pace and doing whatever it is that you want to do, whether that's talking, kissing, or more. Whatever you want, I'm yours for the taking."

Ainsley opened her mouth to say something. Kate watched as she appeared to change her mind and simply stood there, looking at her. Ainsley closed her mouth and smiled softly.

"Simple question, Ainsley," said Kate in a low voice as she placed a hand behind Ainsley's neck to pull her even closer. "What do you want?"

Kate smiled as Ainsley's eyes pupils dilated before she leaned forward and kissed her.

Ainsley pulled Kate tightly against her. It felt, at that moment, like she was kissing Kate with every ounce of pent-up desire that she'd been harboring.

Ainsley broke the kiss and pulled in a ragged breath. "Are you sure you want this?"

Kate crushed her lips back to Ainsley's with a moan. Ainsley's hands roamed over Kate's body, running up and down her sides and hips. Kate gripped the loops of Ainsley's jeans and walked them both slowly back toward the room they had been given without breaking their connection. As they reached the door, Ainsley's hands found their way to the front of Kate's blouse, which she rapidly unbuttoned.

While Kate was shrugging out of her blouse, she missed the open doorway and backed into the wall beside the door instead. Ainsley smirked as she pulled away. "A little distracted, huh?"

Kate opened her mouth to reply, but broke off with a moan as Ainsley pressed a leg between her thighs and used her body to push Kate against the wall. As Ainsley's mouth moved to her neck, Kate finally said, "You are very distracting."

Ainsley pulled her away from the wall. "Hopefully, in a good way." Holding her hips, she pushed Kate gently toward the waiting bed.

Kate turned their bodies so that the back of Ainsley's knees hit the mattress, and the other woman fell backward. "Definitely in a good way."

"I'm surprised," said Aigle as the two Nymphs and Agatha walked away from the guest house where the Nymphs had housed Kate.

"About?" asked Agatha.

"That you haven't told either of them the consequences of using an apple from the Garden," said Erytheis.

"They don't need to know," said Agatha, "and none of you will tell them."

"It's a life for a life," said Aigle, "and the Balance will come calling."

"And when it does, I'll pay the price," said Agatha resolutely as she began to walk away from the two Nymphs. "I owe them both that.

ACKNOWLEDGEMENTS

I am certain that writing and finishing this book would not have happened without the positive influence of so many individuals who have left a lasting impression on my life.

I have to start by thanking Ms Morley. She was an incredible teacher, who nurtured my love of fantasy novelsat an early age. Without the enthusiasm she brought to immersing her studentsin the fantasy worlds she read to us, I would not have fallen in love with thegenre, and I doubt I ever would have gone on to write this novel.

I also want to thank my mother, Gai, for ensuring that this spark continued to grow. She took every opportunityto do whatever she needed to do to enrich my life and education, even if thatmeant sacrifices for herself. I could not thank you enough for alwayssupporting my love of learning and doing what you could to support me.

I could not have finished or gone through with getting this novel published without the unfailing support of Erin. I will never have enough words to express my gratitude for your continued encouragement of me, personally and professionally. You are the person I come to when I want to share good news, when I needed help picking myself off the ground and when I need someone to tell me that I need to stop overthinking things. You are a true friend, and I am a better person for having met you.

Another person whose support and encouragement that I will always be exceptionally grateful for is Suzi. You started as a colleague but quickly became a person I considered to be a trusted friend, who I have relied on to support me and push me when I need it. I think we can both agree that your approach will never be considered as conventional, but you have found a way to not only ground me through a challenging time and help me find both a sense of calmness and a level of self-assurance that I have often lacked. I doubt that I would be where I am currently, personally or professionally, without you and I could not be more appreciative of you coming into my life.

Finally, thank you to Alana Lambert, Jess Chaplin, Luke Harris and Claire Bradshaw for all of your help in making this second edition of Holly and Oak: Season One a reality.